NOT A HAPPY FAMILY

Shari Lapena

PENGUIN BOOKS

TRANSWORLD PUBLISHERS
Penguin Random House, One Embassy Gardens,
8 Viaduct Gardens, London SW11 7BW
www.penguin.co.uk

Transworld is part of the Penguin Random House group of companies
whose addresses can be found at global.penguinrandomhouse.com

Penguin
Random House
UK

First published in Great Britain in 2021 by Bantam Press
an imprint of Transworld Publishers
Penguin paperback edition published 2022

A CIP catalogue record for this book
is available from the British Library.

ISBN
9780552177047 (B format)
9781529177114 (A format)

Typeset in 11.75/15.5pt Sabon by Jouve (UK), Milton Keynes
Printed and bound in Great Britain by Clays Ltd, Elcograf S.p.A.

The authorized representative in the EEA is Penguin Random House
Ireland, Morrison Chambers, 32 Nassau Street, Dublin D02 YH68.

Penguin Random House is committed to a sustainable
future for our business, our readers and our planet. This book
is made from Forest Stewardship Council® certified paper.

MIX
Paper from
responsible sources
FSC® C018179

To the heroes of the pandemic – the scientists, the medical personnel, the frontline workers everywhere – thank you

All happy families are alike; each unhappy family is unhappy in its own way.

Leo Tolstoy, Anna Karenina

Prologue

THERE ARE MANY expensive houses here in Brecken Hill, an enclave on the edge of Aylesford, in the Hudson Valley. Situated on the east side of the Hudson River, about a hundred miles north of New York City, it's like the Hamptons, but slightly less pretentious. There's old money here, and new. Down the long private drive, past a clump of birches, there it sits: the Merton home, on its vast expanse of lawn, presented like a cake on a platter. A glimpse of swimming pool to the left. Behind is a ravine, and thick trees on either side of the property guarantee privacy. This is prime real estate.

It's so still and undisturbed. A weak sun is out, interrupted by scudding clouds. It's four o'clock in the afternoon on Easter Monday; elsewhere, children are greedily finishing off their chocolate bunnies and foil-wrapped eggs, gauging what's left and

1

eyeing how much remains in the baskets of their siblings. But there are no children here. The children have grown up and moved away. Not far, mind you. They were all over just yesterday, for Easter Sunday dinner.

The place looks deserted. There are no cars in the driveway – they are shut away behind the doors of the four-car garage. There's a Porsche 911 convertible; Fred Merton likes to drive that one, but only in the summer, when he throws his golf clubs on the back seat. For winter, he prefers the Lexus. His wife, Sheila, has her white Mercedes with the white leather interior. She likes to put on one of her many colourful Hermès scarves, check her lipstick in the rearview mirror, and go out to meet friends. She won't be doing that any more.

A house this grand, this polished – glossy white marble floor beneath an elaborate, tiered chandelier in the entryway, fresh flowers on a side table – you'd think there must be staff for upkeep. But there's only one cleaning lady, Irena, who comes in twice a week. She works hard for the money. But she's been with them so long – more than thirty years – that she's almost like family.

It must have looked perfect, before all this. A trail of blood leads up the pale, carpeted stairs. To the left, in the lovely living room, a large china lamp is lying broken on the Persian rug, its shade askew. A little farther along, beyond the low, glass coffee table, is Sheila Merton in her nightclothes, utterly still. She's dead, her eyes open, and there are marks on her neck. There's no blood on her, but the sickening smell of it is everywhere. Something awful has happened here.

In the large, bright kitchen at the back of the house, Fred Merton's body lies sprawled on the floor in a dark and viscous pool of blood. Flies buzz quietly around his nose and mouth. He's been viciously stabbed many, many times, his fleshy throat slit.

Who would do such a thing?

Chapter One

Twenty-four hours earlier

DAN MERTON SHRUGS on a navy blazer over an open-necked pale-blue dress shirt and a smart pair of dark jeans. He studies himself critically in the full-length mirror in the bedroom.

Behind him his wife, Lisa, says, 'Are you okay?'

He smiles wanly at her via the mirror. 'Sure. Why wouldn't I be?'

She turns away. He knows she doesn't relish the prospect of Easter dinner at his parents' house any more than he does. He turns around and looks at her – his pretty, brown-eyed girl. They've been married four years, and in that time there have been challenges. But she has stood by him, and he knows he's lucky to have her. She is his first experience of unconditional love. Unless you count the dogs.

5

He tamps down a twinge of uneasiness. Their financial troubles are a source of stress, a constant subject of discussion. Lisa always talks him around, though, and makes him believe things will turn out all right – at least while she's still in the room. It's when she isn't there that the doubts creep in, the crippling anxiety.

Lisa comes from hardy, middle-class stock – that was a strike against her from the outset, but he didn't care; his parents are snobs, but he is not – so she never had great expectations. When they met, she didn't even know who he was, because they didn't travel in the same circles.

'She's the only one who will have him,' he overheard his younger sister, Jenna, say to his older sister, Catherine, when they didn't know he could hear them.

Perhaps that was true. But his marriage, at least, has been a success – they have all had to admit it. And his family have grown fond of Lisa in spite of themselves and their prejudices.

'Are you going to try to talk to your father?' Lisa asks now, apprehension on her face.

He averts his eyes, closing the closet door. 'If the opportunity presents itself.'

He hates asking his father for money. But he really doesn't see that he has any other choice.

*

Catherine Merton – she did not take her husband's surname – looks forward to Easter dinner at her parents' place every year. And all the other occasions when they gather to celebrate holidays at the lavish house in Brecken Hill. Her mother will get out the special plates and the silver, and there will be a huge bouquet of fresh-cut flowers on the formal dining table, and it will all make Catherine feel elegant and privileged. She is the firstborn, and favourite, child; they all know it. She is the high-functioning one, the only one their parents are actually proud of. A doctor – a dermatologist rather than a cardiac surgeon – but still, a doctor. Dan has been a bit of a disappointment. And Jenna – well, Jenna is Jenna.

Catherine puts in a pearl earring and wonders what surprise Jenna might have in store for them today. Her little sister lives in a small, rented house on the outskirts of Aylesford and travels into New York City frequently to stay with friends. Her lifestyle is something of a mystery and causes their parents considerable distress. Dan says Jenna is out of control, but Catherine knows better. Jenna uses her lifestyle as a *means* of control. She has the power to shock and she doesn't mind using it. Jenna is certainly not well behaved, like Catherine. Not respectable or predictable. No, she is an outlier. When they were kids, she would do anything on a dare. Now, their father is always threatening to cut off Jenna's allowance, but they all know he won't do it because she'd move back home and they'd never be able to stand it. The family suspects drugs and promiscuity, but they never ask because they don't really want to know.

Catherine looks up from the seat at her mirrored vanity as her husband, Ted, walks into their bedroom. He's been rather subdued all day – his subtle way of showing his displeasure, although he would never admit it. He doesn't want to go to Easter dinner at her wealthy parents'. He chafes at their expectation of it, every holiday. He doesn't like the tension rippling beneath the surface during these meals. 'God, how can you stand it?' he always says as soon as they're in the car heading back down the driveway.

She defends them. 'They're not that bad,' she always replies, trying to make light of it as they speed away. Now, she gets up and goes over to him and kisses him on the cheek. 'Try to make the best of it,' she says.

'I always do,' he replies.

No, you don't, she thinks, turning away.

'Fuck, I really don't want to go to this,' Jenna says to Jake, who is sitting in her passenger seat as she drives toward Brecken Hill. He had taken the train in from New York City and she'd picked him up from the Aylesford station. He's going to stay the night at her place.

'Then pull over,' Jake says, coaxing, stroking her thigh. 'We can waste some time. Smoke a joint. Get you to relax.'

She glances at him, raises an eyebrow. 'You think I need to relax?'

'You seem a bit uptight.'

'Fuck you,' she says playfully, with a smile.

She drives farther until she finds a turnoff she knows and abruptly takes it. Her car bumps along the road until she pulls over and stops under a large tree.

Jake is already lighting up a joint, sucking in deeply. 'We're going to reek when we get there,' she says, reaching to take it from him. 'Maybe that's a good thing.'

'I don't know why you want to antagonize your parents so much,' Jake says. 'They pay your bills.'

'They can afford it,' she says.

'My wild child,' he says. He leans forward and kisses her, running his hands under her black leather jacket, up underneath her top, stroking her lightly, obviously feeling the buzz already. 'I can't wait to see what kind of people spawned you.'

'Oh, you'll gag. They're so self-righteous you'd

expect a pulpit to appear every time they open their mouths.'

'They can't be that bad.'

She takes another deep drag and hands him the joint. 'Mom's harmless, I guess. Dad's an asshole. Things would be easier if he wasn't around.'

'Parents – they fuck you up,' he says, quoting the poet Philip Larkin, getting it wrong.

He gets most things wrong, Jenna thinks, looking at Jake through a haze of smoke, melting into the feel of his fingers on her nipple. But he's entertaining, and decent in bed, and that's good enough for now. And he's got the right look. Terribly sexy and rough around the edges. She can't wait to introduce him to the family.

Chapter Two

ROSE CUTTER HAS done something stupid. And the thought of what she's done, and what she must do now, is always on her mind. She thinks about it late at night, when she should be sleeping. She thinks about it in the office, when she should be working. She thinks about it when she's trying to numb herself by watching TV.

The prospect of sitting through Easter dinner with her mother and her Aunt Barbara, pretending everything is fine, seems almost more than she can manage. Her mother will see that something is wrong. She notices everything. She's remarked often enough that Rose looks tired lately, that she's lost weight. Rose always brushes the concern away, tries to deflect the conversation to something else, but it's getting harder and harder to do. She has actually started to visit her mother less often, but she can't skip Easter dinner. She studies herself in the mirror. It's true that her jeans, once snug, seem to hang on her. She decides to compensate by putting on a bulky red sweater over her shirt. It will have to do. She brushes her long brown hair, puts on some lipstick to brighten up her wan face, and attempts a smile. It looks forced, but it's the best she can do.

When she arrives at her mom's house, it begins right away, the motherly concern, the questions. But her mother can't help her. And she can never know the truth. Rose got herself into this mess all by herself. And she will have to get herself out.

Ellen Cutter takes one look at her daughter and shakes her head. 'Look at you,' she says, receiving her daughter's coat. 'You're so pale. Barbara, doesn't she look a bit pale to you? And honestly, Rose, you're getting so thin.'

Barbara rolls her eyes at her and smiles at Rose. 'I think you look great,' she says. 'Don't listen to your mother. She's such a worrywart.'

Rose smiles at her aunt and says, 'Thank you, Barbara. I don't think I look *that* bad, do I?' She turns to look at herself in the hallway mirror and fluffs up her bangs a little.

Ellen smiles too, but inwardly she's dismayed. And her sister sends her a quick glance that confirms she's noticed the changes in her niece, despite what she just said. Ellen's not imagining things – Rose *does* look worn out. She's lost her sparkle lately. She tries not to worry, but who else is she going to worry about? She's a widow, and Rose is her only child. Barbara doesn't have any kids, so there aren't any nieces or nephews for her to fuss over. Ellen is really rather alone in the world, except for these two, and her friend Audrey. 'Well, we're going to have a lovely dinner,' Ellen says. 'Come into the kitchen, I'm just about to baste the turkey.'

'What have you been up to?' Ellen hears Barbara ask Rose as they make their way into the other room.

'Not much,' Rose says. 'Just work.'

'That doesn't sound like you,' Barbara says. 'What do you do for fun? Do you have a boyfriend these days?'

Ellen furtively watches her daughter's face as she tends to the turkey, the smell of the roasting meat familiar and comforting. Rose used to be so popular, but she doesn't talk about friends or boyfriends any more. It's all just work, work, work.

'No one at the moment,' Rose says.

'I guess running your own law practice is pretty demanding,' Barbara acknowledges with a smile.

'You've no idea,' Rose agrees.

'There's such a thing as work-life balance,' Ellen suggests gently.

13

'Not if you're a young attorney,' Rose says.

But Ellen wonders if there's more to it than that.

Audrey Stancik has been knocked sideways by a nasty spring flu. She didn't bother to get the flu shot this year and she heartily regrets it now. Inside her modest home, she sits in bed in her most comfortable, faded pyjamas. Her hair is tucked back in a headband, but even ill, her manicure is perfect. She's propped up by pillows, the television on in the background, but she's not really watching. There's a wastebasket full of soiled tissues next to the bed and a box of fresh tissues on her nightstand, beside the framed photograph of her daughter, Holly. She feels utterly miserable – her nose is running like a tap and she's achy all over. Audrey was supposed to be celebrating Easter dinner at her brother Fred's place with the family, and she had been *particularly* looking forward to it this year. She would have enjoyed it much more than usual, knowing what she knows. She's going to miss that delicious meal with all the fixings, and her favourite, Irena's lemon pie. It's really a shame; Audrey enjoys her food.

But other than having the flu, Audrey is quite happy these days. She's expecting a windfall soon. A *significant* windfall. It's too bad someone has to die for her to get it.

She's going to be rich. It's about time.

Chapter Three

CATHERINE STANDS ON her parents' doorstep with Ted beside her, buzzing a little with nerves. She rings the doorbell. It's always like this – wondering how everyone is going to get along, hoping for the best. But she's not going to allow anyone to ruin the day for her.

She and Ted have a lovely home in Aylesford, but it's nowhere near as impressive as this. They have the kind of house two professional incomes – a dermatologist and a dentist – can afford. Her parents' home, where she and her siblings grew up, is more of a mansion. As the eldest, she would like to have this house when her parents are gone. She would like to live here, in Brecken Hill, in comfort and wealth, and host her siblings for holiday dinners, her own children around her. This is what she fantasizes about – and in her fantasy she's never very old. Not much older than she is now. Certainly not as old as she would be if her parents lived a long life and died of natural causes. But then that's the point of fantasies; by definition they are never realistic. She wants the house and everything in it – the dishes, the antiques, the art. Her parents have never promised her the house, or even hinted that they would leave it to her. But they wouldn't leave it to Dan – he wouldn't want it anyway. Jenna would probably trash the place, or if she didn't, her friends would. Her mother would never inflict Jenna and her lifestyle on their wealthy neighbours, Catherine is sure of that.

The door opens and her mother is there, welcoming them in with a smile. She's wearing black trousers and black heels, a white silk blouse, and an orange-and-pink Hermès scarf around her neck. Catherine briefly studies her mother's face, looking for signs of what she herself will look like when she's older. She sees watery blue eyes, good skin, well-cut hair. Her mother has aged rather gracefully – but money helps.

'Hi, Mom,' she says, leaning in to embrace her mother. It's a polite hug rather than a heartfelt one.

'Hi, dear. You're the first,' she says, turning to greet Ted. 'Come on in. I'll get you something to drink.'

She bustles into the dining room to the right of the foyer, saying, 'What would you like? Champagne?'

Her mother always serves bubbly on holidays. 'Sure,' Catherine says, taking off her spring coat and hanging it in the closet as her husband does the same. They never take off their shoes.

'Ted?'

'Yes, sure,' he says, smiling agreeably.

He always starts off well, Catherine thinks; it's only after a bit of time that he begins to feel the strain.

Sheila pours champagne into flutes, and they take their fizzing glasses across the wide entry hall through to the living room on the other side and sit on the plush sofas, the spring sun slanting through the large bay windows. The view out over the lawn is lovely, Catherine thinks every time. And the gardens have begun to bloom with daffodils and tulips. She would do more with the garden, if it was hers. 'Where's Dad?' she asks.

'He's upstairs, he'll be here in a minute,' her mother says. She smiles tightly, lowering her voice and putting her champagne flute down on the coffee table. 'Actually, there's something important I want to talk to you about, before your father comes down.'

'Oh?' Catherine says, surprised.

Something passes across her mother's face, uneasiness perhaps. Catherine's not sure what, but it puts her on guard. And then the doorbell rings.

That can only be Dan, she thinks. Jenna is always late.

As if reading her mind, her mother turns her head toward the front door and says, 'That must be Dan.'

She gets up to answer the door while Catherine raises her eyebrows at her husband. 'I wonder what she wants to talk about?' she whispers to Ted.

Ted shrugs and sips his champagne. They wait until Dan and Lisa join them in the living room, Catherine and Lisa quickly hugging, while the men nod greetings. Dan and Lisa sit down on the sofa opposite, while their mother fetches them glasses of champagne. Catherine thinks Dan looks more tense than usual. She knows he's been struggling. She wonders if her mother is going to let them in on whatever the secret is too. But when her mother rejoins them, she directs the conversation to the general and super-ficial, and Catherine follows her lead.

The doorbell rings again a few minutes later – three short, sharp bursts – announcing Jenna. Their father has still not appeared; Catherine wonders uneasily if something's wrong.

They remain in the living room, listening to her mother and Jenna at the door. 'And who have we here?' her mother asks.

Great, Catherine thinks sourly. Jenna's brought someone. Of course she has – she almost always

18

does. Last time it was a 'girlfriend', and they'd wondered through the entire gathering if she was just a friend, or perhaps a lover; it was hard to tell. They'd all been a little uncomfortable as Jenna and her friend draped themselves over each other, and they'd never really found out. Catherine makes a face at Ted and listens.

'Jake Brenner,' a man's voice answers, deep and confident.

'Welcome to our home,' her mother says, overly polite, a trifle cold.

Then Catherine hears the heavy tread of her father coming down the elaborate front staircase. She stands up and takes a big swallow of champagne, gesturing at Ted with her chin to get him on his feet. He stands reluctantly, switching his champagne flute to his left hand. Together they move toward the foyer.

Catherine acknowledges her father first. As he reaches the bottom of the stairs, she steps forward and hugs him. 'Hi, Dad, Happy Easter.'

Her father hugs her briefly, and as she steps back, he says his hellos and reaches out and shakes hands firmly with Ted. There's nothing warm about it; it's rather formal. Dan and Lisa hang back in the living room and attention shifts to the couple standing at the door. Catherine notices the heavy black eyeliner around Jenna's eyes and the new purple streak in her hair. Even so, she's a striking beauty. Tall and lean in her customary tight black jeans, heeled boots, and black leather biker jacket, she looks like something out of the edgy New York music scene, and Catherine briefly feels the usual stab of irritation – or maybe it's jealousy. Catherine could never pull that off. Then she reminds herself that she would never want to. Catherine has her own look – tasteful, classic, expensive – and she's happy with it. It reflects who she is.

Jenna is a sculptor, and a good one. But she's not serious enough about it to be successful. She's more like a talented dilettante, a party girl looking for an excuse to hang out in New York City. She knows her parents are afraid that the New York art scene will ruin her. None of Jenna's works are on display in her parents' house; they find them too obscene. Catherine knows her parents are in an awkward position – they want to be proud of their talented daughter, they want her to be successful, but they're embarrassed by what all that obvious talent produces.

Jake looks like somebody Jenna would like. Dark and sexy and in need of a shave. He's wearing jeans and a T-shirt and a battered brown leather jacket. Catherine can smell the weed coming off the pair of them from her position at the foot of the staircase. Their father gives them both a stony stare.

'Hi, Dad,' Jenna says breezily. 'Jake, meet my dad.'

Jake just nods laconically, spliffed out, doesn't even step forward and offer his hand to shake. He's tall and lean, like Jenna, and, Catherine thinks, far too laid-back for the situation. He has no manners.

'Come with me. There's champagne,' Sheila says, heading into the dining room.

Fred Merton glances at Catherine as if to say, *Who the hell is he and what is he doing in my house?* Then he greets Dan and his wife.

A short time later, Dan stands in the living room, sipping his champagne, and feigning interest in the gardens beyond the window. All the women are in the kitchen, getting the meal ready to bring to the table. They have been joined by Irena, the former nanny, now cleaning woman, who has been invited to dinner. And to clean it all up afterward. Ted is gamely involving the rather *louche* Jake in conversation on the sofa in front of the living-room window, while Fred, standing beside Dan, listens. They have learned that Jake is a 'serious visual artist' with various unnamed jobs in the gig economy that keep him from creating his own work. Dan can't discern whether Jake is the real thing or a fraud, a wannabe. Knowing his sister, he could be either the next Jackson Pollock, or some loser she picked up last night at a party and spontaneously invited to their family dinner the next day.

Dan moves closer to his father and says in a low voice, 'Dad, I was hoping maybe we could talk, after dinner, in your study.' He meets his father's eye, but then looks away. His father intimidates him. Dan has always felt, as the only son, that enormous pressure was placed on him. He was supposed to carry the family mantle, take over the business someday. He'd done his best to rise to the challenge – he'd worked hard. But his father, who'd made millions in robotics, had recently – and abruptly – sold the company rather than let Dan take over. He'd done everything asked of him – he'd been employed there in various capacities from the time he was in high school, expecting it to be his one day. He'd earned his MBA. He'd worked his ass off. But his father didn't like the way he did things, and he was controlling and pigheaded, always dangling carrots and snatching them away. The sale of Merton Robotics had gutted Dan, left him unemployed and unmoored, and shattered his confidence. He still doesn't know what he's going to do. That was six months ago, and he's been floundering ever since, getting himself into financial trouble. His job search so far has yielded nothing, and he's getting desperate.

He's never resented his father more than he does right now, this very minute – it's because of his father that he's in this mess, and he doesn't deserve it. Dan even wonders whether his father meant to sell the business all along.

'I'm a businessman first and foremost,' he'd said to Dan the day he told him the shocking news that he was selling Merton Robotics. 'A damned good one. This is a very good deal for me, an offer I can't refuse.'

He hadn't even considered what it might mean for his son.

Now, his father responds, more loudly than necessary, 'What do you want to talk about?'

Dan feels a sudden flush starting up his neck. So much for trying to be discreet. He's aware that the conversation between Ted and Jake has stopped. His father always humiliated him when he got the chance. He did it for sport. Dan feels the heat spread across his face. 'Never mind.' He won't talk to his father today. He no longer has the stomach for it.

'No, don't do that,' his father says. 'Don't start something you won't finish. What did you want to talk to me about?' When he doesn't answer, his father says bluntly, 'Let me guess. You need money.'

A feeling of impotent rage floods through Dan, and he wants to punch his father in the face. He doesn't know what stops him, but something always does.

'Yeah. I don't think so,' his father says cruelly.

Just then his mother's voice calls, 'Dinner's on the table. Come be seated, please.'

Dan shrugs past his father, face burning, and makes his way into the dining room. He's lost his appetite.

Chapter Four

IRENA DOES MOST of the work, bringing the food quietly and efficiently to the dining room – the vegetables, potatoes, side dishes and sauces, the gravy – while Sheila carries in the roast turkey on an ornate platter and carefully places it near Fred. Irena wonders when it will get to be too much for her. The bird is obviously heavy and Sheila's not getting any younger. She fears the day when Sheila twists an ankle in those heels and goes down with the turkey on top of her. Fred always carves; it's something he takes seriously, as the man of the household. Fred stands, while they all sit, waiting. He wields the carving knife while telling some story, pausing to make a point. He doesn't care that the food is getting cold.

Fred is at the head of the table, with Sheila at the opposite end. Catherine, Ted, and Lisa are on Fred's right, while Jenna, Jake, and Dan are on his left. Irena is closest to the kitchen, shoved in kitty-corner between Dan and Sheila.

It's too much trouble, Sheila says, to add another leaf to the table, although it would be Irena doing it. If Audrey were here – Fred's sister – the leaf would be added. But Audrey is not here tonight; she has a spring flu.

While Fred carves, Irena observes the others at the table without anyone taking notice. It's easy enough to do if you're the hired help who has been with the family since the children were in diapers. No one pays much attention to her, and she knows all of them so well. Sheila is hiding a tremor; she's clearly worried about something. Irena knows about Sheila's new anti-anxiety meds in the bathroom medicine cabinet. It's hard to keep secrets like that from the cleaning lady. She's wondering why Sheila has started taking them. Dan is a dusky red, as if he has suffered another rebuke, and he alone is not watching Fred carve the turkey. Jenna has brought another plaything with her – a man, this time. And Catherine – well, Catherine is luxuriating in the fine china and crystal and the glint of the silver. She's the only one who seems to be enjoying herself. Ted is on his best behaviour; Irena can sense his restraint.

Irena feels a tug at her heart as she watches them

all. She's fond of the children, and worries about them, especially Dan, even though they have grown up and moved out. They don't need her any more.

The food is served, and the meal begins. Everyone digs in – dark meat and white, stuffing and scalloped potatoes, cold ham, rolls and butter, salads and sauces. And they talk, just like any other family. Fred is going on about a friend's new yacht. Irena notes that he is drinking a lot of wine – the best Chardonnay from the cellar – and quickly, which is never a good sign.

Jenna has finished her meal. She places her knife and fork diagonally across her gold-rimmed plate and casts her eyes around the table. Dan has been subdued; she notes that he hasn't said a word. His wife, Lisa, sitting across from him, has kept a worried eye on him. Jenna suspects Dan and their father already had words earlier – there's a familiar tension in the air. Her mother seems to be chattering more brightly than usual, a sure sign that something is wrong. She feels Jake's right hand creeping up her thigh under the tablecloth. Catherine seems her usual self – such a princess, always, in her pearls, her conventionally handsome husband chewing politely next to her. Her father has been drinking wine steadily and seems like he has something on his mind. She knows that look.

27

Then he taps his glass with his fork to get everyone's attention. He does this when he has an announcement to make, and he's a man who likes to make announcements. He has such a monstrous ego. He enjoys dropping bombshells and watching the reaction on everyone's faces. It's the way he ran his business, apparently, and it's the way he runs his family. Now, all eyes turn to him uneasily. Even Dan's. Jenna knows Dan's had a shitty time of it. Surely there's nothing more he can do to Dan. So maybe it's her turn. Or Catherine's. She finds herself tensing.

'There's something you should know,' her father says, looking at each of them around the table.

Jenna catches Catherine looking at her as if she's thinking the same thing – *it's you or me*. Their father takes his time, drawing out everyone's discomfort. Then he says, 'Your mother and I have decided to sell the house.'

Catherine then. Jenna quickly glances at Catherine. She looks as if she's been sucker-punched in the stomach. She obviously had no idea this was going to happen, and it has floored her. Her face has gone slack, her expression flat. They all knew Catherine wanted this house someday. Well, it looks like she's not going to get it.

She looks across to her mother, but Sheila is looking down, avoiding her daughter's eyes. So this is why all the bright chatter, Jenna thinks. She knew this was coming. Jenna feels a surge of rage. Why is he so bloody mean? Why does her mother let him get away with it?

Catherine attempts to compose herself, but she's not fooling anybody. 'Why would you sell it? I thought you loved this house.'

'It's too big for just the two of us,' Fred Merton says. 'We want to downsize, get something smaller. Too much upkeep on this place.'

'What do you mean, upkeep?' Catherine says, her voice growing bolder, her anger showing. 'You don't even do any of the work yourself – you have a gardening company, a snow removal service, Irena does all the cleaning. What upkeep?'

Her father looks at her as if he's just now noticing her distress. 'What, did you want it for yourself?'

Jenna sees the wash of pink spread across Catherine's fair skin.

Catherine says, 'It's just that . . . we grew up in this house. It's the family home.'

'I've never thought of you as sentimental, Catherine,' their father says, casually refilling his wine glass.

Catherine's face is now an angry red. 'What about Irena?' she asks, glancing at their old nanny at the other end of the table, then back at her father.

'What about her?' He speaks as if she's not at the table, as if she's not in the room.

'You're just going to let her go?'

Her father puts his wine glass down on the table with a *clunk* and says, 'I imagine we'll keep her, in a reduced capacity. But Catherine, she only comes here two days a week as it is. It's not going to kill her.'

'She's part of the family!'

Jenna sneaks a glance at Irena. She's perfectly still, watching their father, but there's a flash to her eyes. Catherine's right, Jenna thinks – surely they owe her something. She practically raised them.

'I'm sorry to upset your expectations,' their father says, not looking sorry at all. 'But the decision has been made.'

'I had none,' Catherine says tartly.

'Good,' their father says. 'Because let me tell you something about expectations. It's better not to have them. Because you will be disappointed. Just like I expected Dan here to take over the family business someday, but I sold it rather than watch him run it into the ground.'

Lisa gasps audibly. Dan looks at his father, his face white, his mouth set in a grim line. Their mother is shaking her head, almost imperceptibly, as if telling her husband not to go there. He ignores her, as always. She is too weak for him, she always has been, Jenna thinks. At times they have all hated her for it. For not standing up for them, for not protecting them. Even now, it's as if their mother isn't even

30

there. He has made this decision without her, despite what he says. Jenna can sense Jake beside her, watching in embarrassment. His hand has dropped away from her thigh.

But their father is just getting started. Happy Easter to all. This one will be memorable. 'And Jenna here,' he says, turning his heavy gaze on her.

She waits for it. She's been the object of his wrath before. She will not shrink before him. He's just a bully. A contemptible bully, and they all know it.

'We had such high hopes for you too,' he says, leaning toward her over the table and glaring at her. 'All that supposed talent – what a waste. How much longer do you expect me to support you?'

'Art takes time,' she fires back.

'You've been such a disappointment,' he says dismissively.

She pretends to ignore it, even though it hurts to hear him say it.

'As your parents, we had expectations too,' he says. 'It cuts both ways. We expected more of our children. We wanted to be proud of you.'

'You should be,' Catherine snaps at him. 'There's lots to be proud of. You just can't see it. You never could.'

He replies, his tone patronizing, 'It's true, we're proud of *you*, Catherine. You're a doctor, at least. But where are my grandsons?'

31

There's a short, shocked silence.

'I can't believe this,' Ted says, surprising everyone. He stands up abruptly. 'We're leaving.' He takes Catherine by the elbow and she rises beside him, unable to meet anyone's eyes. Together they leave the table and march around Fred's back and out to the foyer.

Fred says, 'Yes, run away – that's very mature.'

Sheila pushes back her chair and hurries after Catherine and Ted. The others remain at the table, still stunned.

Then Dan rises and, throwing his napkin down like a gauntlet, leaves the table as well, Lisa rushing after him.

Jenna says, 'We're leaving too.' She gets up and Jake follows obediently. They will all miss dessert. From the entryway, Jenna glances back over her shoulder into the dining room. Irena has disappeared into the kitchen, but her father is still sitting alone at the head of the table, tossing back a long drink of wine. She despises him.

She turns her back on him. Catherine is pulling on her coat while their mother tries to get her to wait until she can pack some pie to take home. 'No, it's okay, Mom. We don't want any pie,' Catherine says.

'Thank you for dinner, Sheila,' Ted says. Then Catherine and Ted are out the front door as fast as they're able.

Dan kisses his mother hastily on the cheek and he and Lisa depart just as quickly. The door closes behind them. Then Irena unexpectedly comes down the hall from the kitchen, puts on her coat, and leaves without a word, as Sheila watches in surprised silence.

And then it's just her and Jake, alone in the house with her parents. Jenna changes her mind; she turns back to face her father.

Chapter Five

CATHERINE SOMEHOW MAKES her way to Ted's car in the driveway without breaking down, but as soon as she gets into the passenger seat and fastens her seat belt, the tears start to flow.

Ted turns to her in concern. He leans over and pulls her into him to comfort her. For a moment, she presses her face against his chest. That comment – *where are my grandsons?* – cut her to the quick. They've been trying for a baby for almost two years now. It's a sensitive subject. Her father doesn't know that, but he might have guessed. He's so cruel, she thinks, and so adept at finding vulnerabilities. And the house – she's furious they're selling it. It's not because of the upkeep. He's selling it so that she can't have it. Just like he sold the business so that Dan couldn't have it.

She pulls away from Ted so that he can drive. He

fastens his seat belt and quickly starts the car, throwing it into reverse. He turns the car around, and speeds down the driveway, engine revving. For once she's as eager to get away as he is. She takes a deep breath and says, 'You're right, I don't know how I stand it. Although that was much worse than usual.'

'Your father is a miserable prick. He always has been.'

'I know.'

'And your mother – for Christ's sake, what's wrong with her? Has she got no spine at all?'

They both know the answer to that.

'I'm sorry about the house,' he says as he calms down and the car slows. 'I know how much you wanted it.'

She stares miserably out the windshield at the road ahead. She can't believe it's never going to be hers.

'Is that what she wanted to tell you?' Ted asks.

'What?'

'When we first arrived, your mother said there was something she wanted to talk to you about.'

'Your guess is as good as mine.'

'Your family is like a fucking soap opera. What more could there be?' Ted says.

'Maybe she's ill,' she says. 'Maybe that's why they're selling the house.'

Lisa doesn't even want to ask. She's afraid of what she might learn. But on the drive home she screws up her courage and asks Dan, 'Did you get a chance to talk to your father, before –'

'No,' he says curtly. Then he glances at her, softens his voice. 'I tried, but he was in no mood. If I'd known what was coming, I wouldn't have bothered.'

She looks out the window as her husband drives. 'He's such a shit,' she says venomously, knowing her husband is thinking the same thing. She feels sorry for Catherine – he was awful to her. But as much as she feels bad about that, some small part of her is glad – or maybe relieved – that he has turned on one of his other children for once. It's reassuring. It makes it look less like Dan's fault that Fred sold the family business. She's tried to keep the faith, but lately it's been hard. Watching her husband flounder, unemployed, without direction. He's done something unwise with their investments. Is Dan a good businessman or not? She doesn't really know any more. But she has doubts.

When she married him four years ago, he had a good position in Fred's company, with a generous salary, bonuses, and a bright future. He was never happy there – his father made his life miserable at work – but they thought Fred would retire and that Dan would run the company someday. The world was their oyster. When Fred sold it out from under

36

them a few months ago, it was like – it was like a death. And Dan still hasn't gotten over the grief. She's done her best to comfort and support him, to prop him up, to help him find a new path. But he has always struggled with depression, and since the business was sold, it has become that much worse. Some days she hardly recognizes him.

Now she says, 'That was a low blow, about the grandsons.'

'Yup,' Dan agrees.

'Do you think he knows that they've been having trouble conceiving?'

'I doubt it. It's not like she'd tell him. She might have told Mom, but she would have sworn her to secrecy.'

'Catherine told me in confidence. She said she wasn't going to tell your mother, but I wonder if she did.'

Dan glances over at her. 'She told you because you're kind. You're right – she wouldn't tell them. It was probably a lucky guess.'

She's silent for a moment. 'She wanted the house, didn't she?'

Dan nods. 'She's always wanted the house. I don't care, one way or the other. The place could burn down as far as I'm concerned.' His voice turns dark. 'It's not like we have a lot of happy memories there.'

She looks at him more closely. 'Are you all right?' she asks.

A car is coming toward them. It passes and the road is empty in front of them again.

'I'm fine,' Dan says, rigid at the wheel.

'Okay.' She watches him uneasily.

What are they going to do? They'd been banking on Dan's father loaning them some money to tide them over until Dan got himself together. But that's not going to happen.

Chapter Six

WHEN DAN AND Lisa arrive home they talk for a while, then Lisa retires to the den to read. Dan doesn't join her. He can't sit still, and he can't focus. He hasn't been able to focus on much of anything these days, other than his problems. He thinks about those endlessly, obsessively, but not productively. Now, after what happened at his parents', he feels the urge to do something drastic, something final – anything to find a resolution.

Dan keeps these thoughts to himself.

He pours himself a whiskey in the living room and paces restlessly. He doesn't bother turning on the lights, and the room slowly grows dark.

He can't see his way through to a new beginning. He still feels as if he's in shock, that he hasn't recovered from the pain of his father telling him he was selling the business. At first, he'd hoped the new

39

owners would keep him on, at least for a year or two. He briefly nursed a private ambition of rising in the company his dad had sold and taking it to new heights. But he'd been told his services wouldn't be required, and that was the second blow. His father had sneered, 'What did you expect?'

Lisa hadn't taken it well, although she'd tried valiantly to pretend otherwise. She has always been his rock.

If he doesn't find gainful employment soon, they will be in serious trouble. He has an MBA. He has good experience. He needs an executive position, and those aren't so easy to come by. He can't just go work in a car wash.

Unwisely, last fall he'd taken a big chunk of money out of their investment portfolio – over the objections of his financial adviser – and put it in a private mortgage that guaranteed a much higher rate of return. But then his father had sold the business and he'd lost his job. And unlike his previous investments, which had some flexibility about withdrawals, he can't get the money out until the mortgage term is up. And now his father has screwed him again – won't even give him a short-term loan.

There's one thing that keeps him going, that gives him hope for the future. He's got his inheritance to look forward to – but how long before he gets that?

He needs the money now. His parents are worth a fortune. Their wills distribute the money equally among their three children. At least that's what they've been led to believe, even though his parents have always played favourites, Catherine being the clear front-runner. Dan is the least favourite, and he knows it. They do a big song and dance about Jenna all the time, but he knows that she comes in second, their beautiful, 'talented' daughter, despite her sometimes appalling behaviour.

If his father was a normal father and not a complete bastard, he could ask him for an advance on his inheritance now, and get it. That's what a real dad would do. He could maybe start his own business. But he can't even get a goddamned loan from his father. His father has ruined him, and he's enjoyed doing it.

Dan slumps into an armchair and sits in the dark for a long while, mulling over his shitty situation. Finally, he gets up and pops his head in the den and says to Lisa, 'I'm going for a drive.' He often does this at night. It relaxes him. Some people run, he drives. It's soothing. It feeds some need in him.

She puts her book down. 'Why don't you go for a walk instead?' she suggests. 'I can come with you.'

'No,' he insists, shaking his head. 'You read your book. You don't need to wait up. I just want to clear my head.'

Once he's in the car, he turns on the ignition and turns off his cell phone.

Lisa listens to the front door close and turns her attention back to her novel, but soon puts it down again. She can't concentrate. She wishes Dan wouldn't go out for drives at night like this, especially after he's had a drink. Why does he do it? Why does he prefer to go for long drives rather than spend his time with her? She knows it's a habit, that it helps him wind down, but she wishes he would find some other way to deal with stress. Walking or running would be better than driving. They've got a perfectly good exercise bike in the basement.

She understands his anxiety, though – she's stressed too. If Fred doesn't loan them money soon, they'll be in real trouble. If only Dan had found another job, they wouldn't be in this position. She'd gone to college, she could get a job, but when she suggested it, he seemed wounded. He didn't like how it would look. He's got his pride. A lot of good that's doing them now.

Once she starts worrying, she can't help going down the rabbit hole. She doesn't know how his job search is going because he doesn't tell her, and he's vague whenever she asks him. She knows he signed up with an executive search company – a headhunter – and they got him a couple of interviews early on, but there hasn't been much lately. He spent weeks fiddling with his résumé upstairs in his office, but she can count on one hand the number of times he's dressed in a suit for an interview. They've been 'exploratory' interviews to assess fit. She doesn't know if he's done any follow-up interviews at all. Why isn't he getting more calls from the headhunter? Are things really as slow as he says?

She casts aside the cosy throw, gets up, and leaves the den. She climbs the stairs to the second floor and makes her way to his office at the end of the hall. This is his private space. She's never done this before, never snooped. She knows it's crossing a line, but she can't help herself. She flicks on the lamp on his desk rather than the overhead light, in case he comes home suddenly.

His laptop is closed. She opens it, but she has no idea what his password is. She quickly gives up and closes the lid. She sees his day planner on the desk and pulls it toward her. She looks at today's date. Sunday, April 21. The pages for this past week are blank. She turns the page – nothing there for next week either. She pages forward – there are no appointments, other than one with the dentist in three weeks. Then she goes backward from today's date. Those pages are blank too, except for a doctor's appointment. But she was certain he had interviews, at least two of them, in March. She distinctly remembers him dressing in his steel-grey suit, looking very dapper, and going out. She recalls another day he left in his navy suit – both times were just last month, but there's no record of either appointment in his planner. Maybe he doesn't note things down in his diary – maybe it's all on his phone? But there's a dentist appointment in the diary. And that doctor's appointment from a couple of weeks ago. She goes back months. There are only two other appointments noted, both with his headhunter. She remembers how hopeful she'd been in those early days that he'd find a good job and, best of all, not with his father. She focuses on the diary again. There's nothing since those two initial meetings with the headhunter almost six months ago.

Her heart sinks. Has he been lying to her? Dressing up in a good suit and tie and carrying his slim, expensive attaché case to go sit and have coffee alone somewhere for a couple of hours?

When Catherine and Ted returned home from the awful Easter dinner, they'd binge-watched something on Netflix to take their minds off things. Now, as the closing credits roll upward on the screen, Ted turns to his wife and asks her if she'd like to watch something else. He thinks she still looks too wound up to sleep.

'I'm not tired,' she says.

'Me neither. Do you want me to make you a drink?'

She shakes her head dismissively. 'No. But you go ahead if you want.'

'I won't if you don't.'

'I wonder,' his wife says, 'if there *was* something else Mom wanted to talk to me about.'

He can hear the worry in her voice. What a particularly shitty Easter, he thinks. Ted says patiently, 'Why don't you go over and see her tomorrow? It's Easter Monday, you've got the day off. You can find out then. No point in working yourself up any more tonight.' But he knows his wife. She's like a dog with a bone when she's got something on her mind. She won't let it go. She gets a bit obsessive about things. Like pregnancy. But he's heard that many women get like that when they can't conceive. It's a fixation with a ticking clock attached.

He thinks about what it's been like for her the last few months. The cycle monitoring – running into the fertility clinic first thing in the morning, before work. Having her blood taken, her egg follicles monitored. His own role hasn't been as onerous, only the awkwardness of providing a semen sample for testing. The first three months of cycle monitoring, armed with the knowledge of perfect timing, they had done it the old-fashioned way – at home in bed. But last

45

month they stepped it up. It was the first time they tried artificial insemination. He went in at the appropriate time to provide another sample, but other than that, there wasn't much for him to do. He hopes it works and these interventions can stop soon, rather than becoming even more intrusive. If nothing else, it's messing up their sex life.

'I think I'll just call her,' Catherine says, breaking into his thoughts.

'It's late, Catherine,' he says. 'It's after eleven.'

'I know, but she won't be asleep yet. She always reads at night.'

He watches as she picks up her cell phone from the coffee table and calls her mother. He hopes it will be a short, reassuring call, then they can go to bed. But Sheila had said it was important. He tells himself it was probably about selling the house, and there's nothing else.

'She's not answering her cell,' Catherine says, turning to him in concern.

'Maybe they've gone to bed and she left it downstairs. Try the landline.'

Catherine shakes her head. 'No. I don't want to chance speaking to my father.' She seems to be considering something. 'Maybe I should go over there,' she says.

'Catherine, honey,' he protests. 'You don't need to do that. She probably just left her phone somewhere – you know what she's like.' But Catherine looks worried. 'She probably wanted to talk to you about the house,' Ted says. 'You can wait till tomorrow.'

But Catherine says, 'I think I'll just pop over there.'

'Really?'

She comes close to him. 'I won't be too long. I just want to talk to Mom, find out whatever it was she wanted to tell me. Otherwise I'll never be able to sleep.'

Ted sighs. 'Do you want me to come with you?' he offers.

She shakes her head and gives him a kiss. 'No. Why don't you go to bed? You look tired.'

He watches her go. Once her car has disappeared down the street, he turns away from the door, and as he passes by on his way upstairs, he notices that she's left her cell phone on the hall table.

Chapter Seven

DETECTIVE REYES OF Aylesford Police stands on the drive surveying the mansion in front of him. It's Tuesday after the Easter weekend, shortly after 11:00 a.m., and they've been called out to what's been described as a bloodbath.

Detective Barr, his partner, stands beside him, following his gaze. 'Sometimes having a lot of money can be a bad thing,' she says.

The place is busy. The ambulance, patrol division, and the medical examiner's office have all arrived within the last few minutes. The scene has been marked off with yellow tape. The press has begun to gather at the end of the drive, and soon, no doubt, the neighbours will appear.

A uniformed officer from patrol division approaches. 'Morning, detectives,' he says. Reyes acknowledges him with a nod. 'The scene is secure,' the officer informs them.

'Tell me,' Reyes says.

'Victims are an older couple, Fred and Sheila Merton. One in the living room, one in the kitchen. They lived alone.' He glances at Detective Barr, no doubt noticing her fresh skin and still bright blue eyes.

Reyes smiles ever so slightly; he knows Barr's stomach is stronger than most. She has a keen curiosity about murder scenes, bordering on the macabre. It comes in handy. But he wonders what will happen if she ever has a family – she's only thirty. Will she still stick pictures of corpses and crime scenes up on her kitchen wall? He hopes not. Reyes has a wife and two kids at home and if he did something like that his sensible wife would file for divorce. He tries to keep a balance, tries not to bring his work home with him. Not that he always succeeds.

The officer says, 'The cleaning lady found them. She called 911 at ten thirty-nine this morning. She's in the patrol car, if you want to talk to her.' He indicates the car with his chin, then turns back to Reyes. 'It looks like they've been dead a while.'

'Okay, thanks.' Reyes and Barr leave the cleaning lady for now and make their way to the house.

Another officer is stationed by the front door, keeping track of who goes in and out. He tells them to be careful of the bloody footprints. Reyes and Barr pull on booties and gloves and enter the front foyer. As soon as he steps carefully inside, Reyes smells the blood.

He looks around slowly, getting his bearings. There's a single set of fresh, bloody footprints leading from the kitchen he can see at the back of the house, and down the hall, toward them, fading as they approach the front door. Another less-distinct set of bloody footsteps seems to head from the kitchen up the carpeted stairs.

He looks to his left, into the living room, sees a broken lamp on the floor. Beyond that, a technician is kneeling next to the body of a woman. Avoiding the bloody footprints, Reyes walks over, Barr following, and squats down beside the technician. The victim is wearing a nightie and a light bathrobe. He sees the marks around the woman's throat, the tell-tale bruising, the eyes flecked with red. 'Ligature strangulation,' Reyes says. The technician nods. 'Any sign of what she was strangled with?'

'Not yet,' the other man says. 'We've barely started.'

Reyes notes that her ring fingers are bare, spots a cell phone flung under an end table, and stands up. He waits as Barr takes a closer look and tries to imagine what went on in this room. She opens the door, Reyes thinks, realizes her mistake, flees into the living room. There's a struggle. Why didn't her husband hear anything? Perhaps he was asleep upstairs, and the sound of the lamp falling and breaking was muffled by the thick carpet. Barr rises from her study of the body and the two of them return to the foyer. From there, Reyes glances into the dining room, sees the drawers of the buffet pulled open and left hanging. At the end of the long hall that runs straight to the back of the house from the foyer, he sees figures in white suits moving around in the kitchen. He walks forward soundlessly in his booties, close to the wall to avoid the bloody prints, Barr right behind him.

It's a bloodbath, all right. The sight and smell of it briefly overwhelm him. For a moment he holds his breath. He glances at his partner – her sharp eyes are taking everything in. Then he focuses on the scene before him.

Fred Merton lies on his stomach on the kitchen floor, his head turned to the side, in blood-soaked pyjamas. He's been stabbed multiple times in the back and his throat appears to have been slit. Reyes counts the stab wounds as best he can, leaning over the body. There are at least eleven. A frenzied, violent crime. A crime of passion, perhaps, rather than a robbery? Unless it was a thief with some unresolved anger issues. 'Christ,' he mutters. Out here, no one would hear them scream. He looks up and recognizes May Bannerjee, the head of the forensics team, a very capable investigator. 'Any idea how long they've been lying here?' Reyes asks her.

'I'd say it's been at least a day,' Bannerjee tells him. 'We'll know more after the autopsies, but my guess is they were murdered sometime Sunday night or early Monday morning.'

'Any sign of the murder weapon for this one?' Reyes asks, as he casts an eye around the kitchen. There's no bloody knife anywhere that he can see.

'Not yet.'

He tries to decipher what might have happened. Barr is making her own silent study of the scene. There's a tremendous amount of blood spatter, on the walls, the ceiling, the island. Reyes looks down at the smeared floor and the bloody trails leading out of the room. 'What does this look like to you?' he asks Bannerjee.

'My guess – the killer wore thick socks, maybe more than one pair – and no shoes. Possibly booties on top. That way we can't get any usable prints, or even a reliable shoe size.' Reyes nods. 'You can see he went to the cupboard under the sink – there's blood all over it. He entered the dining room from here.' She points to the entry in the kitchen that opens directly into the dining room, separate from the main hall. 'He also went into the study, off the kitchen.' She points her head toward the other side of the house. 'And he went down the hall and upstairs – looks like he tore the place apart after the murders looking for cash and valuables, then exited out the back. We can see the foot smears and there's blood on the back doorknob and on the patio. There's a bloody spot on the back lawn where he probably changed his clothes; after that, nothing.'

'How did he get into the house? Any sign of forced entry?'

'We're still going over the perimeter, but nothing obvious so far. The cleaning lady said the front door was unlocked when she got here, so maybe the female victim opened the door.' She turns toward the kitchen sink under the window. 'Some pretty obvious fresh, clear footprints from the body to the sink, and then out to the front door – those will be from the cleaning lady.'

The victims were in their nightwear, possibly already in bed, Reyes thinks. Sheila Merton might have put on her robe and come downstairs to open the door to the killer. She was obviously killed first, as there was no blood transferred to her from the murderer, who would have been drenched in it after killing the husband. They need to find out what, exactly, has been taken. The cleaning lady might be able to help with that.

'What do you think?' Reyes asks, turning to Barr.

'It seems unnecessarily brutal for a robbery. I mean, did they have to stab him that many times?' Barr says, staring at the butchered body on the kitchen floor. 'Maybe it's just supposed to look like a robbery, and it's not a robbery at all.' Reyes nods in agreement. Barr adds, 'And they really went to town on him, compared to her. Overkill, I'd say.'

'Indicating that the rage was for him, not her.'

'Maybe. And she was just there, in the way.'

'Although strangulation is also quite personal,' Reyes says. 'Let's talk to the cleaning lady.' As they exit the house and walk toward the driveway, Reyes's eye is drawn upward to the dark shapes circling above them. Five or six large birds are gliding on the currents, high in the air.

'What are those?' Barr asks, shielding her eyes and staring up at the hovering birds.

'Turkey vultures,' Reyes says. 'They probably smell the blood.'

Chapter Eight

IRENA SITS ALONE in the back seat of a patrol car, hunched over in her spring jacket, trying to get warm. It's a bright day, but it's only April and still cool. Or maybe it's the shock. She's shivering and she feels nauseated too. She can't stop thinking about Fred and Sheila. All that blood, the stench of it. The look on Sheila's face, staring up at her, as if she wanted to say something. Sheila probably knew who her killer was, but she's not going to be able to tell anyone.

Irena trembles and waits. She notices there is blood on her shoes.

One of the officers opens the car door and pops his head in. 'The detectives would like to talk to you now, if that's all right,' he says.

She nods and gets out of the car. Two people are walking toward her – a tall, dark-haired man probably about forty, and a woman who is shorter and younger. Both are in plain clothes. Irena swallows nervously.

'Hello,' the man says. 'I'm Detective Reyes and this is Detective Barr of Aylesford Police. I understand you found the victims.' She nods. 'Do you mind if we ask you a few questions?'

She nods again, then realizes this is confusing and says, 'I don't mind.' But she is shaking like a leaf.

Reyes turns to Barr and says, 'There's a blanket in the trunk, can you grab it?'

She lopes off, returning with a navy wool blanket, which she drapes over Irena's shivering shoulders.

'It's the shock,' Reyes tells her. He raises his eyes to the yard and says, 'Why don't we go sit in the gazebo – we can talk there.'

They make their way across the lawn to the pretty structure, where she settles on a bench, hugging the blanket around her, and faces the two detectives. She used to play in here with the children, a long time ago.

'Can we have your name, please?' Barr asks.

'Irena Dabrowski.' She spells it out, watching the female detective write it down. Irena may have a Polish name but her English is perfect and unaccented. Her parents came here when she was a baby.

'I understand you're the Mertons' cleaning lady,'

Reyes says. She nods. 'How long have you been working for them?'

'A long time,' she begins. 'I started when their first child was born. I was a live-in nanny here for many years – till the last child went to school. Then I continued on as housekeeper, and then as their cleaning lady. I come in twice a week now.'

'So you know the family well.'

'Very well. They're like my own family.' She realizes she should probably be crying, but she just feels numb. Irena breathes in fresh air, trying to dispel the smell of blood.

'It's okay,' Barr says gently. 'Take your time.'

'I just can't believe it,' she says eventually.

'When was the last time you saw the Mertons alive?' Reyes asks.

'It was on Sunday, at Easter dinner. I was here all day Saturday, cleaning. They were having the family for Easter, and Sheila wanted the place spotless. I had extra polishing to do. And then I came back on Sunday, to join them for dinner.'

'Who came to dinner?'

'The kids were all there. Catherine, the eldest, and her husband, Ted. Dan, the middle one, and his wife, Lisa. And Jenna, the youngest. She brought a boyfriend. They always come home for holiday meals – it was expected. Usually Fred's sister, Audrey, comes too, but she wasn't there on Sunday.' She looks up at them. 'Do the kids know yet?' she asks the detectives. 'Have they been told?'

'Not yet,' Reyes says.

'They'll be absolutely devastated,' she says.

'Will they?' Barr says, looking out from the gazebo to the house, which is worth millions.

What an extraordinarily tactless thing to say, Irena thinks. She glances at Reyes as if to convey this thought to him. Barr doesn't miss it and she doesn't seem to mind.

'I imagine they stand to inherit quite a lot of money,' Barr says.

'I suppose so,' Irena agrees coolly.

Reyes says, 'So you came here this morning – was it to clean the house?'

She averts her eyes and looks at the house instead. 'Yes. I usually do Mondays and Thursdays, but Monday was a holiday, so I didn't come in till today.'

'Take us through what happened when you got here. Every step.'

She breathes deeply and exhales. 'I drove in at just after ten thirty. It was very quiet, none of the cars were in the driveway. I knocked like I usually do, but no one answered. I let myself in – the door was unlocked, so I assumed they were home.'

'Go on.'

'As soon as I got inside, I noticed the smell and

saw the blood in the hallway. I was afraid. I saw the lamp on the floor, and then I saw Sheila.'

'Did you go near her body?'

She nods, remembering. She notices that her hands are still trembling in her lap. 'But I didn't touch her. Then I went to the kitchen, and – I saw him.' She swallows, forcing the bile down.

'Did you go inside the kitchen?' Reyes asks.

She suddenly feels dizzy. 'I'm not sure.'

'It's just that there's blood on the bottom of your shoes,' Barr says.

She looks at Barr, startled. 'I must have – it was so shocking, but yes, I remember now – I walked up to Fred and looked down at him.' She swallows again.

'Did you touch him, or touch anything in the kitchen?' Reyes asks.

She looks at her hands in her lap, turns them over, as if looking for telltale blood. They're clean. 'I don't think so.'

'You didn't walk over to the sink?' Reyes presses.

She feels confused now. 'Yes – I was afraid I was going to throw up. I did throw up, in the sink. And I washed it down.'

She knows she's being a little unclear, but what do they expect? She's never been in this situation before. It's completely unnerved her.

'It's okay,' Reyes says. 'Do you know if the

Mertons had any enemies? Anyone you can think of who might do this?'

She shakes her head. 'No, I don't think they did.' She pauses and adds, 'But you never really know, do you?' She looks at them. 'I mean, I just come in to clean the house now. I don't live here any more.'

'What about security?' Reyes asks. 'Was there any?'

'No. There are some security cameras set up around the house, but they've never worked, as far as I know. They're just for show.'

Barr asks, 'Did they keep any valuables in the house?'

Irena looks back at her, thinking that this young detective must be a bit of an idiot. 'The house is full of valuables. The paintings are worth quite a lot, the silver, her jewellery, and so on.'

'What about cash?' Reyes asks.

'There's a safe in Fred's study, on the first floor at the back of the house. I'm not sure what they keep in it.'

'We'd like you to go through the house with us and take a quick look to see if anything is missing. Do you think you can do that?'

'I don't want to go back into the kitchen,' she whispers.

'I think we can skip the kitchen, for now,' Reyes

says. 'Is there anyone else who works on the property, a gardener, perhaps?'

She shakes her head. 'They use a service.'

'You wouldn't happen to have contact info for the three children, would you?' Barr asks.

Irena reaches for her phone. 'Yes, of course.'

Chapter Nine

REYES WATCHES AS Irena stares down at the body of Sheila Merton, her hand covering her mouth. Finally, she says, 'She always wore two large diamonds – her engagement ring and another on her right hand.' She looks up at him. 'They're gone.'

A quick tour of the house in the company of the cleaning lady reveals a fuller picture. The silver is missing from the dining room, but none of the paintings, even the most valuable ones, have been touched. Fred's study has been ransacked, but the safe, hidden behind a painting of a landscape, appears to have escaped the intruder's notice. Still, they will have to get it opened.

Reyes and Barr climb the staircase to the second floor, stepping carefully to avoid the blood trail. A chandelier hangs down in the centre, and as Reyes draws level with it, he notes the absence of dust.

They enter the master bedroom – it's at the front of the house, with floor-to-ceiling windows overlooking the lawn and gardens. It's a large room, with a king-size bed and matching walnut dressers. The drawers have been pulled open roughly, clothes spilling out. A handbag has been dumped haphazardly onto the unmade bed, some smears of blood on its pale leather surface. Fred's and Sheila's wallets have been emptied of cash and credit cards and flung to the floor.

The jewellery box on Sheila's dresser is open and askew, as if someone had pawed hurriedly through it. The bloody smudges confirm it. Reyes stands beside Irena and together they look down into the empty velvet interior. 'She had some diamond dinner rings, some pricey earrings and bracelets, some pearls – but she might have kept those in the safe downstairs,' she tells them. 'The insurance company will have a record.'

The detectives thank Irena once they are back outside. As they head to their car, Reyes thinks, We'll catch them when they try to use the credit cards or fence the jewellery. Whoever it was took only things that were easy to carry, easy to convert to cash.

But it was such a savage crime. Perhaps it wasn't primarily a robbery at all.

*

The detectives pull up outside Catherine Merton's downtown medical practice. Reyes has sent a pair of uniforms to the homes of each of the other siblings to do the dreaded dead knock – to inform them of the murder of their parents before they hear it on the news. Neither Dan nor Jenna Merton have a workplace at the moment, according to Irena.

It's a busy clinic, with several different practitioners sharing space. The detectives find the front desk on the third floor, show identification, and ask for Dr Catherine Merton. The receptionist's eyes widen when she sees their badges. 'I'll get her for you,' she says, and leaves the desk.

When she returns, she says, 'If you don't mind waiting in Room C just down this hall – she'll join you in a couple of minutes.'

Reyes and Barr make their way to the examination room. They don't have to wait long.

There's a light knock on the door and then a woman in her early thirties, wearing a white coat, enters the room. Reyes studies her carefully. She's pleasant-looking, with regular features. Her black hair is shoulder length, parted at the side, and she wears pearls around her neck. Her eyes are full of inquiry.

'I'm Dr Merton,' the woman says. 'My receptionist said you wanted to see me?'

Reyes introduces them and says, 'I'm afraid we have some terrible news.' She seems to falter. 'Perhaps you should sit down,' he suggests, and Catherine sinks into a plastic chair, while he and Barr remain standing.

She looks up at them and swallows. 'What is it?'

'I'm afraid it's your parents. They've been found dead in their home.' He lets this sink in.

She stares back at him in disbelief. 'What?' she gasps.

Reyes says as gently as he can, 'They were murdered.'

Her shock seems genuine. They wait as she processes the news. Finally, she asks, appalled, 'What happened?'

'It looks like a robbery gone wrong,' Reyes says. 'Money was taken, credit cards, jewellery.'

'I can't believe it,' she says. She looks up at him and asks fearfully, 'How did they die?'

There's no easy way to say it, and she will find out soon enough. 'Your mother was strangled; your father was stabbed, and his throat was slit,' Reyes says quietly.

'No . . .' Catherine Merton whispers, shaking her head mournfully, her hand pressed up against her mouth as if she might retch. When she's able, she asks in a choked voice, 'When – when did this happen?'

'We don't know yet,' Reyes says. 'Ms Dabrowski found them, around eleven o'clock this morning. She mentioned that there was a family dinner on Easter Sunday?'

She nods. 'Yes. We were all there on Sunday.'

'And was everything fine then?'

'What do you mean?' she asks.

'Was there any sign of anything being wrong? Did your parents seem different, nervous, like anything was bothering them?'

'No. Everything was the same as usual.'

'What time did you leave their house?' Reyes asks.

'About seven o'clock,' she says distractedly.

'Did you have any contact with your parents anytime after that?'

She shakes her head. 'No.' She's staring down at her hands in her lap now.

'We think they were killed sometime later Sunday night, or early Monday morning,' Reyes tells her.

'How much money do you think your parents were worth?' Barr asks bluntly.

Catherine looks up at her, taken aback. 'They were wealthy. I don't know how wealthy, exactly.'

'Ballpark?' Barr says.

'I don't know. You'd have to ask their lawyer,' she says. 'Walter Temple, at Temple Black.' She rises from the chair. 'I – I have to talk to my brother and sister.'

66

Reyes nods. 'They're being informed now as well,' he says. 'We're so sorry for your loss.' He hands her his card. 'We'll be in touch shortly, of course, about the investigation. We'll see ourselves out.'

Chapter Ten

CATHERINE WATCHES THEM go, then closes the door of the examining room and collapses back into the chair. She can hardly catch her breath. She feels light-headed, queasy, unable to think. She has patients waiting, and Cindy at the front desk will wonder what's happened to her. She must pull herself together.

This is so difficult. She wonders what the detectives thought of her. She'd lied to them. Could they tell?

She must talk to Dan and Jenna. She'll have Cindy reschedule her patients. They'll understand once they find out why. No one would expect her to carry on with work after what's happened. She hears a light tap at the door. 'Yes?' she says.

Cindy opens the door tentatively. 'Are you okay?' she asks, clearly worried. 'What's happened?'

Her voice leaden, Catherine says, 'My parents have been murdered.' Cindy's eyes widen in horror and disbelief. She's speechless. Catherine says brusquely, 'Can you please reschedule all my appointments? I'm going to need a few days off. I have to leave.'

Catherine walks hurriedly past Cindy to her own office to hang up her white coat, put on her trench coat, and grab her handbag. She strides right past the patients in the waiting room without acknowledging them and out of her practice, into the elevator, and straight out to her car in the parking lot. Once she's seated inside the car, she grabs her cell phone out of her purse. Her hands are shaking. She takes a deep breath and calls Ted.

Fortunately, he's not with a patient and he answers. 'Yes?'

She tries to stifle a sob, but it escapes.

'Catherine – what's wrong?' he asks quickly.

'The police were just here, at my office.' She's beginning to panic now. Her breathing is fast and ragged. 'My parents are dead. They've been murdered. In their house.'

There's complete silence on the other end of the phone for a moment; Ted is obviously stunned. 'That's – that's – oh, Catherine, how awful. What happened?'

'They think it was a robbery,' she says. Her voice sounds strained to her own ears.

'Stay there,' he says. 'I'll come get you.'

'No, don't do that. I have to – I'll go to Dan and Lisa's. They'll know by now. Maybe you could meet me there? And I'll call Jenna, tell her to join us.'

'Okay,' he says, his voice tight. 'This is – it's unbelievable. I mean – you just saw them on Sunday night.'

She hesitates and says, 'About that.'

'What?'

'We need to talk.'

'What do you mean?'

'Just – don't tell anyone that I went over there later that night, okay? I – I didn't tell the police. I'll explain.'

Jenna wakes blearily to the sound of her phone buzzing. She opens one eye, sees the empty space where Jake should be – it's his bed, his apartment, his sexy scent on the sheets – and then reaches for her phone on the floor. Jesus, it's late. Jake must have gone to work and let her sleep. It's her sister, Catherine. She accepts the call. 'What?' she says.

'Jenna – have the police spoken to you yet?'

'What? No. Why?'

'Where are you?'

She can hear the distress in her sister's voice. 'I'm at Jake's, in the city. Why?'

'Oh. I have some bad news.'

70

Jenna sits up in the bed, brushing her hair back from her forehead. 'What?'

'Mom and Dad are dead. They've been murdered.'

'Fuck,' Jenna says. 'For real?' Her heart is suddenly racing.

They talk briefly – Catherine telling her to meet them at Dan's – then Jenna gets out of bed, throws on some clothes, and goes into the kitchen to leave a note for Jake. But he's already left one for her.

Hi Gorgeous,

Stay as long as you want. Or come down to the studio when you wake up. XO

She decides against a note. Better to tell him over the phone.

Through the kitchen window, Lisa sees Catherine's car pull into their driveway. Dan has been hovering anxiously, waiting for her. Lisa turns around and glances at her husband. He's been so agitated since they got the news, and now that Catherine has arrived he looks like he's about to jump out of his own skin.

She walks toward the front door, but Dan brushes past her, opens it, and meets Catherine outside on the driveway.

Lisa hears Catherine say, 'Let's get inside.'

Catherine looks pale and distressed. She's obviously been crying, Lisa thinks. She hears the sound of another car and they all look to the street – Lisa recognizes Ted in his sports car, the top down on this pleasant April day. Catherine doesn't wait for her husband, just walks straight into the house, and Dan follows. Lisa waits for Ted and wordlessly they go inside. Ted, too, seems shaken.

The distress coming off Catherine is upsetting to Lisa, who absorbs other people's stress like a sponge. She goes to Catherine – whom she thinks of as a sister – and gives her a warm hug, feeling her own eyes filling up in sympathy. They all make their way into the living room.

'Jenna is on her way,' Catherine says. 'I called her to join us, but she's in the city. I had to tell her.' Catherine slumps into an armchair and drops her purse at her feet.

Lisa glances at Dan as she sits down on the sofa – he's pacing around the living room, his movements jumpy. Ted goes to stand beside Catherine and rests his hand protectively on her shoulder.

Catherine says, bluntly, 'They were probably murdered on Sunday night.' Catherine looks at Dan as she says it. There's something in the way she's looking at him that Lisa doesn't like.

'I can't believe it!' Dan exclaims.

Lisa watches him, disturbed at how high strung he is.

'I know,' Catherine says. 'I can't believe it either. But two detectives just came to my office.' Her voice is a bit shrill. 'They're opening a murder investigation.'

'Jesus – this is – *surreal*,' Dan says, stopping suddenly.

Lisa gestures to him to come sit beside her and he does, dropping heavily onto the sofa.

Catherine stares at them. 'Did they tell you that Irena is the one who found them?'

Dan nods nervously from the sofa. He grabs Lisa's hand and clutches it.

It's finally hitting her. *They're both dead*, Lisa thinks. She can't believe it either. She can't believe their good luck. This changes everything. She glances at her husband. Maybe things aren't so bad after all. Maybe they're rich.

Dan asks, 'What did the detectives say?'

'They seem to think that it was a robbery that turned violent.' There's a tinge of hysteria in Catherine's voice. 'Mom was strangled. Dad – Dad's throat was slit, and he was stabbed.'

'My God,' Dan says, standing up again suddenly and running a hand through his dark hair. 'That's horrible. They didn't tell us that.'

Lisa looks back at Catherine in horror. They

73

hadn't heard those details from the officers at the door, only that Fred and Sheila had been murdered, not how. Now she feels like she's going to be sick.

Dan hesitates, then turns to Catherine. 'But – you know what this means,' he says.

Lisa watches her husband, trying to keep down the bile with a hand pressed against her mouth.

'What?' Catherine says, as if she isn't following him.

'We're free. All of us, we're free of him.'

Catherine's face falls; she looks appalled. 'I'm going to pretend you didn't say that,' she says repressively. 'And I would keep thoughts like that to yourself.'

Lisa watches uneasily, the sick feeling growing in the pit of her stomach. She wishes Dan had more of Catherine's self-control. Lisa is pretty sure the same thought was one of the first things to cross Catherine's mind when she heard the news, but she has more sense than to admit it.

Chapter Eleven

AS LISA DEPARTS for the kitchen to make coffee, Dan says to Catherine and Ted, 'Poor Irena.'

'It must have been awful, finding them,' Catherine agrees, staring into space. Then she looks up at Ted, and Dan sees his hand squeeze her shoulder reassuringly.

'What happens now?' Dan asks.

'I don't know,' Catherine says.

Her uncertainty makes him feel momentarily unglued. If Catherine doesn't know what to do, how will they manage?

But then Catherine seems to pull herself together. 'We have to plan a funeral.'

'Right,' Dan says. He hadn't thought of that.

'And the detectives will want to talk to all of us,' Catherine says.

'Talk to *us*,' Dan repeats. 'Why?' Why is she

looking at him like that? '*I* didn't do it,' Dan protests. They look at him in surprise. Why did he say that? He needs to get a grip. Catherine is watching him closely and Ted is regarding him uneasily.

Suddenly exhausted, Dan collapses onto the sofa and leans his head back. He falls into a sort of pleasant reverie. His parents are dead. No more family dinners. No more asking for money and being told no. No more demeaning digs from his father in front of other people. And, once the funeral is over and things settle, there is the estate to be dealt with. He wonders who the executor is. Probably Catherine. Or maybe his father's lawyer, Walter. One thing is certain, it won't be him.

All that lovely money coming their way. He can feel his chest expanding with happiness. Catherine can pretend all she wants, but he's sure she's as happy about this as he is. She can have the house now; she can take it as part of her share. He wants his in cash. Lisa will be relieved that they're out from under his father's crushing heel at last, out from under all this debilitating financial stress. They can be happy again. And Ted – Dan has no doubt that Ted is as delighted as the rest of them, despite the fake look of concern on his face. He couldn't stand their father. And Ted appreciates the finer things; Dan has always been rather jealous of Ted's sports car, a BMW Z3 convertible. But he always told himself that that's what dentists do – they buy sports cars to compensate for how boring and unpleasant their job is. Now Ted can retire if he wants to. And Jenna – she won't even pretend to be sorry they're gone.

The truth is, they're all so much better off now that their parents have been murdered. No long years – perhaps decades – of waiting for their inheritance. No more jumping to their father's tune, no endless years of depressing, dutiful visits to old-age homes. They've been spared all that. They can start to *live*. If it wouldn't be so unseemly, they really ought to be having a celebration. He feels like popping a bottle of champagne into the fridge.

Ted is distracted from his study of Dan when Lisa returns with a tray of coffee cups, milk, and sugar. There's a weird vibe in the room and it's making him uncomfortable. Also, he's been thinking about what Catherine said to him on the phone. Why does she not want anyone to know that she went over there later that night? Surely she's being foolish about this. Of course she must tell the police – it will help them to better establish a timeline of what happened. He'll have to talk to her about it as soon as they get home.

He tries to read Lisa's face as she places the tray on the coffee table, but it's hidden by her thick, brown hair swinging forward. Dan is being a bit odd – he seems overexcited, and Ted wants to know if he's the only one who's noticed. He looks from Dan to Catherine, wondering how well he understands either of them. They shared an unusual childhood, Catherine, Dan, and Jenna. A childhood of privilege and pain. Of their parents withholding love and playing favourites. From what Catherine tells him, it has caused long-standing rifts and rivalries among them, but it also binds them in some strange way too. Ted doesn't have any siblings, he doesn't know how it works. Catherine has tried to explain her relationship with her brother and sister to him, but as an only child, it's hard to grasp. There are things going on here that he just doesn't get. Catherine reaches for a coffee, and they each busy themselves with their cups for a moment.

Dan says, 'We should call Irena. Ask her to come over.' He picks up his coffee – his cup trembles a little as he brings it to his mouth. 'After all, she's family, she should be here at a time like this.' Then he looks apprehensive and says, 'It's strange that she didn't call us, don't you think?'

'I'll call her,' Catherine says, digging in her purse at her feet for her cell phone.

This is another thing Ted has never really understood – the relationship of the rich to their hired help. They say Irena is like family. But from what he's observed, Fred and Sheila treated her like a domestic worker and not much else. Irena had left with the rest of them when Easter dinner blew up – she'd sided with the kids. They, at least, seem to think of her fondly. Catherine has told him that Irena practically brought them all up. She was much more hands-on than their own mother. He wonders if Irena, too, will be secretly pleased at the turn of events, once she's over the shock. She will be out a client, but maybe there is something for her in the wills.

The wills. That's what they're all thinking about. Even though no one has mentioned it yet. He wonders who will be the one to finally bring it up. Jenna, probably.

Being pleased that someone is dead isn't something you admit to, but Ted knows you can be glad when someone dies. When his own father died of cirrhosis of the liver, Ted was twelve years old and mostly relieved. His mother was perfectly appropriate as the grieving widow, but when they were home alone at night, and he was in his bedroom, he would hear her humming about the house, sounding happy for the first time in years. He'd be the first to admit that the world is better off without certain people in it.

Catherine puts down her phone. 'Irena said she'll come right over.' She adds, 'And when Jenna gets here, we can start making plans for the funeral.'

79

Dan nods and says, 'Since she found them, maybe Irena can tell us what's going on over there. What the police are saying.' He looks back at them all, at their silence. 'What, aren't you curious?'

Ted *is* curious. He suddenly wonders who killed Fred and Sheila, if it was a robbery at all. He wants to know what Irena can tell them – he's sure they all want to know. He finds himself looking at Dan and wondering. He remembers the exchange between Dan and his father on Easter Sunday in the living room, the flush of impotent rage creeping up Dan's neck. Ted knows about Dan's financial troubles – Catherine has told him. Lisa has been confiding in her about how strapped they are for cash. And he knows Catherine has been worried about Dan lately.

He wonders when, exactly, Fred and Sheila were killed. He thinks back to Sunday night, after that miserable family dinner. Catherine had gone back over there, and he'd gone to bed. When she got home, he doesn't know when, he was asleep. He woke briefly as she crawled into bed beside him.

'Go back to sleep,' she whispered.

'Everything all right?' he murmured.

'Yes, everything's fine.' She kissed him and turned on her side.

The next morning she'd told him at breakfast that she and her mother had talked the night before. She explained that her mother had left her cell phone downstairs, and that's why she missed her call.

'What did she want to talk to you about?' he asked.

'She wants me to talk to Dad about Jenna. He wants to cut off her allowance, and she asked me to intercede. She doesn't want Jenna moving home.' Now, Ted looks at his wife and feels his stomach curdle a little. It's just occurred to him that she might have missed the murders by a short time. What if she'd arrived there in the middle of it?

She'd be dead too.

Chapter Twelve

AUDREY IS FEELING much better, having mostly recovered from her nasty flu. The only sign of it is a lingering redness around her nose. She's in the car on her way to the grocery store to pick up some milk and bread. She has the radio on, and she's humming along when the news comes on. The lead story is about a wealthy couple murdered in Brecken Hill. She turns the volume up. That's a little too close to home, she thinks.

There is no name or address given for the victims. She pulls over into a plaza and calls Fred to see what he knows about it. When there's no answer on the landline, she tries his cell, which goes to voice mail. Still, she's not really concerned. She doesn't live far away, although her home is in a much less wealthy neighbourhood, and out of curiosity she decides to head to Brecken Hill.

She drives through the familiar winding enclave of wealthy homes. It's only when she's approaching Fred and Sheila's house that she sees all the activity. There are police cars stationed at the end of the driveway, and as she tries to pull in, her heart thumping hard now, she's turned away. She catches a glimpse of an ambulance and other vehicles up closer to the house, yellow tape, and swarms of people, and it suddenly hits her.

She has to pull the car over to the side of the road for a few minutes to process it, her hands trembling on the steering wheel. Fred and Sheila are the murdered couple. It seems impossible. Fred, murdered. He's the least likely murder victim she can imagine – he's always been so powerful, so intimidating. He must be furious, she thinks.

This changes things. She's going to get her windfall a little sooner than she expected.

She reaches for her cell and calls Catherine's house – she doesn't have her cell number. There's no answer, but Audrey realizes she'd be at work. She forgets about the groceries. She decides to drive to Dan's house first since there's no answer at Catherine's. If there's no one there, she'll try Catherine's. She knows there will be a gathering of the family at either Dan's or Catherine's, and no one is going to tell *her*.

*

After leaving Catherine Merton's office, Reyes and Barr return to the crime scene. The vultures are still circling overhead, dark against the pale-blue sky. Reyes catches Barr glancing up uneasily at the birds. He spots the medical examiner, Jim Alvarez, and he and Barr walk over to speak to him.

'Quite a messy one,' the ME says, as Reyes nods agreement. 'We'll move the bodies in a bit, get to the autopsies later this afternoon. Probably start with the female.' Alvarez adds, 'Why don't you come by tomorrow morning, we should have something for you by then.'

Inside the house, in the kitchen, Reyes approaches May Bannerjee. Fred Merton is still lying on the kitchen floor. 'Anything interesting?' he asks, Barr at his elbow.

'I think we found the murder weapon for him,' Bannerjee says. 'Here, take a look.' She leads them over to the sink and shows him a knife in a clear evidence bag lying on the adjacent counter. 'It's the carving knife from the knife block there,' she says, pointing to it. 'It was all cleaned up and put back in the knife block.'

Reyes glances down at the knife and then at the knife block. 'You're kidding.'

'Nope.'

'Any prints?'

'No. It's been thoroughly washed and wiped

down. But there are still microscopic flecks of blood – it's harder to wash those away. We'll know for sure in a bit.'

Reyes looks at Barr, who is as surprised as he is. This doesn't fit with the kind of crime scene they found here. You would expect the killer to take the knife and throw it away somewhere where it will never be found – in the Hudson River, for instance. Why clean and return the knife to its place? 'Any sign of what was used as the ligature on the wife?'

'No, but we're still looking. Anyway, I'm not finished about the knife,' Bannerjee tells him. 'Look, here,' she says, squatting down and pointing out some markings in the blood on the floor. 'The knife lay on the floor beside the body for quite a while – you can see the outline of it, where the blood dried. It was there for perhaps a day or more before it was picked up, cleaned, and returned to the block.'

'What?' Barr exclaims.

'So – not by the killer,' Reyes says.

Bannerjee shakes her head. 'Not unless he came back, and there's no evidence of that.'

'The cleaning lady,' Barr says. 'Her bloody footprints go right to the sink.'

Reyes nods thoughtfully. 'Maybe she did it. And there's only one reason she would do that.'

Barr completes his thought. 'To protect somebody.'

85

Reyes bites his lower lip. 'What about the rest of the house?' he asks.

'We've got several sets of prints to eliminate – probably from family over for dinner on Easter, and the cleaning lady.' She adds, 'Won't get any tyre tracks off that paved drive.'

'Okay, thanks,' Reyes tells her. 'Let's take a closer look around,' he says to Barr. They head back upstairs. There are two technicians in the master bedroom, still dusting for fingerprints. One of them looks up when he sees the detectives. 'Blood smears but no prints on the wallets, handbag, drawers, and the jewellery box – whoever it was wore gloves.'

Reyes nods, unsurprised, and he and Barr move into the en suite bathroom. Reyes opens the medicine cabinet with his gloved hands and looks at the medications on the shelf. There's an assortment – the kinds of things you'd expect to find in the medicine cabinet of an older couple. There's a prescription for strong pain medication for Fred. He picks up another vial, for Sheila Merton. He checks the date. The prescription was filled less than two weeks ago. *Alprazolam*. He turns to Barr. 'Do you have any idea what Alprazolam is?'

She looks at the vial in his hand and nods. 'Xanax. It's a powerful anti-anxiety medication.'

'Look at the date,' Reyes says. 'What was Sheila so anxious about lately?' He places it back inside the cabinet and Barr notes the name of the medication and the doctor who prescribed it in her notebook.

Together they systematically go through the rest of the house, but other than the downstairs and the master bedroom, the place appears to be untouched by the intruder. On the same floor as the master bedroom is a spare bedroom, another bathroom, and another large room with an attached sitting room and an en suite bath that used to be Irena's when she lived with them. They know this from their earlier walk-through with Irena. Reyes enters Irena's old bedroom now, his mind turning to the cleaning lady.

She moved out long ago. The dresser drawers are empty, the closet is bare; there are no books, no trinkets on the shelves, nothing in the adjoining bathroom or sitting room. The rooms haven't been inhabited for years. He wonders what it was like for Irena when she lived here. It's a luxurious suite, but she was still the hired help. Ready to wake up in the night if one of the children called out in their sleep and needed to be soothed. Up early to get the breakfasts ready, to make the school lunches. Then the cleaning, taking orders. He wonders how close Irena really was to the family. Perhaps she was closer to some of them than others. What were the dynamics here? Do any of the adult children confide in her? He thinks about the carving knife, returned to its place.

He turns away from the room and climbs up the stairs to the third floor. These are the children's old rooms. There are three spacious bedrooms up here, a former playroom, and two bathrooms. They have been emptied of anything from the Mertons' childhoods. They have been done over as attractive guest rooms, redecorated so they look like they never had children living in them at all. Reyes thinks of his own cluttered house and wonders where all their stuff is – their pictures, sports equipment, books, school projects, Lego models, dolls, stuffed animals. Is it all packed away in the basement somewhere?

'Not exactly sentimental, were they,' Barr says.

Chapter Thirteen

JENNA HAS HAD the entire drive up from New York City to think. Her parents are dead, and this changes things profoundly. For all of them.

She thinks about how it will affect her first. She will get a third of her parents' estate. It's a lot of money. She doesn't know how much exactly or how long it takes to settle an estate and get it paid out. She knows it takes a bit of time, but how much time? Presumably the allowance she is currently receiving will continue until she gets her share. She's going to be rich. She can buy a place in New York, a studio maybe, on the Lower East Side.

She thinks of Dan next. Of the three of them, he is the weakest. Emotionally, mentally. She has always wondered if it's because of how they were brought up, or whether he was just born that way. They're all so different, and yet they all grew up in the same fucked-up family. But they weren't treated the same, so there's that. Maybe Dan's scars run deeper. But now their father can't hurt him any more. He'll be rich. He won't have to work at all if he doesn't want to.

It's funny how they all turned out. Catherine, the oldest, is the most conventional. Hardworking, conservative, not wanting to rock the boat. Of course she became a doctor. Of course she wants the house. She wants to become their mother. Okay, maybe that's a bit harsh.

People think there's no harm in Catherine, but Jenna knows better.

People also think that Dan was given every opportunity to succeed, but Jenna knows that isn't really the case. It was more like he was sabotaged by their father at every turn. Their mother wasn't that interested in them. She could be warm sometimes, and occasionally fun, but she would also simply disappear whenever things got demanding or difficult or tense. Not that she'd go anywhere, she just disappeared inside herself. She could detach herself from any situation. Poof, and she was gone. She never stood up to their father; she failed to protect them and they resented her for it. It was pathetic really, Jenna thinks, how much they all craved her attention, how they continued to turn to her, knowing she'd let them down. They all hated their father.

She's glad he's dead. She's certain the others feel the same way.

It's awful, the way they died. But it's for the best really. It's a lot of money, and it's theirs now. If their parents hadn't been murdered, they would probably have lived for a long time.

As she drives north on the highway toward Aylesford, the city falling behind, her thoughts turn to Jake. She and Jake hadn't left the house right after the others on Sunday. They'd stayed longer, and there had been an argument. She'd called Jake while leaving his apartment on her way to her car. She'd cried down the line, made a big deal about how her last words with her parents had been harsh, and how much she regretted it. Then she worked in that it would be best if nobody knew about that argument, better to say, if anyone asked, that they'd left right after everybody else, and that he'd been with her all night. It would just be easier.

Jake had been supportive. He told her not to worry. He has that manly, protective streak in him, and she kind of likes it.

She remembers the night they met, about three weeks earlier – in a loud, pulsing, underground nightclub. She'd gone into the city to party with friends. She was spaced out on Molly, drinking heavily, but she looked good on the packed dance floor and she knew it. She likes to enjoy herself;

she'll admit she's a bit of a hedonist. She caught him watching her from the sidelines. She stumbled over to the bar. He bought her a drink. She guessed from the smell of him – paint and turpentine – that he was an artist, and she found herself attracted to him right away. He was sexy and brooding and didn't talk too much and he wanted to take her home with him. She was more than willing, but she wasn't ready to leave. She told him to wait for her and went back out onto the dance floor with her friends, where she proceeded to strip off her tight T-shirt and dance topless. She likes to push the boundaries, likes to get a reaction. She's an artist, after all; she's supposed to challenge the status quo. She knew he was watching her. Everyone was watching her. When a bouncer tried to give her a hard time, Jake made his way over to her, wrapped his leather jacket around her – her T-shirt was lost somewhere, trampled underfoot – and took her home.

She's so lost in thought that she arrives in Dan's suburb in Aylesford before she knows it. And maybe she's been pressing the gas to the floor, anxious to get there. She sees Catherine's car in Dan's driveway and spots Ted's on the street – they must have arrived separately. She recognizes another car parked on the street – Irena's old clunker. But then she sees another car she recognizes and feels a stab of annoyance. It belongs to her aunt Audrey, her father's irritating sister. What the fuck is she doing here? They don't want her here. Not yet.

She parks her own car on the street and walks up the driveway. She can see them all gathered in the living room through the large window. She doesn't bother to knock, but walks right in. They're expecting her.

As soon as she enters the room, it's obvious she's interrupting something. Catherine is seated in an armchair, her face strained; Ted is by her side, on a dining-room chair that's been pulled up next to her. Lisa and Dan are on the sofa together, united in a look of dismay, and Irena is sitting in another armchair, her face set like stone. Audrey, who is in another dining-room chair that has been brought in, appears to have just broken off in the middle of saying something.

'Jenna!' Catherine says, standing up. She comes over and gives Jenna a quick hug. 'You got here fast.'

Irena rises and hugs Jenna as well. Audrey folds her arms across her chest. She looks like she's irritated at the sight of Jenna, but still, she seems – *triumphant*. What's going on here?

Lisa brings in another chair from the dining room, and Jenna sits down.

A tense silence has fallen over the room.

Catherine says, 'Audrey was just telling us that Dad changed his will before he died.'

Audrey Stancik looks around the room at all these spoiled children, so smug, so entitled, so sure they're going to get what they think they're owed. But now it's her turn. *She's* the one who's going to get what should be coming to her. Despite the circumstances, she can't suppress a smile.

Jenna is now regarding her with open hostility. They were all unhappy to see her, even if they initially made a feeble attempt at pretending otherwise. But Fred was her only brother. He was all the family she had left, other than her own daughter. She doesn't consider the rest of them family.

Now Jenna says, her voice cold, 'What the fuck are you talking about?'

Audrey regards her with dislike. She has never got on with Jenna, who does whatever the hell she wants, with flagrant disregard for how it affects anybody else. Now she enjoys taking some of the wind out of her sails. She doesn't bother to hide her glee. 'In fact, he did it last week.'

She watches Jenna's eyes flicker to Catherine, then Dan. She's already dropped this little bombshell on the others, and it got a similarly disturbed reaction from them.

'What the fuck is this?' Jenna says to Catherine.

Jenna doesn't even have the decency to direct the question to her, Audrey thinks sourly. Well, it's always been that way, hasn't it? They've always treated her as the unwanted outsider, the hanger-on, the poor relation outside their little club. It infuriates her. They don't have any idea what she and her brother went through, what she did for him. They've never had to grow up. They have no clue.

Catherine turns to her. 'Tell her, Audrey, what you told us.'

Audrey sits back in her chair and crosses one leg over the other. She's going to tell them again, for Jenna's benefit this time. Although it's shocking and upsetting, what's happened to Fred and Sheila, she can't help smiling a little – this is her moment, after all. She says, 'I visited your father just over a week ago, on Monday. He called me and asked me to come to the house. We had a long discussion. He told me he was going to change his will – that he would see Walter and do it later that week. Sheila already had a significant amount to live on until she died, and to leave as she wished, but regarding the bulk of his estate – half would go to me and the rest would be split among the rest of you.'

'I don't believe that!' Dan exclaims vehemently, from the sofa. 'Why would he do that?'

'It's what he wanted,' Audrey says firmly, turning on Dan. 'There's still plenty to go around.' But she knows they're greedy and they want as much as possible for themselves. And they don't want her to have any of it.

'I don't believe it either,' Jenna says. 'You're just making this up! You've always wanted Dad's money.'

Audrey wants to hiss back at her, *Look who's talking, you greedy bitch*, but instead she takes a deep breath, allows her smile to widen, and says, 'Your mother was there too. She didn't like it, but there wasn't much she could do about it. She'd already signed a postnup agreement for what she got years ago; he could do what he liked.'

'This is fucking unbelievable!' Dan bursts out angrily, standing up suddenly. Audrey jumps a little in her chair.

Catherine interjects. 'Let's just all calm down, please. Dan, sit down.' He sinks back onto the sofa. Catherine says, 'As far as I know, I am the executor of our parents' estates. I will call Walter and find out what the wills contain. I'm sure there will be no surprises,' she says meaningfully, looking at Audrey. 'But I'm not going to do it this minute. Our parents have just been murdered – how would it look?'

That's Catherine for you, always concerned about how things look – the complete opposite of her sister, Audrey thinks. But she's right – it would be inappropriate to call the lawyer a couple of hours after the discovery of the bodies. She surveys them all with distaste. They were always brats as children, and they haven't changed any as adults.

Fred could be cruel; she knows that as well as anyone. Audrey, his little sister, is probably the only person alive who really understood him, knew what he was made of. She looks around the room at each of them – Catherine, Dan, and Jenna. The news on the radio suggested that it was a violent robbery, but what if it wasn't? *What if it was one of them?*

She sees them now through new eyes. She's never really had to consider it before. But now she thinks about the family taint – the streak of psychopathy that has run through the Merton family. She wonders if it lurks hidden inside one of them.

Perhaps she should be more careful, she thinks uneasily.

Chapter Fourteen

IN THE EARLY afternoon, Rose Cutter steps out of her storefront office on Water Street to grab a coffee. There's a coffee-maker in the office, but her nerves are on edge and she needs to get out for a brisk walk. She slips into her favourite café. There's a short line of people in front of her, and she waits impatiently. A television is on behind the counter of the coffee shop, the volume off, and while she waits for her latte, she sees the images of a mansion swarming with police and reads the silently scrolling text beneath. *Fred and Sheila Merton found murdered in their home.*

As she picks up her coffee to take back to the office, her hand is shaking, and she can't make it stop.

Finished with the house, Reyes and Barr canvass the area around the Mertons' home for anyone who might have seen something around the time of the murders. They approach the house on the east side of the Mertons', which is also at the end of a long drive. Reyes steps out of the car and notes that, from here, the Merton house can't be seen at all. The lots are enormous, the houses too far apart, and there are thick stands of trees between them.

Reyes rings the doorbell, while Barr surveys the property.

A woman answers the door. She's in her sixties and seems anxious at the sight of them. They show their badges and introduce themselves.

'I saw it on the news,' she says.

'Maybe we should sit down?' Reyes suggests.

She nods and leads them into a large living room. Then she takes a cell phone out of her sweater pocket and texts someone. She looks up at them. 'Just asking my husband to join us.' Soon enough a man comes down the stairs and into the living room. They introduce themselves as Edgar and June Sachs.

Reyes asks, 'Did you see or hear anything unusual on the night of Easter Sunday, or early Monday?'

Mrs Sachs looks at her husband and shakes her head. 'We can't see or hear the neighbours from here.'

Her husband agrees. 'It's very quiet around here, very private. I didn't notice anything.'

Mrs Sachs tilts her head for a second, as if she's just remembered something, and says, 'I did see a pickup truck go by that I didn't recognize. It went past here, away from the Mertons' place.'

'About what time was that?' Reyes asks.

'I don't know. We'd gone to bed. But I woke up because my legs were aching and got up to take some Advil. I happened to look out the front window of the bedroom and noticed the truck. I have no idea what time it was. Sorry.'

'What time did you go to bed?'

'Around ten. So it was sometime after that. I often wake up in the night and have to take something for my legs.'

'What did the truck look like?' Reyes asks.

'It was quite distinctive. Not really the kind of vehicle we see around here. I know what everybody drives and nobody has a truck like that. And we all use the same gardening service, with white trucks, and it wasn't one of those. It was dark – black, maybe, and it had yellow and orange flames along the side, like those old Hot Wheels toys.'

Reyes thanks them for their time, and he and Barr speak to the other neighbours. There's only one home on the other side of the Mertons' house, and that's where the road ends. There had been no visitors there that night, and no one had seen a truck at all. Nor had anyone in the other neighbouring houses. Reyes wonders briefly if the pickup was a figment of Mrs Sachs's imagination. One neighbour volunteered that he'd recognized Jenna Merton's Mini Cooper go past his driveway away from the Mertons' when he was out walking his dog on Easter night, just after eight o'clock. Barr makes a note. Reyes and Barr head back to the police station. It's mid-afternoon, and they're both starving. They stop at a favourite lunch spot and grab sandwiches and coffee on the way – ham and cheese for him and chicken salad for her.

Catherine watches out the large front window of Dan and Lisa's house as Audrey gets in her car and drives away. She takes a deep breath and then turns to face the rest of them.

They're all relieved that Audrey has gone, but their relief is tinged with worry. They look at one another in concern. Catherine leans back in her chair and closes her eyes for a moment, exhausted.

Jenna begins, 'You don't honestly believe her, do you? She's just saying that to try to guilt us into giving her some money.'

'I don't know,' Catherine says, lifting her head and opening her eyes. 'You know what Dad was like the last time we saw him. He was horrible to everyone. He said they were going to sell the house.' She adds, 'Maybe he did change his will in favour of Audrey. God, I hope not.'

'It's just the sort of thing he would do,' Dan says

angrily. 'Give half his money to someone we don't even like, just so that there's less for us.' He adds pettily, '*He* didn't even like her.'

'Well, I'm not buying it,' Jenna counters. 'She's making it up. If he'd just changed his will in her favour, he would have told us all about it at Easter dinner – and he would have enjoyed it.'

'Good point,' Catherine agrees. They had always been led to believe, in an offhand way, that the estate would be split equally among the three children, but what if things had changed? Catherine realizes she has no real certainty at all about what the wills contain. She observes the rest of them. 'Look at us,' she says after a moment. 'The way we're talking – as if all we care about is money.' That falls a little flat. She leans forward. 'Look, we have to pull together.' She turns toward Irena, who has been almost mute since Audrey arrived; before that, she'd given her account of what happened that morning at the crime scene. 'You said the police seemed to think it was a robbery that got violent, but they're still probably going to question all of us.' She looks at each one of them in turn, even giving her husband a warning glance. 'I suggest you keep your feelings about our father to yourselves. Let's try to look like a functional family. And try not to look too happy about the money.' She adds, 'And none of us speaks to the press, got it?' They all

102

nod agreement. 'Now, we have a funeral to sort out. And it has to be done properly.'

They spend the next hour coming up with a plan for the funeral. They would like it to be held at St Brigid's, the church her parents attended. They expect a large crowd. They will be laid to rest in the cemetery nearby, the one rich people use, the one with all the mausoleums.

Catherine will say a few words at the funeral service, as the eldest. They discuss where to invite people to go afterward. The obvious place would have been the family home – it's the only one of their places large enough for it, but it's an active crime scene, so it's out. They decide on the golf and country club their parents belonged to. They can do the food too. Catherine will call them and the church, first thing tomorrow.

Finally, she gets up to leave, feeling completely drained. It's hard to believe it's only four o'clock in the afternoon. She thinks she will remember the day her parents were discovered dead as one of the longest days of her life. But she must still talk to Ted when they get home. Where no one else can hear what they say.

Chapter Fifteen

AUDREY HAD DRIVEN away from the unpleasant scene at Dan's house directly to the home of her closest friend, Ellen Cutter. They've known each other for decades, from back when they both worked for her brother at Merton Robotics in the early days of the company. Ellen knew Fred well, having been his personal assistant for many years, although it was a long time ago.

When Audrey arrived, Ellen was expecting her – she'd already heard about the murders on the radio. They processed the shocking news over coffee in Ellen's sunny kitchen. They didn't know how Fred and Sheila had been killed, as that information hadn't yet been released. The family had told her they didn't know yet. It felt bizarre to Audrey to be doing something she did so often – having coffee at Ellen's – but discussing something so entirely out of the norm. Ellen was clearly shaken by the news of the murders. She already knew that Audrey was going to get half her brother's estate someday, because Audrey had confided in her. Unlike Fred's children, Ellen had been happy for her. But neither of them had expected it to happen quite so soon. Audrey might have said a bit too much about how this would change her life. But she couldn't help it if, even in the midst of such a tragedy, it gave her pleasure to discuss it.

They talked about taking a trip together, a cruise maybe, around Italy. Audrey's treat.

Lisa stands at the front door watching as the others leave. She sees Irena stop at Catherine's car, as Ted saunters to his own vehicle, farther away. He leans against it and lights up a cigarette. Jenna joins him and lights up, too, the only smokers in the family. Lisa turns her attention back to Catherine and Irena. They're talking in low voices. What are they saying that they couldn't say inside? She feels Dan behind her, can feel his warm breath on her neck.

Catherine glances back to the house, where Lisa and Dan are watching from the front door, and abruptly stops speaking to Irena and gets into her car. After that, they all drive off – Catherine first in her Volvo, Ted following in his sports car, Irena in her old Toyota. Jenna stays behind, at her own car now, to smoke another cigarette and scroll through her phone.

Lisa turns around suddenly and catches an odd expression on her husband's face, before it quickly vanishes. What was it? But now he's looking at her in his usual rueful way and she can't be sure.

He turns away from her, running a hand through his hair.

She follows him into the kitchen, pours herself another cup of coffee from the carafe. She turns around, her back to the counter, watching him closely. 'Are you all right?' she asks.

He sits down in one of the kitchen chairs, his elbows on the table, hands clasped tightly. 'I'm not sure.'

She thinks about how to put it. 'I know you had your issues with your father. But I also know how much you loved your mother. I can't imagine how difficult this must be.'

Lisa hasn't lost either of her parents yet, and when the time comes, she's sure it will be difficult. She has a good relationship with both of them. Dan's relationship with his parents was complicated. He's told her some stories from his childhood, and she's observed enough since she married him to feel no particular regret that Fred Merton is out of the picture. She's sad about Sheila, though – she liked her mother-in-law well enough. But Dan could never rely on her. Her love was always conditional. Couldn't she see how much that hurt her son?

Life has been so uncertain lately. But this changes things. And maybe Dan will finally be able to bury his parents and what they did to him.

She chews her bottom lip, still looking at him. She wonders if he will break down and cry; if he does, she will go to him, put her arms around him.

Instead, he stares into space. He looks . . . empty. She's never seen him this way before; it makes her uneasy.

She comes over and sits down at the table next to him. 'Dan,' she says, putting her hand on his arm, shaking it a little. He starts and focuses his eyes on hers.

'I keep seeing them,' he says. For a second his face twists.

'What do you mean?' She pulls back instinctively.

'I keep imagining them, Mom strangled, and Dad's throat slit, him stabbed over and over, like Irena said.' His voice holds a tremor. He turns his glazed eyes to her. 'Imagine how much that must hurt.'

She grasps his hand tightly on the table. She feels slightly sick. 'Try not to think about it,' she urges. 'You can't think about that. It's over. They're not feeling any pain now. We have to look forward. Things will be better now, for us.' She doesn't plan on saying it, it's not really appropriate, but it just slips out. 'Once you get your inheritance, we won't have to worry about money any more. Think how much better everything will be.' He nods silently. Encouraged, she leans forward a little and in a softer voice says, 'Maybe we can travel, like we've always wanted to. I know we never really could before, when you were working for your dad – but this could be a new beginning for us.'

He puts his other hand on top of hers and says, 'Yes, a new beginning.' He kisses her. It's a sweet moment; but he breaks off the kiss, sits back in his chair, and says, 'But –'

'But what?'

'What if Dad changed his will?' Dan says, looking worried now. 'We always thought the three of us got all of it in equal shares. What if Audrey gets half, like she says? Or what if I get nothing at all? After everything I've done, after everything I've put up with all these years?'

'Fred wouldn't do that,' she assures him. But it gives her a fright. *Would he, though?* She thinks back to that dreadful Easter dinner.

'And there will be an investigation,' Dan says. 'The police will come here, asking questions, digging into our family. It's going to be awful.'

He seems so agitated, Lisa thinks. 'You just have to get through it, Dan. You'll all get through it. And I'm here for you.'

But his face remains unsettled. 'I'm going to call Walter,' Dan says. 'I don't care about the optics.' He stands up and leaves the room.

A thought scurries across her mind, like a rat scuttling in a corner out of sight. Something that hasn't occurred to her until now. The night of the murders. He'd gone out again, afterward, for a drive. And he'd been gone a long time. She'd lain in bed, awake, waiting for him, but she eventually fell asleep. What if the police ask them about that?

The sound of the front door opening makes her jump. She exits the kitchen and sees Jenna in the hall. She hadn't left with the others after all. 'Dan's calling Walter about the will,' she says. Then she turns and hastens up the stairs toward Dan's office, Jenna quickly following.

Chapter Sixteen

TED IS ONLY moments behind Catherine, following in his own car. He's grateful for the time alone. There's so much to get his head around. Fred and Sheila dead. A murder investigation. His wife lying to the police. Why would she try to hide that she went back over there that night? Why wouldn't she just say so? Her parents were obviously fine when she left them.

So why doesn't she want anyone to know?

He parks in the driveway and lets himself in the house. Catherine is waiting for him in the living room, sitting on the sofa, her eyes downcast.

He stands still at the entry to the room and says, 'Catherine, what is it? What's going on?'

'Sit down,' she says.

He comes in and sits down on the sofa beside her, looking at her in concern.

'I – I think I might have made a mistake,' she

says. She's gripping her hands tightly; the composure she showed at Dan's house is deserting her. 'The detectives asked me if I had any contact with my parents after we left the dinner on Sunday night, and I told them no.'

'Why would you do that?' He doesn't understand.

'I don't know.' She shakes her head as if she can't understand it herself. 'It was a knee-jerk reaction. I just said no. I guess – I guess I didn't want them to see me as a suspect.'

He stands up now in consternation and looks down at her. 'Catherine – that's ridiculous. Why would they suspect you? It was a robbery.' She looks up at him, and she's more distraught than he's ever seen her.

She says, her voice rising, 'You weren't there when they told me. The way they looked at me, as if they were suspicious.' She starts talking faster, rushing her words. 'They're going to think it was one of the family, they're going to suspect all of us, sooner or later, because of the money. I didn't want them to know I went back over there that night – it would look . . . bad.'

He shakes his head. 'It doesn't look bad. You wanted to talk to your mom. You have to tell the police.'

'No, I don't.' She looks at him a bit wildly. 'I can't tell them now. Not after I lied to them!'

'What if they find out anyway?' he protests, genuinely worried now. 'That will just look worse.'

'So, what, I tell them I just *forgot* that I went over there that night? That it slipped my mind? Tell them that everything was fine, I spoke to Mom and left? What if they don't believe me?'

'Catherine! Why *wouldn't* they believe you? Think of what you're saying! You can't honestly think they would suspect you of murdering your own parents!'

She gets up then and walks nervously around the room. She finally turns to him and says, 'Irena told me something, at the car when we were leaving. She wanted to give me a heads-up.'

'What? What did she say?'

'She said the detectives seem to think it might be someone my parents knew.'

'Why would they think that?' he asks, concerned.

'She overheard them say they thought it looked *personal*.'

Ted says, 'She told us that they thought it was a robbery gone wrong.'

She pauses. 'She said they seem to be very interested in the inheritance.'

His mind, unbidden, turns automatically to Dan. Surely . . .

She fastens her eyes on him, and she looks deadly serious. 'I don't want those detectives to know I was there that night. And Dan and Jenna – they

112

can't know I went over there that night, that I kept it from the police.'

'Why not?'

'I don't trust them,' she says, averting her eyes.

After Audrey is gone, Ellen Cutter sits in the kitchen for a long while, staring at her cup of coffee, thinking about the murders. Now, she gets up and pours her cold coffee down the sink. It's so dreadful that the Mertons have been murdered that she can hardly come to grips with it. She's never known anyone who's been murdered before. It's something that happens to strangers on the news.

It's nice for Audrey, of course, that she's going to be rich. She didn't have to go on about it quite so much, though.

Ellen's mind turns to Catherine Merton, who is one of her daughter's closest friends. What a shock this must be for her and her siblings. They will all be wealthy now, although not quite as wealthy as they expected.

Ellen wonders if Rose has heard the news. She picks up the phone to call her.

At the Aylesford police station, Reyes and Barr establish a team to handle the Merton homicides. The two detectives will get some help from patrol division, but the investigation will fall mostly to them. It's not a big department. Reyes assigns a small team to search the area surrounding the Merton house for any sign of discarded bloody clothing from the killer, or the ligature used on Sheila Merton. They will gradually widen the search to include the nearby Hudson River, wooded areas, local dumpsters. They put out a police bulletin about the pickup truck they are trying to locate.

They review all the background information on the family they can find, but there isn't much. Fred Merton was an extremely successful businessman, and he and his company have been covered extensively in the media. But there's very little about the family. They seem to have been very private. Reyes wonders what secrets they might have.

Chapter Seventeen

REYES AND BARR get into Reyes's car and drive to one of the nicer parts of Aylesford, a suburb of doctors, lawyers, and executives, with large detached homes on tree-lined streets. It's upscale, but it's no Brecken Hill.

'Rich people,' Barr says. 'They never think they have enough. They always want more.'

'Know a lot of rich people, do you?' Reyes says, smiling.

'Not really, no,' she admits.

He pulls up on the street outside the home of Dan and Lisa Merton. It's a comfortable two-storey house of yellow brick, well maintained, as all the properties here are. A garden of shrubs and spring flowers runs along the front of the house beneath a large window looking into the living room.

Reyes and Barr walk up to the front door and

knock. The door is opened by a petite, attractive woman with brown hair and brown eyes.

'Lisa Merton?' Reyes asks.

She nods, looking apprehensive. Reyes produces his badge and says, 'I'm Detective Reyes, and this is Detective Barr. May we come in?' He can hear a television on somewhere.

'Yes, of course,' she says, drawing back and letting them in. She turns her head and calls, 'Dan!'

Dan Merton appears in the front hall. He's of medium height and build, with receding black hair. Very average-looking. Right behind him is a woman, probably in her mid-twenties, tall and slim and dressed all in black. She's rather striking.

Reyes holds up his badge once again and repeats the introductions. 'You're Dan Merton?' Dan nods.

'I'm Jenna Merton,' the other woman volunteers.

She doesn't look anything like her older sister, Reyes notes, who in contrast is quite conservative. He remembers the pearls around the older sister's throat, showing beneath the white doctor's coat. Jenna has a slash of purple in her black hair and dramatic eyeliner. There are no signs of that makeup being ruined by recent tears. 'May we sit down?' Reyes suggests.

'Of course,' Lisa says, flustered. She leads them all into the living room, where they each take a seat – Reyes and his partner in the armchairs, the other three sharing the sofa.

'I'm so sorry for your loss,' Reyes begins. He takes a moment to regard them carefully. Dan Merton seems tense. His sister less so, but she's watching him as carefully as he's watching her. 'We're investigating the murder of your parents,' Reyes begins.

Dan says quickly, 'We want you to catch whoever did this horrible thing as quickly as possible. I still can't believe it. I mean – we're all just devastated.'

Reyes notes the curious echo; that's what the cleaning lady had said.

'We just have a few questions,' Reyes says, 'for now. As I'm sure you know, we've already spoken briefly to your sister, Catherine.'

'Of course.' Dan waits, poised to answer, as if he's on a quiz show.

'Did your parents have any enemies that you know of?' Reyes asks, looking from Dan to Jenna and back again.

'Enemies?' Dan repeats nervously. 'No.'

'Please consider the question carefully,' Reyes says. 'Your father was a wealthy man, a successful businessman, I understand. Might he have angered someone?'

Dan shakes his head. 'My father's business was completely above board, detective. I would know – I worked there. I was practically his right-hand man. And besides, he was retired; he sold the business several months ago.'

'I see,' Reyes says. 'Do you know if anything was bothering either of your parents recently? Did they seem worried about anything?'

Dan shakes his head, his mouth turned down in a frown. 'Not that I know of.' He looks at his sister.

'How would I know?' she says, shrugging. 'I didn't see them that often.'

'It's just that your mother had recently started taking anti-anxiety medication,' Reyes says. They look back at him in apparent surprise. 'No idea why that might be?' Dan and Jenna shake their heads. 'The last time you saw them was for Easter dinner on Sunday, is that right?' Reyes asks.

'Yes,' Dan says. 'We were all there. Me and Lisa, Catherine and her husband, Irena, and Jenna and – what was his name again?'

'Jake,' Jenna says.

'What time did you leave that night?' Reyes asks.

Dan says, 'Catherine and Ted left first, around seven. Lisa and I were right behind them, and I saw Irena come out after us.'

'And you?' Reyes says, turning to Jenna.

'We left a couple of minutes later,' she says.

Reyes notes the lie. He knows she didn't leave until after eight o'clock. He lets it go, for now. 'Any of you see them or talk to them after that?' They shake their heads. 'And nothing struck you as being out of the ordinary that evening?' He adds, 'They

118

were likely murdered sometime later that night.' Nothing is said, but Reyes can feel something change in the room. He'd bet dollars to doughnuts *something* was off that night.

'Nothing happened at Easter dinner?' Barr presses.

She must sense it, too, Reyes thinks.

'No,' Dan says, frowning again, shaking his head. 'Just a regular Easter dinner. Turkey and pie.'

'Same as ever,' Jenna agrees.

Reyes glances at Lisa. She seems frozen in place, her gaze locked somewhere in the air between him and Barr.

Reyes lets a long silence stretch out until everyone but he and Barr is uncomfortable.

Dan says, 'Anyway, it said on the news that it was a robbery that turned violent – that their money and jewellery were stolen. Isn't that what it was?'

'That's one possibility,' Reyes says.

Then he asks them about the money.

Irena sits in her favourite armchair in her small bungalow as evening falls, her fat tabby cat on her lap, a second-hand Anthony Trollope novel open facedown and ignored on the arm of the chair. She can't concentrate on the book. She can't think about anything but Fred and Sheila, the human carnage on the kitchen floor, sticky with Fred's blood. She'd washed that floor too many times to

119

count over the years. The kids used to play on those tiles while she baked cookies.

What a good thing that we can't see the future.

She can't stop thinking about them, those children she brought up while Fred and Sheila couldn't be bothered. What will happen to them now? Of course the kids will be suspects. There's a lot of money at stake. As long as they all keep their mouths shut and don't start pitting themselves against each other, all might still be well. It's important that the detectives don't find out what things were really like in the Merton family.

It was always a dysfunctional household, but she stayed because the kids needed her. She had been there, watching over them, protecting them. Guiding them, trying to help them be better.

And now she has interfered with a murder scene.

Once they've seen the detectives to the door, Jenna, Dan, and Lisa stare at each other for a moment without speaking, as if nobody wants to be the first to voice an opinion. They need to dissect what just happened. They return to the living room.

'God,' Dan says, striding across the room. 'I need a drink.' He pours himself a glass of whiskey at the credenza that serves as a bar. He turns his head to ask, 'Anybody want one?'

Jenna and Lisa both say no. He comes back to

the sofa and slumps onto it, and Lisa sits down beside him.

Jenna throws herself into an armchair – the one recently vacated by Detective Reyes – and says, watching her brother, 'They have to do their job, you know. They have to ask questions.'

'Fuck!' Dan says.

'What's wrong, Dan?' Jenna asks.

'They obviously think it's one of us. All that about how much money Dad was worth and who gets it.' When he picks up his glass his hand is trembling slightly.

Jenna glances at Lisa – she's noticed it too.

'They're probably going to think it was me,' Dan says. 'It won't matter that I'm completely innocent! Everyone knows how Dad sold the business out from under me, ruining my life. They'll find out soon enough. And they'll find out –' He stops suddenly.

'Find out what, Dan?' Jenna asks. She darts another look at Lisa, whose face is pale.

He hesitates and then admits, 'That we don't have any money.'

Jenna is surprised to hear this. She studies him for a moment before saying, 'Well, you're unemployed. Of course times are tough right now. Anyone would understand that. You can't actually be *broke*. You must have savings. They're not going to think you're a murderer.'

He shakes his head, agitated now. 'It's worse than you think. Before Dad sold the company and I lost my job, I made an investment. Most of our savings are tied up in it and I can't get the money out for another six months. I've tried. And the rest we've spent, to live on.' He adds, 'We've been living off credit cards.' Then he takes another drink, finishing off his glass and slamming it down onto the coffee table.

Lisa seems to shrink deeper into the sofa, and Jenna notices that she doesn't look well.

Dan turns to his wife miserably and says, 'I'm sorry. I'm such a fuckup.' Then he clutches his head in his hands.

Chapter Eighteen

ON WEDNESDAY MORNING at 9:00 a.m., Aylesford Police hold a press conference about the Merton murders. It's a sunny spring day, and it's held outside, in front of the station.

Interest is strong. Not only the news outlets are present, but many people who live in the area have come in person to hear what he has to say. Reyes suspects that they are hoping to learn that an arrest is imminent. They're going to be disappointed.

He steps up to the podium and waits for the photography to die down and for the crowd to settle. Then he says, 'Thank you for coming. I am Detective Eric Reyes of Aylesford Police. We are conducting an investigation into the murders of Fred and Sheila Merton in their home in Brecken Hill. Their bodies were discovered there yesterday. At this time, we appeal to the public for any information leading to the arrest and conviction of the person or persons responsible for the murders of Fred and Sheila Merton. In particular, we are interested in speaking to anyone with knowledge of a pickup truck, dark in colour with orange or yellow flames on the side panels, that was seen driving away from the direction of the Mertons' property on the night of Sunday, April twenty-first.' He takes a breath and continues. 'We are encouraging members of the public to call the tip line.' He recites the number slowly and repeats it. 'We will not rest until the perpetrators of this awful crime are brought to justice. Thank you.'

Reyes steps away from the podium. The reporters start calling out questions, but Reyes turns his back and walks inside the station.

Audrey Stancik watches the press conference on television. It reveals precious little. There was more information in the *Aylesford Record* that morning. Some enterprising reporter had found out that the bodies were discovered by Irena, and that Sheila was strangled and Fred was stabbed numerous times and his throat slit. So now she knows. Reading that, Audrey found herself shaken. The house had been ransacked and valuables were missing. There were no further details. When Audrey had been at Dan's the day before, no one had told her that Irena had found them, and how they'd been killed. And Irena was *right there*. She'd had to get it from the newspaper.

Audrey gets in her car and drives downtown to see her brother's lawyer, Walter Temple. She doesn't have an appointment, but she's sure he won't turn her away, not under the circumstances. She simply can't wait another moment.

Walter sees her right away. They've known each other for many years. They greet each other solemnly. He tells her how sorry he is about Fred and Sheila. But the attorney seems noticeably ill at ease, and it makes Audrey nervous.

She summons her courage and says, 'Fred came to see you last week about his will, didn't he?'

She's expecting a quick confirmation, but Walter averts his eyes and starts straightening the edges of the papers on his desk. She's worrying in earnest now. He clears his throat and says, 'I was away all last week unexpectedly. I didn't see him.'

She feels the blood drain from her upper body; Walter's face swims in front of her eyes. 'What?'

'Apparently he wanted to see me, but as I was unavailable, he made an appointment for this week – he was supposed to see me today, at ten o'clock. But he died before . . .' His voice trails off delicately.

Audrey sags in the chair, all her hopes shipwrecked. 'But that can't be,' she protests. 'He promised he would do it last week.'

'Yes, he did try to come in, but I was away on business. I'm sorry.'

'Maybe he saw another lawyer?'

'Apparently not, no.'

'He was going to change his will,' she says, her voice rising, all her plans crashing to pieces around her. 'He promised me. He was going to change it so that I got half and his kids shared the other half. And if I died before him, my share was to go to my daughter.'

Walter looks back at her in obvious discomfort, but it's nothing to what she's feeling. 'I'm truly sorry, Audrey. But he died before he could make any changes to his will. He couldn't have known what was going to happen –'

She sits there stunned, not moving, disbelief turning to rage. It was her one shot at having something for herself, and for her daughter. And now it's gone, just like that. Just like Fred. And now all his hard-earned money is going straight to his three spoiled, undeserving kids. 'She knew!' Audrey cries.

'What?' the attorney says, startled.

'*Sheila* knew. She knew Fred was going to change his will to give me half. She was there – and she didn't like it. She never liked me.' He's clearly uncomfortable, wanting no part of this. 'You know what must have happened, don't you?' she says. He meets her eyes warily. 'She told the kids what their father was going to do. And one of them murdered them both before he could do it.' She adds bitterly, 'And they never saw it coming.'

'That's absurd, Audrey,' Walter says, turning pale.

She gets up abruptly and leaves the office without another word. Descending in the elevator, in her fury, she's certain. Sheila must have told one of them. Which one? Or maybe she told all of them. And one of them murdered Fred and Sheila without a shred of regret.

She's going to figure out who if it's the last thing she ever does. And they will pay.

Reyes and Barr drive to the medical examiner's office, not far from the police station. He parks in the lot and they enter the low brick building.

The two detectives make their way to the autopsy room. The sight of the gleaming metal counters below the high row of windows, the bodies resting on the matching metal tables, the awful smell – Reyes never really gets used to it. He slips a cough drop into his mouth. He glances at Barr, but she seems unbothered. Sometimes he wonders if she has any sense of smell at all, or if it's impaired somehow.

One of the forensic pathologists, Sandy Fisher, is standing over a body, garbed in full protective gear. 'Good morning, detectives,' she says.

They've come right in the middle of her work on Fred Merton, Reyes notes. The body cavity is still open, and there's a stomach sitting on the weigh scales. He turns away, focusing on the covered corpse farther down the room, behind the pathologist. That must be Sheila Merton.

'I've finished with her,' Sandy says, nodding over her shoulder, 'but I still have a lot to do on this one.'

She steps away from the open corpse and beckons them over to the other body. The pathologist's assistant pulls down the cover from Sheila Merton's corpse to reveal her upper body. 'Pretty straightforward,' Sandy begins, as they stare at the unfortunate woman. 'Ligature strangulation, most likely with something very smooth, like an electrical cord.'

'And there's no sign of it anywhere, or of it having come from anywhere inside the house,' Reyes says thoughtfully. 'So whoever killed her likely had it with him. There was no sign of a break-in – he might have known it would probably be Sheila who would answer the door.' He pauses for a moment, gazing at Sheila Merton's dead face. 'Someone showed up on that doorstep wearing gloves, thick socks and no shoes, holding something in his hands to strangle her with. Then, when she was out of the way, he grabbed the knife in the kitchen and waited for Fred.'

Barr nods thoughtfully. 'Possibly someone who knew them, knew the house.'

Reyes asks, 'Time of death?'

'Well, you know that's always just a rough esti-mate,' Sandy says. 'But my best guess is somewhere between ten o'clock Sunday evening and six o'clock Monday morning.' She adds, 'I'll know more when I've finished with him. But I can confirm that the knife from the kitchen block was indeed the murder weapon.'

Chapter Nineteen

BACK AT THE station, Reyes and Barr learn that none of the security cameras at the Merton house were working. The cleaning lady was right. The safe has been opened, and seemed undisturbed. There was no jewellery inside. The preliminary forensic report offers little new information to help them. Reyes scans it quickly. There are numerous sets of finger-prints in the house, especially in the kitchen, which you would expect after a dinner party. Prints will be obtained from each of the family members and Irena today for exclusionary purposes – perhaps there will be a strange print that they can't place, but Reyes is not expecting it. The killer was obviously very care-ful. They'll have to track down Jake as well.

Reyes grabs his jacket off the back of a chair and says to Barr, 'Come. We're going to talk to Fred and Sheila Merton's lawyer.'

They drive the short distance downtown. It comes as no surprise that Fred Merton used one of the top firms in Aylesford. Walter Temple is busy when they arrive, but a flash of their badges does the trick. 'He'll see you now,' the receptionist says after only a couple of minutes and leads them to his office.

Walter Temple extends his hand to each of them as they introduce themselves and offers them each a seat before sitting down behind his desk. 'I imagine you're here about Fred and Sheila,' he says.

Reyes nods. 'Yes. We're investigating their murders.'

'I'm just gutted by this,' the attorney says, visibly distressed. 'Fred was a friend, as well as a long-time client.'

'What can you tell us about him?' Reyes asks.

'Fred Merton was a hugely successful businessman. He made a fortune in robotics, then sold his company – Merton Robotics – for another fortune last year. His net worth, at the time of his death, after taxes, was roughly twenty-six million dollars.'

Reyes says, 'That's a great deal of money.'

'It is,' the lawyer agrees. 'Sheila leaves about six million as well.'

'Did Fred Merton, or his wife, Sheila, have any enemies that you know of?'

The lawyer leans back in his chair and averts his

eyes, looking down at the blotter on his desk. 'No, I don't think so. They were well liked, respected. Fred could be very charming.' He lifts his eyes and adds, 'They were good people. My wife and I dined with them regularly.'

'Did you notice anything different about either of them recently? Did they seem worried about anything? Mention anything unusual?'

The attorney shakes his head and frowns. 'Not that I noticed. But you should ask my wife. She's much more perceptive about these things, although she never mentioned anything to me. She and Sheila were close. My wife – Caroline – she's at home, if you'd like to speak to her.' He writes out his address for them and hands it to Reyes.

Reyes asks, 'Who inherits the Merton fortune?'

'I suppose I can tell you that,' the attorney replies. 'Sheila's wealth goes equally to their three children. Under Fred's will, there are a couple of specific bequests, but the bulk of the estate is to be equally divided among his children.'

'What were the specific bequests?'

'One million to Fred's sister, Audrey Stancik. One million to the long-time housekeeper, Irena Dab-rowski.' The attorney clears his throat. 'There's something else you should know,' he says. 'There are four children named in Fred's will, not three. Fred included a child he had fathered out of wedlock as one of the equal beneficiaries. A woman by the name of Rose Cutter.' He adds, 'This is going to come as a rather unpleasant surprise to the legitimate children. Probably a nice surprise for her, though. I don't think she has any idea.' He asks, 'Would you be able to put off talking to her until the other children get the news from me? That will probably be early next week, after the funeral.'

'I think we can do that,' Reyes says, beginning to rise from his seat.

'There is one other odd thing,' the lawyer says, and Reyes sinks down again. 'Dan Merton called me yesterday afternoon. Fred's sister, Audrey – apparently she was over at Dan's house yesterday with the family after the news of their deaths got out. She told them that Fred had changed his will to give her half.' He chews his lip and adds, 'She was just here this morning, and told me the same thing. She was quite adamant that he'd meant to do it last week.'

Reyes raises his eyebrows, sceptical.

'I know, it sounds unlikely, but I was called away suddenly all last week, and when I got back, I noticed that he'd tried to see me. When I was unavailable, my secretary made an appointment for him to see me this week. That appointment was to be this morning, at ten o'clock. I guess we'll never know for sure.'

*

After the detectives leave, Walter remains at his desk, reflecting uneasily on the situation. He's rather disturbed by what Audrey had said. And the detectives being here – well, he's a corporate and estate attorney, he's not accustomed to dealing with detectives conducting a murder investigation.

He hadn't exactly been forthcoming with the detectives, not wanting to speak ill of the dead. He hadn't said anything that was untrue. Fred could certainly be charming, and he didn't have any enemies that Walter knew about, but he did have an edge to him. Fred wasn't always a fine fellow.

He hadn't told the detectives everything Audrey had said, either – accusing Fred's own children. It was too awful to mention. Too awful to imagine.

Chapter Twenty

WALTER'S WIFE, CAROLINE Temple, is visibly upset
about the violent murder of the Mertons. She insists
on serving tea to the detectives in proper china
cups, as if to pretend everything is normal. But
Reyes understands – there's nothing normal about
being interviewed by homicide detectives in your
living room for a woman like Caroline Temple.

'How well did you know Sheila and Fred?' Reyes
asks.

'We knew them socially for many years – decades,
actually.'

'Your husband said you and Sheila were close.'

'Did he? Well, it probably looked that way to
him. But we weren't particularly close. She wasn't
one to bare her soul. Walter was friends with Fred,
but to be honest, I didn't care for him.'

'Why didn't you like Fred?' Barr asks.

She hesitates a moment and says, 'You know men.' She gives an apologetic glance at Reyes. 'It's all about business and golf. They don't really get into the personal stuff. But Sheila told me things that made me dislike him.'

'Such as?' Reyes asks.

'I don't think he was an easy man to live with. He had a mean streak.' She takes a sip of her tea. 'I mean – the way he sold the business out from under his son!' She tells them all about it, how hard Dan had worked, how upset he'd been, how he hasn't found subsequent employment. How Fred told them he did it so that Dan wouldn't run his business into the ground. 'People don't treat their kids that way. Sheila wasn't happy about it, I can tell you that.'

'Did she try to change his mind?' Reyes asks.

'Nobody could change Fred's mind. He was stubborn. I doubt she even tried. She never stood up to him.'

Barr asks, 'Did Sheila seem particularly worried lately?'

'Actually, yes,' Caroline says. 'She told me that she'd started taking medication for anxiety.'

'Did she tell you why?' Barr presses.

Caroline shakes her head. 'No. I tried to get her to open up, but Sheila – she'd offer a bit and then withdraw. Stiff upper lip and everything. Me, I'm a puddle when I'm upset.' Caroline pauses, as if remembering something. 'She did tell me, the last time I saw her, that the kids weren't going to be happy about their father's will – that it wasn't going to be what they expected.'

Reyes flicks a glance at Barr. 'How so?'

'I don't know. She wouldn't tell me any more than that. As I said, she was rather private.' She stops to pour more tea and then continues. 'The kids didn't get along with their father, and it seemed to be getting worse. None of them liked him – she told me that. Fred seemed to enjoy mistreating them. The only thing he cared about was himself.' She leans forward, about to impart something important. 'Between you and me,' Caroline says, 'I'm pretty sure Fred Merton was a psychopath. Apparently lots of very successful businessmen are.'

Ted hasn't gone into work at his dental practice this morning. He's stayed home to offer emotional and practical support to his wife as she arranges a double funeral. Catherine is constantly on the phone, and people are coming to their door, offering condolences and leaving food. There are so many interruptions that Catherine is complaining that it's hard to get anything done. Her laptop is open on the coffee table to catch any news updates on the murders.

Ted tries to help as much as he can, as he studies

his wife and frets about what to do. He's certain the police will want to formally interview her, and possibly him, as well. What the hell is he going to tell them? If he can't get Catherine to change her mind, does he lie too? Say she was home with him all night? He doesn't like it. He thinks she should come clean with the detectives.

But she's already lied to them. Such a stupid thing to do – and he's angry at her for it. He doesn't understand her reasons. From what he can see, if the detectives think it's one of the adult children, Dan is the most obvious suspect. He was behaving a little strangely yesterday. But one could argue that Catherine is behaving strangely too.

He thinks about the phone call. She called her mother's cell phone on Sunday night, from her own cell. There will be a record of it. Won't they ask her about that? They will see the time of the unanswered call and might think her parents were dead already, when Catherine and he both know that they were alive for some time after that. All of this runs through his mind as he stands on the door-step accepting a covered dish from family friends.

He sees Jenna's car pull up on the street while he manages some pleasantries to the well-wishers. They are beginning to leave as Jenna reaches the door, but then they have to hug her and offer their sympathies all over again.

'How's she doing?' Jenna asks him when they're finally gone.

She means Catherine. Ted looks at Jenna with new eyes, wondering why his wife is afraid to trust her. What history do they have? 'Okay, considering,' Ted says. 'I'm glad you're here. How are you doing?'

'Better than Dan.' She walks past him and enters the house, and Ted follows her into the living room.

'We should talk,' she says, glancing between him and Catherine.

'What's wrong?' Catherine asks, alert to trouble.

'The detectives came by Dan's place yesterday after you left, while I was still there. They asked us a bunch of questions. It was fine, but Dan seemed to fall apart after they left.' She sits down beside Catherine on the sofa and says after a moment, 'Do you think he could have done it?'

Ted watches as Catherine averts her eyes and says, 'I don't know.'

Ted swallows, feels slightly sick.

'Me neither,' Jenna admits. There's a long, fraught silence. Finally Jenna says, 'I think he's losing his grip. He seems convinced they're going to think it was him. Because of Dad selling the business. And – did you know that he's got no money?'

Catherine looks at her now and nods wearily.

'You knew? I didn't. He says the police are going

to come after him and they're going to go into it with blinders on and convince themselves that he did it, and they won't be able to see anything else.'

Ted clears his throat and suggests, 'Maybe he should get a lawyer?'

Catherine turns to him and nods. 'Maybe. In the meantime, we say nothing.' She turns to Jenna and looks her in the eyes. 'Okay?'

Jenna nods. 'Okay.'

'You didn't tell them about what happened at Easter dinner, did you?' Catherine asks.

'Of course not.'

'Good.' She seems to relax a little. Then Catherine says, a furrow in her brow, 'Dan isn't wrong to be worried. Yesterday, as we were leaving his place, Irena told me she thinks the police might not believe it was a robbery at all. They might suspect it was one of us.'

'Why didn't she say that to all of us?' Jenna asks.

'She probably didn't want to upset Dan.'

Ted watches Jenna nod. 'I imagine Dan has told you the good news?' Jenna asks.

'What good news?' Catherine says.

'He called Walter yesterday, after you left, before the police arrived.'

'What?' Catherine says sharply.

Ted can tell by her tone that Catherine isn't happy about it.

'Dad didn't change his will to benefit Audrey. He'd made an appointment, but he hadn't done it before he was killed. So there's that.' She adds, with a smirk, 'I wonder if Audrey knows yet?'

Chapter Twenty-one

JENNA HAS OFFERED to visit the florist, mostly to get out of the house. She wants to get away from Catherine. Something about the way Catherine takes charge of everything irritates her, even though Jenna certainly doesn't want to take on management of the funeral arrangements herself.

As Jenna drives downtown to order the flowers – from the same florist that used to deliver fresh bouquets to her parents' house on a regular basis – her thoughts turn to what Irena told Catherine. So the detectives already suspect it was one of them. Because of the inheritance, obviously. But is there something more? What did Irena hear, exactly? She decides that after her business at the florist, she will pay Irena a visit and ask her herself.

The bell on the door to the flower shop tinkles when Jenna enters. Inside, she is assaulted by a riot of colour and the sweet, pleasant smell of fresh plants. She spends some time choosing a number of arrangements for the front of the church – lilies and roses. She knows Catherine will be pleased. When she's finished, Jenna leaves the shop and is surprised to spot Audrey across the street, staring at her. She wonders if Audrey is following her, whether she already knows she's not going to be rich after all.

Jenna gives Audrey a smile and a flippant wave, then turns her back on her.

At the station, Reyes and Barr are digging through background information on the Mertons' adult children. Catherine and her husband, Ted, are quite well off – but they'll be in another league entirely with the inheritance.

Details of Dan Merton's financial situation reveal signs of desperation, however. He has not worked in six months – since his father sold his company. He and his wife, who doesn't appear to have a job either, must have been living on savings. They have recently been using new credit cards to pay the minimums on other credit cards that are maxed out. His parents' deaths could not have come at a better time, Reyes thinks cynically.

The youngest, Jenna, seems to live from month to month, relying mostly on the generous allowance provided by her parents, occasionally selling some pieces of her art for modest amounts. There are no signs of any recent problems she might have had with her parents. But she'd lied about when she and her boyfriend had left the house on Easter Sunday. Why?

Who he finds most interesting right now is Irena Dabrowski, the cleaning lady. She cleaned the knife to protect someone. It was rather foolish of her, but she wouldn't have been thinking clearly. Obviously she thinks the murders were committed by someone close to Fred and Sheila, someone she cares about, most likely one of the kids.

He wants to know why.

Irena puts down the phone, unhappy. She has been asked to come to the police station to answer a few questions. There's an unpleasant surge of adrenaline coursing through her body.

She notices Jenna's car drive up as she locks her bungalow behind her.

'Irena!' Jenna calls, getting out of her car and approaching her. 'Do you have a minute?'

'I'm on my way out,' Irena says, as Jenna reaches her and gives her a brief hug.

'Where?'

'One of those detectives just called me; they want to ask me some questions.'

'What are you going to tell them?' Jenna asks bluntly.

'Nothing,' Irena replies. 'I have nothing to tell them. Why would I?'

'Good.' Jenna studies her. 'I was over at Catherine's this morning,' she says. 'She said you told her that the police might suspect one of the family. What did they say, exactly?'

Irena shifts her eyes away. She doesn't want to talk about this right now. 'It's just – they made a big deal about the money.'

'Of course they're going to make a big deal about the money,' Jenna reassures her. 'But that doesn't mean anything. It was probably a robbery.'

'I heard them say that Fred and Sheila might have known their killer.' Irena feels dizzy, saying this to Jenna.

Jenna looks at her intently. 'Why do they think that?'

'They think Sheila must have opened the door to whoever it was, and it was late at night.'

'So? That was Mom for you, she'd open the door anytime, to anyone, you know that.'

Irena nods. 'But it was so violent.' She stops there. She doesn't want to describe it, doesn't want to relive it. 'They thought it might be – personal – somebody they knew.'

Jenna seems to consider this information.

Irena says, 'I have to go.'

'Come back to Catherine's as soon as you're done and tell us what they say,' Jenna says.

'All right.'

'Irena?' Jenna says as Irena turns away. She turns back. 'Catherine and I are worried about Dan.'

Chapter Twenty-two

DAN IS IN the garage tinkering. Despite his education and his executive ambitions, he actually likes getting his hands dirty, fixing things. He likes to keep busy, his mind occupied. Right now, he has the ride-on mower up on a hoist and he's checking the blades. He loves the comforting smell of the garage, the oil on the cement floor near his head, even the old grass stuck to the mower blades, but it's not enough to keep his mind off everything that's happened.

He can't stop thinking about the detectives who were in his house late yesterday afternoon with their questions and their insinuations. He knows what they're thinking. What worries him most, right now, is the opinion they formed of him. How did he come across to them? Did he look as agitated as he felt? Did he look as if he had a guilty conscience?

Lisa is the only one he can talk to about this, the only one he can trust completely. He's afraid to ask Jenna; he's afraid of what she might say.

'I know this is difficult,' Lisa said quietly to him in bed the night before, 'but they're not going to think it was you.'

'What if they do?' he whispered. He could feel panic twisting in his guts.

She looked at him, her brown eyes wide. The lights were off but a faint glow from the moon filtered into the room. 'Dan, you went out again that night, after we came back from your parents'. Where did you go?'

He swallowed and said, 'I just went for a drive. Like I always do.'

'Where?'

'I don't know. I don't remember. Just around. I needed to clear my head. You know I like to drive when I have a lot on my mind.'

'When did you get back?'

'I didn't check the time. Why would I? It was late, you were asleep.' He knew he sounded defensive. She must have been asleep, he told himself, if she didn't know.

'The police are going to question us. We have to get our story straight.'

She was offering – was she offering? – to lie for him. 'What?'

'I mean – I think you should tell them you were home all night, with me. And I'll back you up.'

He nodded, grateful. 'Okay.' This was something that had been bothering him. She'd solved this problem for him, and he hadn't even had to ask. A small relief.

She touched his face with both hands. 'You need to relax. You didn't kill them. No matter what you felt about your father, I know you're a good man.' She looked deeply into his eyes. 'You could *never* do something like that.' She gave him a little smile and kissed him briefly on the lips. 'Everything's going to be all right. And when this is all over, you'll get your inheritance, and we can put all of this behind us.'

Now Dan stares up into the darkness of the mower blades. He tries to think about the money. The freedom he will have. He tries to imagine a bright future.

Audrey fumes in her car in the parking lot in front of the police station, her hands clenching the steering wheel. She thinks of that smile on Jenna's face outside the flower shop. They must know by now that Fred didn't change his will. She'd like to kick something, but it's hard to do that when you're sitting in the driver's seat. She thinks about getting out and kicking her own tyres, but she doesn't want to draw attention to herself. Her breathing is fast and shallow and she's fighting tears – she still can't believe it. To have something she'd counted on snatched away like that – just because Walter was away that week. She's absolutely enraged.

But no, that's not right. She hasn't had wealth beyond her wildest dreams snatched away from her *because Walter was away.* It's because Fred was murdered, in cold blood, before he could see Walter, and there's fuck all she can do about it now. She's pretty sure she knows why. She just wants to know who.

The promised money is gone. It's going to go to those bloody kids. She can taste the bitterness in her mouth. She's always wanted to be rich. That's what growing up in poverty does to you. Fred managed it, she didn't. This was her last chance.

Audrey wants to know who murdered Fred and Sheila. She wants to know who, exactly, has screwed her out of millions of dollars.

She's been sidelined by the family, shut out. They aren't going to tell her what's going on. As soon as she arrived at Dan's house yesterday, they'd all clammed up.

The police seem mostly concerned about this truck. She hopes the detectives don't waste a lot of time on that. Of course valuables were taken – the murderer would disguise it as a robbery. They're not going to make it obvious. But thieves don't slit a person's throat and stab them countless times. Whoever killed her brother clearly hated him.

She sits outside the police station now, watching to see if any of the family are going in for questioning. Surely they would be formally interviewed? Surely the day after the bodies were discovered is not too soon. She keeps her keen eyes trained on the police station, wondering if she'd missed anything already.

After a while, she sees a familiar woman walking up the front steps of the station. Irena has arrived.

Detective Reyes watches Irena Dabrowski settle into her chair. They're in one of the interview rooms, bare but for a table and chairs. Barr is beside him, and she offers Irena water, which she declines.

Irena's face is lined; her brown hair, pulled back in a short ponytail, is greying. Her hands are strong and rough-looking, devoid of rings, nails short and unpainted. A cleaner's hands.

Reyes sits, taking his time. He says to her, 'Thank you for coming in. You're here voluntarily, of course. You can leave at any time.'

She nods mutely, pulling her hands into her lap below the table where he can't see them.

'Now, you were the live-in nanny at the Mertons' house many years ago.'

'Yes, I told you that.'

'How many years were you the live-in nanny?'

She appears to think. 'I started soon after Catherine was born, so about thirty-two years ago. Dan came along two years later. And Jenna another four years after that. I lived in the house until Jenna started school, so altogether, probably about twelve years.'

'So you know them all pretty well,' Reyes says mildly.

'Yes, I told you – they're like my own family.'

'And are you still close to them?'

'Yes, of course. But I don't see them as much as I once did.'

Reyes asks, 'Would you say you were closer to the children or to the parents?'

She looks as if the question has made her uncomfortable. 'The children, I suppose,' she answers.

Reyes waits for her to say more. Silence is a great tool. He watches her think.

'Fred and Sheila were my employers – they kept me at arm's length, in a way.' She smiles a little. 'Children don't do that. And they were all good, affectionate children.'

'Were there any problems in the family?' Reyes asks.

'Problems?' she repeats.

And right away, he knows there were problems,

and he wants to know what they were. 'Yes, problems.'

She shakes her head. 'Not really. I mean, nothing out of the ordinary.'

'We know that Fred Merton had a falling-out with his son, Dan,' Reyes says. 'What can you tell us about that?'

'It wasn't a falling-out, really. Fred got an exceptionally good offer for his company that he felt he couldn't refuse, so he sold it. He was all about making the right business decision.' She presses her thin lips together. 'I know Dan was very disappointed.'

'How did the girls get along with their parents?' Reyes asks.

'Very well,' Irena says.

'Did anything unusual happen at that Easter dinner?'

She shakes her head. 'No, not at all.'

'Why did everyone leave so quickly?'

'I'm sorry?'

Reyes knows that she's trying to buy time. 'Catherine and her husband and Dan and his wife and you all left within a couple of minutes of each other.'

She shrugs. 'It was time to go, that's all.'

'And you didn't stay to clean up? Wouldn't that be expected?'

She bristles. 'She'd given it to me as a holiday.

They invited me to Easter dinner. She didn't expect me to stay and clean up.'

Reyes sits back in his chair and gives her a long, level gaze. 'You seem very protective of the Merton kids,' he suggests. She doesn't reply. 'Maybe we should go over it again – what happened when you found the bodies.' He listens as Irena describes her discovery of the bodies the previous morning. When she's finished, Reyes says, 'I think you've left something out.'

'I'm sorry?' she says again.

He watches her face flush slightly. He says, 'The bit about how you picked up the murder weapon off the floor, cleaned it at the kitchen sink, and put it back in the knife block.'

Chapter Twenty-three

IRENA HAS GONE quite still, and he knows he has hit the mark.

'I didn't,' she says, but it's a weak attempt.

He leans forward then, closing in on her, his arms on the table. 'We know you did. The forensic evidence shows it. The blood had dried around the knife on the floor for at least twenty-four hours. Your footprints led right past the body to the sink. The knife was scrubbed clean and put back in the knife block. But we know it was the murder weapon.' She sits unmoving, like an animal aware of a predator, her hands in her lap. 'The question I have is why did you do that?'

She becomes flustered. 'I don't know why. I was in shock. I saw the carving knife on the floor. I recognized it. It's been in the family for decades.

I just picked it up and washed it and put it back. It was habit, I guess.'

Reyes smiles at her. 'And we're supposed to believe that?'

'I can't help what you believe,' she says.

'I'll tell you what I believe,' Reyes says slowly. 'I believe you arrived there, found Sheila dead and Fred awash in blood, saw the carving knife on the floor, picked it up, put on the pair of rubber gloves we found under the sink, and scrubbed the knife thoroughly in case the killer had left prints on it. Because you wanted to protect the person who did it. Which makes us think that you believe that the killer is one of the children.'

'No,' she protests.

'We could charge you, you know.'

She remains silent, staring at him.

He leans back in his chair again, giving her some room. 'Is there anything you want to tell us now?'

'No.'

'The thing is,' Reyes says, 'whoever the killer was, he or she was quite careful and wore gloves. You needn't have interfered with the murder scene after all.' She looks back at him, her face rigid. 'Thanks for the tip, though.'

As she rises to leave, Barr says, 'We'll just get your fingerprints before you go – we need them for exclusionary purposes. We have to do everybody.'

Irena exits the police station and makes her way to her car as if she can't get there fast enough. Once she is in the car, though, she sits still for a few minutes, gathering her thoughts. She takes deep breaths, resting her head back against the headrest. She closes her eyes. *What has she done?*

Finally, she starts the car with trembling hands and drives to Catherine's house. This is going to be difficult, and she's dreading it.

When she arrives, she sees that both cars are in the driveway and Jenna's is parked on the street in front. There's no sign of Dan's vehicle. She gets out of the car and approaches the familiar front door.

It's Ted who answers her knock, his handsome face grave.

'Come in, Irena,' he says. 'Jenna said you'd be coming over.'

Catherine stands up when Irena enters the living room; Jenna is already on her feet, over by the window. All three of them look at her expectantly. She is the first to be interviewed by police at the station; they want to know what happened. They know they will be next. The room is charged with tension.

Catherine gives her a quick hug and says, 'Come sit down and tell us everything.'

No sooner is Irena seated in an armchair than she blurts out, 'I'm sorry.'

They all look at her in alarm.

She tells them what she did with the knife, and that the police know, and watches their faces flood with confusion, then disbelief.

Catherine says, 'Why? Why would you do that?' She seems astonished and angry.

When Irena can't find the words, Jenna answers for her, blunt as always. 'Because she thinks it was one of us.'

Irena can't meet anyone's eyes. She sits in silence, staring at the floor.

For a moment everyone seems to forget to breathe. At last Catherine says, 'Irena, surely you don't believe that.'

Irena is silent. She doesn't know what to say.

'So,' Jenna prods, 'which one of us do you think did it?'

Irena evades the question. She looks at each of the sisters in turn, wanting to be forgiven, knowing that she won't be. 'I shouldn't have done it. Now the police seem to think it was one of you kids. I'm sorry.'

Catherine, Jenna, and Ted all stare back at her in dismay.

'Thanks a lot,' Jenna says.

*

Audrey, from her vantage point in the parking lot in front of the station, had watched Irena hurry to her car, looking more upset than when she arrived. Then she'd sat there for a long time, as if she were shaken and trying to pull herself together. Finally she drove off, leaving Audrey desperate to know what had happened inside the station.

Now, Audrey badly needs to pee but she doesn't want to leave her post in case she misses something. But it's not long until she sees Dan's car enter the parking lot. He pulls up near the entrance. He gets out of the car, alone. He doesn't glance her way or notice her at the back of the lot. Once she sees him go up the steps and into the station, she knows she's got a bit of time. She glances at her watch, gets out of the car, and walks quickly to a doughnut shop down the street. She uses the bathroom, buys herself a chocolate doughnut and a coffee, and gets back to her car in the space of ten minutes.

They bring Dan Merton into the same interview room they had used to question Irena a short time before. He's dressed in clean jeans, an open-necked shirt, and a navy blazer. He wears an expensive-looking watch. He looks like he comes from money – he has that careless way with expensive things, Reyes thinks, the assurance that comes from growing up with a good wardrobe. He wears his clothes well, but everything else about him seems uncomfortable, unsure. He takes a seat and clears his throat nervously, his fingers tapping on the table.

'Dan,' Reyes says, 'we just want to ask you a few questions. You're here voluntarily; you can leave at any time.'

'Of course,' he says. 'Happy to help. I want you to find out who did this terrible thing. Any luck on the driver of the truck yet?'

Reyes shakes his head and sits back in his chair. As always, Barr is beside him, watching everything, evaluating, a shrewd second pair of eyes. Reyes says, 'Now that you've had some time to think, do you have any idea who might have murdered your parents?'

Dan frowns and shakes his head. 'No. I can't imagine why anyone would do this.' He adds awkwardly, 'I mean other than for the obvious reason of robbery.'

Reyes nods and asks, 'How did you feel when your father sold Merton Robotics?'

Dan Merton's face flushes. 'What's that got to do with anything?'

'I'm just asking.' Reyes watches Dan's hands fidget on the table.

'I wasn't happy about it, to be honest,' he admits. 'I'd worked hard in that company for years with the expectation it would be mine someday. He sold it without even considering what it would mean to me.' He stops suddenly, as if he's said too much.

Reyes nods. 'It seems like a shitty thing to do.'

Dan looks at him as if he's deciding to drop some of his defences. 'Well, he could be a shitty person sometimes. But I had nothing to do with this.'

'I'm not saying you did,' Reyes assures him. 'We're just trying to get a full picture of the background here.' He pauses and goes on. 'Because of the sale of the business, I understand you are now in some financial difficulty. Do you want to tell us about that?'

'No, not particularly,' he snaps. 'I don't see how that's relevant.'

'You don't?' Reyes says. 'You have a grudge against your father, you're in financial difficulty, and you now stand to inherit a very large fortune.'

Dan flicks a nervous glance between him and Barr. 'Do I need to get a lawyer?'

'I don't know. Do you?'

'I had nothing to do with this,' Dan repeats more stridently. He rises from the chair. 'I'm not answering any more questions. I know my rights.'

'You're free to go,' Reyes agrees, then looks over at Barr. 'We just need to get you fingerprinted first.'

Chapter Twenty-four

'YOU WALKED OUT? Why?' Lisa asks, concerned.

She watches Dan carefully as he tells her about the interview at the police station. They're in the kitchen, seated at the table. His leg is jiggling nervously. As she listens, her own anxiety surges. The look of near panic in his eyes unnerves her. He tells her he has to get an attorney.

She swallows, her mouth dry. She thinks he's probably right. Even though this is outrageous – Dan couldn't harm a flea. But what if his fears are justified, and they zero in on him because of the circumstances, and they can't find the guy in the truck, and they try to make Dan look guilty just so they can get a conviction? People are wrongfully convicted all the time. How can this be happening?

And she's going to have to lie to the police.

'How will we pay for an attorney?' she asks, worried.

Dan looks at her, his eyes wild. 'Catherine will help,' he says. 'She has to. She can afford it. And she won't want the precious family name dragged through the mud. She'll want the best that money can buy.'

A short time later, Dan drives them the short distance to Catherine's house, his mind racing. He needs to talk to Catherine and Jenna. He turns to Lisa just before they exit the car. 'Don't tell them that I went out that night – that's just between me and you. They don't need to know. What if they let it slip to the police?'

She nods back at him, her brown eyes big.

Ted answers the door and they enter the house. Jenna is there, as expected, but he's surprised to find Irena in the living room as well. Maybe she's helping with the funeral preparations, too, he thinks. 'I've just been interviewed by those detectives,' he blurts out, 'at the police station.' They look back at him warily. He throws himself into an armchair. 'They were acting like they think *I* killed them!'

He notices a glance being shared among the others. Do *they* think he did it too? Surely not. Fear suddenly floods through him. 'What? What is it?'

Catherine says, 'They interviewed Irena this morning too.'

Irena tells him what happened at the police station. Dan hears it all with mounting dismay. He and Lisa sit for a moment in stunned silence, the only sound the ticking of the clock on the mantel.

Then staring at Irena, Dan says, 'Why did you do that? *What have you done?*' He looks around the room at all of them, distraught. 'I have to get an attorney,' he says. 'Today. Except – I can't afford one,' Dan says plaintively, looking directly at Catherine.

'We can help with that,' Catherine says, without even looking at Ted to see what he feels about it. 'Please don't worry about it. I'll pay.' At that moment, Catherine's cell phone buzzes. They all stare at it on the side table. Catherine picks it up.

Audrey is noting how long each of the interviews last. From the short time Dan was in the police station, she concludes that they didn't get much out of him. He probably refused to talk to them. Unlike Irena, Dan had left in a hurry, his car tearing out of the parking lot as if he were angry.

Audrey tries to kill time while keeping an eye on the entrance. She plays with her phone. She risks another pee break at the doughnut store and buys another coffee and hurries back just in time to see

Catherine arrive and park her car. She is also alone. Audrey notes the time – it's almost 2:30 p.m.

How she wishes she could be a fly on the wall in there. What Audrey wants to know more than anything is: *Who knew that Fred planned to put her in his will?*

Catherine seems perfectly composed as she takes a seat in the interview room the day after her parents were discovered murdered. Seeing her now, without her white doctor's coat, Reyes gets a clearer picture of her style. Expensive and classic. She's wearing dark trousers and a printed blouse. No pearls today, but a gold necklace with a diamond at her throat. A diamond tennis bracelet. A designer handbag.

'Can I get you anything? Coffee?' Barr offers.

Catherine smiles politely. 'Coffee would be lovely,' she says.

She is more self-possessed than her brother.

Barr returns with the coffee and Reyes explains that she is here voluntarily and can leave at any time.

'Of course,' Catherine replies. 'I want to help any way I can.' As the interview proceeds, she again denies that anything unusual happened at Easter dinner, despite the apparent mass exodus. She tells him that she and Ted remained at home together the rest of the night.

'We know Dan had problems with his father,' Reyes says. 'That he was having financial problems. You all stand to inherit a lot of money.' Her expression remains impassive. He waits a beat and asks, 'Did Jenna have any problems with your parents?'

She shakes her head, as if impatient. 'No.'

'Did you?'

'No.' She adds spontaneously, 'If anything, I was the favourite.'

Reyes leans back in his chair again. 'So you were the favourite, Dan was the least favourite, and Jenna was somewhere in the middle? Your parents played favourites?' He detects a flicker in her eyes; perhaps she regrets what she said.

'No, it wasn't like that. I shouldn't have said that. It's just that my parents were happy that I was a doctor. Dan – our father had very high expectations of Dan, and he was a bit hard on him. And Jenna – well, they didn't like her art. They felt it was obscene.'

'Obscene?'

'Yes. She does sculptures of female genitalia and the like.'

Reyes nods. 'I see. And that didn't go over well with your parents?'

'Not particularly.' She adds, 'But these were minor things. We were a perfectly ordinary family.'

166

Reyes doesn't respond to that. 'Your former nanny, Irena – are you all close to her?'

'Of course. She looked after us for years. She's like a mother to us.'

'Does *she* have a favourite?'

'Look, I know what you're getting at,' Catherine says, her voice even. 'Irena came over to my place a little while ago and told us about your interview. I can't explain what she did. All I know is, none of us had anything to do with this. And you need to find out who did.'

Catherine leaves the police station with a sense of relief, feeling that the interview went well. She was perfectly relaxed, convincing. She hopes that's the end of it, for her anyway. As she walks into the parking lot she glances up and spots Audrey in her car, alone at the back of the lot. Catherine stops in her tracks for a moment, surprised to see her there. Audrey catches her eye and looks down, as if at a cell phone. For a second, Catherine debates whether to go over and talk to her, ask her what she's doing here. Is she spying on them? Or have the police asked her to come in for an interview?

She walks directly to her own car, her earlier confidence gone.

Chapter Twenty-five

ROSE CUTTER STANDS nervously on Catherine Merton's doorstep. Her palms are sweaty. She wipes them on her skirt and presses the doorbell. She doesn't want to be here, but Catherine surely needs her support.

Rose owes her. Catherine's been such a solid friend, ever since high school, where they met in English class. Catherine hadn't been much of an English student, she was more into the sciences, and she wanted high marks. They'd been paired together on an assignment, and from there, Rose began helping her with her essays. An unlikely friendship flourished and expanded outside the classroom. Catherine was popular by virtue of who she was, and because of her lovely clothes – she could always afford the hottest new styles. Rose was a nobody and had zero fashion sense, which was the kiss of death in high school. She remembers how generous Catherine had been with her, how she'd made it clear to everyone that they were friends, and how differently the other kids treated her after that. Catherine invited her to things – parties, outings – and just like that, she was accepted.

Catherine knew Rose didn't have the advantages she had. She helped her dress better, even giving her some of her own clothes, or taking her to thrift shops to find pieces she could actually afford. Sometimes Rose wondered if she was some kind of project for Catherine, if she'd befriended her out of some sort of rich-person guilt. But she realized after a while that although Catherine appeared to be popular, she was lonely, and with Rose she could be herself. They became close. Catherine wasn't as confident as she seemed to be, and things were difficult at home. She needed a friend as much as Rose did. One day she'd even confided to Rose that she'd been caught shoplifting and told her she thought her father was going to kill her. Rose had been astonished – her parents were millionaires, Catherine could have anything she wanted, and she was shoplifting? It made Rose feel better, because she'd always known how greedy she was herself, and it was nice to know that she wasn't the only one.

They'd stayed in touch while they attended different universities – SUNY for Rose, Vassar for

Catherine – and reconnected when they both found themselves back in Aylesford as adults. The pattern continued. Catherine invited her to social events – sailing at the Hudson Yacht Club, and that charity polo match last year. Things that Rose could never attend or afford on her own. But mostly they met for coffee, or over lunch, and had long talks, sharing details of their lives, reminiscing about fun times they'd had.

Now, Ted answers the door. Rose has seen Catherine and Ted together socially on many occasions. She has always found Ted attractive – tall, broad-shouldered, the strong, silent type. She's glad Catherine has him to lean on. She gives him a tentative smile and says, 'Hi, Ted, can I come in?'

'It's not a good time, Rose,' he says apologetically. 'Catherine's just come back from the police station.'

Rose hears Catherine's voice in the background. 'Is that Rose?' Then Catherine appears at Ted's shoulder, joining him at the door.

'Rose,' Catherine says. She smiles a welcome, but it's a smile that's on the verge of tears.

'Oh, Catherine,' Rose exclaims, reaching out to hug her. She holds her close, breathing in the familiar smell of her. Rose finds herself fighting back tears, and squeezes her eyes shut.

Catherine is a dear friend, but she's always been

jealous of her for having everything Rose doesn't have, all the advantages that money brings. Rose was brought up by a widowed single mother who scrimped and saved her entire life. That Rose has made anything of herself at all, she attributes mostly to her own hard work. She knows that the Mertons weren't a very happy family, but they have millions.

Still, Catherine is her best friend. Rose trembles a little as they embrace. They must not find out what she's done.

Reyes watches Jenna Merton walk into the interview room in ripped jeans and a black leather biker jacket. He's struck again at how different the three Merton children are from each other. He thinks fleetingly of his own two kids – also both completely different from one another in looks, temperament, and interests. And then he directs all his focus on the woman in front of him. After a few introductory matters, he gets right to the point.

'You and Jake Brenner were the last people known to see your parents alive,' he begins.

She raises her eyebrows. 'We were only five minutes behind the others.'

Reyes gives her a long look. 'Except you weren't. You didn't leave shortly after seven o'clock, like the others. You left about an hour later, just after eight o'clock.'

She stiffens slightly but remains silent, as if considering what to say.

He waits. They stare at one another. 'You were seen,' he says, 'by a neighbour walking his dog down his drive shortly after eight o'clock. He recognized your car. He's seen it often enough.'

She takes a deep breath and says, 'Fine, whatever.'

'What happened in that extra hour?'

She frowns, shakes her head. 'Nothing much. We talked a bit. I guess I lost track of time.'

He pushes her on it, but she sticks to her story. He changes tack. 'Did you go out again at all that night?'

'No. We drove back to my place. Jake stayed the night. We went to bed.'

After Jenna has been fingerprinted and left, Reyes says to Barr, 'We have to check all their alibis.'

Audrey almost decides to call it a day. It's uncomfortable – and mostly boring – to sit in a car in a parking lot. She's been here for hours. Catherine had seen her – she'll tell the others that she's keeping an eye on them. Good.

She knows the detectives have spoken to Catherine and Jenna now, as well as Dan and Irena. She thinks that's probably it. She's about to start the car when she sees a familiar figure walking toward the front doors of the police station. She leans closer to the windshield, watching. She recognizes Dan's wife, Lisa. They must be checking up on Dan, seeing if he has an alibi. Pleased, she settles back down in her seat.

Lisa swallows her fear and walks into the interview room. Her heart is pounding. She's taking a risk. Dan hadn't wanted her to come. He told her to refuse, to wait until he had a lawyer. They have an appointment later this afternoon with a top criminal lawyer, Richard Klein, thanks to Catherine.

But she held her ground. 'Dan,' she said, 'I'll go in and tell them you were with me all night. That's it. How will it look if I refuse to talk to them at all?'

So here she is. She knows what to say and what not to say.

They begin with generalities, but Detective Reyes soon says, 'We know *something* happened at Easter dinner. Do you want to tell us about that?'

This is unexpected. She wonders who might have let something slip and shakes her head, frowns as if she doesn't know what he means. 'No, it was a perfectly ordinary Easter dinner.'

'Did you or your husband go out again anytime that night after you returned home?' Reyes asks.

She knew he would ask this; it's why she's here. She says, perfectly convincingly, 'No. After we got home from his parents, we both stayed in. All night.'

Ted is uncomfortable; he can feel himself sweating – under his arms, down his back. He's furious at Catherine for putting him in this position. He couldn't very well refuse to come when they asked him in. Every one of them has been called into the police station today, like ants marching into a picnic. And they're all having their fingerprints taken.

'Just tell them I was home all night,' Catherine said when they were finally alone. 'It's not hard.'

'You should have told them the truth,' he shot back.

'Yes, I probably should have,' she admitted with heat. 'But I didn't. I made a mistake. Now the question is, are you going to make it worse, or are you going to help me?'

He'd agreed that sticking to her original story was probably the best course of action, given the circumstances. So here he is. He's a bit annoyed at her, too, for agreeing so quickly to pay for Dan's legal fees. What if they run into the hundreds of thousands? But it's her money – she's the one inheriting a fortune, not him, so there's not much he can say.

But he's a confident man, and he knows he will be able to come across well in the interview. He knows Catherine didn't murder her parents.

'Thank you for coming in,' Reyes says.

Ted denies anything unusual happened at the dinner that night. They've all agreed to stick to this – that it had been a pleasant evening and there were no conflicts. Finally Reyes asks the expected question. 'After you arrived home from the Mertons' on the evening of Easter Sunday, did you go out again any time after that?'

'No.'

'What about your wife?'

He shakes his head. 'No. She was home with me all night.'

Once Ted leaves the police station, Audrey decides to call it a day. It's been so frustrating to be stuck in the parking lot when all the action is going on inside that building. The only place more interesting today is probably Catherine's or Dan's house, and she can't get inside there either.

She checks her phone one more time and quickly looks at the local online news. Police teams are now conducting a search of the river near Brecken Hill, looking for evidence in the Merton murders. She pulls out of the parking lot.

Chapter Twenty-six

AUDREY STANDS LOOKING out at the Hudson River. A cool breeze is ruffling its dark surface. There's a police boat out on the water, bobbing gently, where divers in wetsuits are at work. Uniformed officers are searching the edge of the river. Audrey can see the two bridges of Aylesford, one to the south of her, one to the north, spanning the river to the Catskill Mountains on the other side. It would be a pretty, peaceful scene, but it's marred by what's going on here.

Audrey is part of a small crowd watching the police activity in the pleasant spring weather. The media is here too. She observes silently for a while, standing near a woman in her thirties who has the demeanour of a professional. Audrey wonders if she might be a journalist. Then she notices the logo of the *Aylesford Record* on her windbreaker, confirming it. 'What are they doing?' she asks the woman.

'It's the Merton murder case,' the woman replies, glancing at her briefly, then turning her attention back to the river. 'They're not saying much, but they're obviously looking for evidence. The murder weapon, probably. The knife.' She's quiet for a moment, then adds, 'And the bloody clothes. A murder that violent, the killer must have had to get rid of his clothes. They must be looking for those too.'

Good point, Audrey thinks to herself. It annoys her that she doesn't know any more about the actual crime than the reporter, and she's family. Fred was her brother, and yet she hasn't been let in on anything. The police are saying nothing, and the family isn't talking to the press. She tries to tamp down the malignant fury she's feeling toward them all.

'Is there anything new?' Audrey asks, hoping the reporter might share some tidbit.

The woman beside her shakes her head and then shrugs. 'I bet they know more than they're letting on. Wealthy family, you know. They always get preferential treatment, more privacy. More respect.'

Without planning to, Audrey says suddenly, 'I know the family.'

The woman turns to her and for the first time looks at her with interest. 'You do? How?'

'Fred Merton was my brother.'

The woman appraises her, as if trying to discern whether she's some kind of crackpot. Maybe she makes a quick judgement about Audrey's age and her appearance and realizes she might be telling the truth. 'Really? Do you want to talk about it?'

Audrey hesitates, casting her eyes to the police boat out on the river.

She shakes her head and turns to go.

'Wait,' the other woman says. 'Let me give you my card.' She hands Audrey a business card. 'If you want to talk, call me. Anytime. I'd really like to talk to you, if you are who you say you are.'

Audrey takes the card and looks at it. Robin Fontaine. She looks up and offers the woman her hand to shake. 'Audrey Stancik. But my maiden name was Merton.' Then she turns and heads back to her car.

Reyes studies the younger man across from him. Jake Brenner has the starving-artist look down – ripped jeans, wrinkled T-shirt, battered leather jacket, two-day-old stubble. He's trying hard to be cool, to look as if he doesn't have a care in the world, but Reyes can tell he's not as comfortable as he would like to seem. He smiles too much, for one thing. And his thumb drums the surface of the table in an irregular, annoying way.

Reyes says, 'Thank you for coming all the way

up from the city to talk to us. How did you get here, by the way?' he asks casually.

'The train.'

Reyes nods. 'We just want to ask you a few questions about the night of April twenty-first, Easter Sunday.' Jake nods. 'You were with Jenna Merton that day, at her parents' house for dinner, is that right?'

Jake looks at them steadily. 'Yes.'

'What was it like, that dinner?'

Jake takes a deep breath in, lets it out. 'Well, it was a bit fancy. I was worried about using the right fork.' He smiles again. 'They have a lot of money, you know. They seemed nice enough.'

'Everybody get along all right?'

He nods. 'I think so.'

'Okay.' Reyes says, 'I understand you and Jenna were the last to leave the house that night.' Jake seems to freeze briefly, then relaxes. Reyes adds, 'We know you and Jenna left about an hour later than the others. Why is that?'

No smiles now.

'What did you and Jenna do in that extra hour inside the Merton house?' Reyes asks conversationally.

'Nothing,' he says, shrugging his shoulders. 'We just talked. They wanted to get to know me better.'

'Really?' Reyes says. He leans forward. 'What did you talk about, exactly?'

Jake swallows nervously. 'Art, mostly. I'm an artist.'

'Was there an argument that night, Jake? Did something happen during dinner? Or maybe after dinner?'

He shakes his head firmly. 'No. There was no argument. We just stayed to talk for a while and then we left. They were fine when we left them, I swear.'

'Let's move on,' Reyes says. 'What did you do after you and Jenna left the Mertons' place?'

'We drove back to her place. I spent the night.'

'Neither of you went out again?'

'No.'

Reyes gives him a long look and says, 'Okay. We'll be in touch.' He sends him off with Barr to be fingerprinted.

When Barr returns, he says to her, 'All three of them have very convenient alibis, don't you think?' She gives him a cynical nod. 'Well I'm not buying it. We need to check them out. See if you can get any video from the Aylesford train station. See if he took a train back to the city that night.' He adds, 'And if not, check the morning video too. I want to be sure.' She nods. 'In the meantime, I'll check in with the ME's office on that second autopsy.'

He glances at his watch – it's almost 5:00 p.m. – and makes the short drive there.

Sandy Fisher, the forensic pathologist, greets him saying, 'I was just about to give you a call.'

She leads him over to Fred Merton's body, which is lying uncovered on a steel gurney. They look down at him.

'Fourteen stab wounds, some of which show real ferocity. But it was the slitting of the throat first that killed him. Grabbed from behind, throat slit left to right – the killer is right-handed – then he dropped or was thrown to the floor onto his stomach and stabbed fourteen times in the back, with decreasing depth, probably because the killer was tiring.' She pauses for a moment and adds, 'A lot of anger there.'

'Yes,' Reyes agrees.

'One more interesting thing,' she says. 'Fred Merton had advanced pancreatic cancer. He was dying anyway. He probably only had three or four months.'

'Would he have known?' Reyes asks, surprised.

'Oh, I would think so, most definitely.'

Reyes makes his way back to his car, thoughtful. That certainly might lend weight to Audrey Stancik's claim that Fred was going to change his will. He wonders who knew that Fred was dying, and what he was planning to do.

Chapter Twenty-seven

IT'S LATE WEDNESDAY afternoon when Dan drives downtown to the attorney's office, Lisa silent in the passenger seat beside him. She'd told him that Ted had gone in for questioning right after her, so he knows they're checking on Catherine's movements that night too. He thinks about that as he pulls into the parking lot of the building housing his criminal attorney. But Catherine isn't in a financial mess. And Catherine didn't have a public falling-out with their father.

They walk through the glass doors of the high-end law firm. It's not the same firm his father used. And this one has the best criminal defence lawyer Aylesford has to offer. They don't have to wait. Richard Klein comes out to meet them and takes them directly to his office.

Dan doesn't notice much about his surroundings.

He focuses on the attorney as if he's a lifeline. Klein will tell them what to do. He will make it clear to the police that he had nothing to do with this. That's his job.

'I'm glad you called me,' the attorney says reassuringly. 'You did the right thing.'

Dan tells the attorney everything – the tense Easter dinner, the discovery of the bodies, what Irena did with the knife, the falling-out with his father, the financial mess he's in, the aggressive way the police questioned him. He doesn't tell him that he went out for a long drive that night, though – that it was a habit of his – and that Lisa lied to the police for him. The attorney listens intently, asking the occasional question.

Klein says, 'So you were home all night. Your wife confirms that.' Dan and Lisa nod. 'Then you don't have a problem.' He leans forward over his desk, lowering his head. 'They're looking at you – and probably your siblings – because of the money. Naturally. But it doesn't matter if they think you had motive if they don't have evidence. We have to see what they come up with.'

'I didn't do anything,' Dan says.

'Right. So there won't *be* any evidence. You don't have anything to worry about. Just sit tight. They can't railroad you if I'm with you.' He adds, 'Don't talk to them again without me there, either of you.

183

If they want to talk to you, call this number' – he slides a card across his desk, after hastily scribbling a number on it in pen – 'it's my cell. Call anytime. Day or night. I'll come.'

'Okay,' Dan says, taking the card.

They sort out the retainer. Dan assures him that it won't be a problem; his sister Catherine has given him a loan. And when this is all over, he thinks to himself, he'll pay her back out of his inheritance. Finally Dan rises to leave, Lisa beside him.

'One more thing,' the attorney says. 'Whatever you do, don't talk to the press. Without evidence, the police can't do much to you, but the press can still destroy you.'

Audrey drives directly from the river to Ellen's place, showing up unannounced. They have that kind of friendship. Both are widows who live alone, so there's no concern about interrupting anything. They often drop in on each other. Audrey has been holding her emotions forcibly in check all day, but at the sight of Ellen's kind and familiar face, she promptly bursts into tears.

'What's wrong?' Ellen asks, alarmed.

Audrey pours it all out – her visit to Walter that morning, how Fred hadn't changed his will in her favour after all, her suspicions that one of the kids murdered their parents before Fred could follow through on his intentions.

Audrey hadn't told anyone except Ellen about her great expectations. She's the only one who knows – the only one to whom she bares her soul.

Ellen is speechless at first, then says, 'Oh, Audrey, I'm so sorry.'

When Audrey eventually stops sobbing, she feels drained, completely worn out.

'You don't really think one of their own kids did this, do you?' Ellen asks tentatively, as if she can't stomach the idea. They all know now how the Mertons were killed; it's all over the news.

'I'm sure of it. And I'm going to figure out which one,' Audrey vows. She adds, 'The police think so too – they've had all of them in for questioning today.'

As evening falls, Catherine joins Ted in the kitchen for supper. No need to cook – the refrigerator is stuffed with offerings. Ted has put out some of the things that he thinks she will like best; it's been a long and challenging day. In addition to the stress of the police interviewing everyone, she's had her hands full dealing with calls from friends of the family. It's been difficult – accepting their condolences while putting off their prurient curiosity. She's been holding herself so tightly all day that now her entire body aches. But she's got the funeral mostly under control – it will be on Saturday, at two in the afternoon. They expect a crowd. Her parents were prominent citizens of Aylesford and the manner of their deaths is going to draw many people who might otherwise have skipped it. After the funeral, there will be a reception at the golf club, with drinks and food – and the expected slide-show of photos running on a loop in the background. And when that's over, Catherine will collapse. She doesn't think she will have time to process anything properly until then. She wonders how it will all hit her when she can finally allow it to.

Ted reaches over to her across the table. 'Are you all right?'

She shakes her head slowly.

'Eat something,' he prods, pointing at the lasagna, her favourite.

She half-heartedly spoons out some of the reheated lasagna onto her plate, adds a bit of salad, and tries to eat. But she begins to tremble. The fork in her hand is wobbling so much she can't bring it to her mouth. She drops it on her plate with a clatter.

'Catherine, what is it?' Ted says.

She blurts it out. 'What if –' She can't continue.

Ted gets up from the table and comes over to sit beside her. He puts his arms around her as she sobs into his chest.

'What if what?' he whispers into her hair.

She looks up at him. '*What if Dan killed them?*'

Ted's feeling of dread surfaces. Catherine's voiced a fear he's mostly tried to ignore since the afternoon before, when Dan had behaved so oddly. He'd been so nervy and agitated, and said such inappropriate things. Now, Ted doesn't know what to say, how to comfort her. He simply holds her. Finally, she pulls away, her face streaked with tears. Her cheeks seem to have hollowed out in the last day and a half.

He strokes her hair. 'Catherine, it's going to be all right,' he says helplessly. 'I love you.' He's never seen her so distraught. 'Come,' he says gently, guiding her back into the living room. They've lost all interest in food. They sink together onto the sofa and she turns to him, her eyes huge, welling with tears. 'He *hated* our father, Ted. You have no idea.'

'But could he *do* that?' he asks, swallowing his revulsion. 'You know him better than I do.'

'I don't know,' she says, her voice hollow. 'Maybe.'

Ted feels a chill run down his back. The thought of Dan strangling his own mother and stabbing his father over and over again in a raging fury and then pretending to be innocent in front of them all is so disturbing that he feels physically sick.

'I don't know what to do,' she whispers.

'You don't have to do anything,' he says. But

187

even as he says it, he asks himself, *What should they do?* If he's a murderer, they can't just continue to let him into their home, surely? He might actually be insane.

'He's right. They're going to think he did it,' Catherine says, agitated, 'and they're going to question me again.'

Ted, deeply troubled, stares blankly out the living-room windows, his arms around her. He sees two people across the street, walking up to the front door of their neighbours'. They look vaguely familiar. Then, with a jolt, Ted realizes who they are. It's the detectives, Reyes and Barr. What are they doing on their street?

And all at once he knows. There's only one reason they would be there.

Catherine must sense his sudden tension because she looks up at him and says, 'What is it?'

She follows his gaze across the street, recognizes the detectives, and inhales a sharp breath.

'Fuck,' Ted says.

'What if someone saw me?' she says, frightened.

Ted's mind is racing. Someone might have seen Catherine go out later that night. She might have been caught somewhere on camera. If the police are checking on her, they might find out the truth. This is what he was afraid of. 'Then you'll have to tell them the truth,' he says slowly. 'That you didn't tell them before because you were in shock, and afraid of what they might think, because of the inheritance. That you went over and saw your parents, they were fine, and you came home again.'

'But . . .' she whispers at him.

Her face has gone shockingly pale, and it frightens him. 'But what?' he asks.

'They weren't fine. They were already dead.'

Chapter Twenty-eight

TED LOOKS BACK at his wife in shock and confusion. 'What?'

'I'm sorry, Ted, I lied to you too.' She's crying again in earnest now, tears coursing down her cheeks.

He pulls farther away from her, staring at her in horror. 'How could they already be dead? And you said nothing?' His heart pounds as he realizes that his wife, the woman he knows so well, came home from seeing that her parents had been brutally murdered and went to bed as if nothing had happened. And then blithely told him the next morning that she'd spoken to her mother, and made up some lie about her mother asking her to intervene with her father on Jenna's behalf. His world spins. 'What the fuck are you talking about?' he gasps angrily.

'Don't be mad at me, Ted!' she begs. 'I didn't know what to do!' She swipes at some tissues from a box on the coffee table and wipes her eyes. She makes an effort to compose herself as he watches her, his heart still beating painfully fast, loud in his ears.

'I went over there to talk to Mom. When I got there, it was late – around eleven thirty. There was still a light on upstairs. So I knocked on the door. Nobody answered, so I knocked again. I knew they must still be up. But I started to think it was strange, because Mom hadn't answered her phone, and no one came to the door. I tried it, and it was unlocked. So I went in. It was dark in the hall, but there was a bit of light in the kitchen. I glanced in the living room and saw a lamp on the floor – and then I saw Mom. She was lying on the floor in the living room.' She starts to hyperventilate. 'I went over to her. She was dead. Her eyes were open. It was horrible.'

Ted sees her obvious pain and fright and listens in dread.

'I wanted to run away, but it was like I was paralysed. I couldn't move. I was terrified. I thought Dad had killed her. That he'd finally snapped.' Her voice breaks. 'I don't know how long I was there. But I didn't hear anything. Then I thought he must have killed himself too.'

Jesus, Ted thinks to himself.

She swallows. 'Somehow I walked down the hall

to the kitchen. I could see then that there was blood on the floor and I avoided it. And then –' She stops.

Ted watches her, stunned. He can't process any of this. 'Go on,' Ted says. 'Tell me everything.'

'I didn't go in, I just stood at the doorway. Dad was on the kitchen floor. There was blood everywhere. The carving knife was there, beside him.' She seems to freeze, as if she's seeing it all again in her mind's eye. As if he's not there at all. The expression on her face makes him queasy.

'Why didn't you call 911?' Ted cries. 'Why didn't you tell *me*?'

'I thought – I thought –' But she can't seem to get the words out.

Ted says it for her, realizing. 'You thought Dan did it.'

She nods almost imperceptibly. She's stopped crying now; she just looks numb. 'I thought Dan came back that night and killed them. I knew he needed money and that Dad wouldn't give him any. And I was afraid.'

'Afraid –'

'That he would be caught.' She turns her eyes on him. 'I just wanted to give him some time – some time to get away, or to clean up . . . I knew he couldn't have been thinking straight.'

'Catherine,' Ted says. He says her name as calmly

192

as he can, but he's shaken to the core. 'Dan should go to jail if he's done this. He's – *dangerous*.'

She covers her face with her hands and sobs. 'I know. But I just can't bear it.' At last she looks up at him and says, as if she's pleading with him, 'He's my little brother. We have to protect him.'

She doesn't say it, but Ted can't help thinking it: *And he's done us all a favour.*

The lights are on in Catherine Merton's house, Detective Reyes notices as he and Barr approach the neighbours' house directly across the street.

They show their badges and are invited inside by the owners, a man and woman in their sixties. Reyes explains that they are investigating the murders of Fred and Sheila Merton, whose daughter lives across the street. Their eyes grow big.

'Were you home on Sunday night?' Reyes asks.

'Yes, but we went to bed early,' the man says. 'Had a big Easter dinner at our daughter's.'

Reyes says, 'Did you by any chance see anyone leave the house across the street – Ted Linsmore and Catherine Merton's house – anytime after seven thirty in the evening on Easter Sunday?'

The two of them look at each other and shake their heads. Before Reyes can even ask the question, the man offers, 'But we have a porch cam and it catches the cars going up and down the street. Do you want to have a look?'

'May we?'

'Sure,' he says, as his wife hovers in the background.

Upstairs there's an office where the security footage can be accessed via a laptop. He goes back to 7:00 p.m. Easter Sunday and then forward. As they watch the black-and-white footage, the occasional pedestrian or car going past, they see Ted's car return and park in the driveway at 7:21 p.m.

They continue watching, fast-forwarding through the footage until Reyes says 'Stop'.

The helpful neighbour goes back a bit then plays it again slowly. At 11:09, they see Catherine's car backing out of the driveway. The video doesn't capture who got into the car, but as it goes down the street, they recognize Catherine, in the driver's seat, alone.

She's lying, Reyes thinks. And her husband is covering for her. He and Barr share a glance over the man's head.

'Let's see what time she comes back,' Reyes says, turning back to the screen.

Catherine stands to the side of the living-room window, careful not to be seen. The detectives have been in the house across the street for a long time. She waits for them to come out. When they do, she catches both of them glancing at her house as they walk to their car. They're not questioning anyone else. They obviously don't need to.

She must have been seen. They must know she went out that night. They know she lied. They know Ted lied. He lied for her, and she knows he's not happy about it.

If they're checking on her, then they're going to check on Dan and Jenna too. Dan says he never left the house that night after he got home from their parents'. Lisa backed him up.

She knows what that's worth.

Dan is in the garage, the door wide open to the street. Soon he sees them. Those two detectives are talking to his neighbours, trying to find out if anyone saw him leaving his house Sunday night. He stands in shadow, terrified.

Maybe no one saw anything.

Catherine had called him on his cell a little while ago, told him what the detectives were doing. Asked him if anyone on his street had cameras. He didn't know. With his luck, somebody would have fucking cameras. He'd told Catherine – he'd told them all – that he'd been home all night. She obviously doesn't believe him, or she wouldn't have called.

Everyone has an alibi, he thinks, but him.

He's beginning to panic. He returns to the house

and finds Lisa in the kitchen, cleaning up. 'The detectives are here,' he says tersely.

'What?' she asks in alarm.

'On the street. Go look out the window,' he says sharply. 'Don't let them see you.'

She throws him a look of concern and creeps over to the living-room window, standing behind the drapes.

He hovers behind her and watches her face change as she realizes what it means.

Ellen Cutter draws herself a bath that evening, humming a little, thinking about Audrey's long visit earlier. Apparently she is not going to inherit a fortune after all. How quickly things change. She'd spoken rather wildly about Fred's children – how they must have found out about his plan to change his will and killed him and Sheila too. Ridiculous, Ellen thinks, adding some bubbles to her bath. That's a bit over the top, even for Audrey, who's always had a vivid imagination.

They have been friends for a long time, but Ellen is feeling just a little bit of *schadenfreude*.

Chapter Twenty-nine

JENNA IS PLEASED to see that for once in her life, Catherine's trademark composure is nowhere in sight. Catherine had called her cell and asked her to come over, even though it's a little late. Her superior older sister is going to pieces in front of her, and Jenna tells herself that she wouldn't be human if she didn't enjoy it, just a little.

Still, what she's hearing is startling. Catherine and Ted have lied to the police. That's not particularly surprising – Jenna has lied to them herself. What's shocking is that Catherine found the bodies that night and didn't tell a soul. Not even her husband. She waited two days and let Irena find them. Catherine says she kept it to herself to protect Dan.

Jenna glances at Ted, who looks grave and preoccupied, and wonders what he thinks of Catherine now. Is she still the woman he thought he married?

How cold-blooded do you have to be to see your parents' murdered corpses and go home and act like everything's fine?

It tells her something about Catherine – she's a great actor. At least up to a point. It looks now like the stress is getting the better of her. 'Do you really think Dan did it?' Jenna asks now.

'That's what I thought at the time,' Catherine says uneasily. 'It's why I didn't say anything that night. But he says he was home with Lisa.'

'Maybe he was,' Jenna says doubtfully.

'Well, we'll find out soon enough,' Catherine says, 'because the detectives are looking for witnesses.'

Jenna says, her voice grim, 'Maybe we should ask Dan point-blank if he did it. Then we'll know what we're dealing with. Maybe we can help him.'

'He's already denied it!' Catherine says. 'And why would he admit it to us? He would never trust us that much.'

'We never did trust each other much,' Jenna says.

'Well, we're adults now,' Catherine says, as if that makes a difference.

But really, Jenna thinks, the stakes are just higher now.

'I'm trusting *you*,' Catherine says, 'with the truth.'

'So,' Jenna asks, 'if the police find out you went out that night, what are you going to tell them?'

Catherine glances quickly at Ted, then back at

her. She swallows. 'Maybe I should tell them the truth. That I went there, they were already dead, I came home and said nothing.'

'They'll want to know why,' Jenna presses.

'I'll tell them I was in shock,' Catherine says.

'For fuck's sake, Catherine, you're a fucking doctor. You need to come up with something better than that.' Catherine is silent. Ted is standing off to the side, anxiously biting his lip. There's a long pause as they consider the options. 'If you don't want them to think you immediately suspected Dan,' Jenna suggests, 'you *could* tell them that Dad told us that night that he was going to sell the house. You could say you were afraid they would think you did it.'

Catherine looks back at her rather coldly.

'I'll back you up about the house,' Jenna says, 'and I'm sure Dan will too. If you didn't do it, you have nothing to be afraid of.'

It seems as if all the air has been sucked out of the room.

Finally, Catherine counters, 'Or I could tell them they were fine, I spoke to Mom and came home.'

Jenna watches Ted. He's clearly uncomfortable with the lie.

'Maybe you should just tell them the truth,' Ted says.

'How's it going to look if I tell them the truth?' Catherine protests. 'They're going to think it was either me or Dan. Even if he was home all night and Lisa vouches for him, they may not believe it.'

Jenna shrugs and says, 'They're going to think it's one of us no matter what.'

'I suppose *you* have an alibi?' Catherine says.

'Yes. Jake was with me at my place all night.'

Much later that night, Ted lies in bed, awake. Catherine hasn't decided what to tell the police, but had agreed when Ted insisted she take a lawyer with her the next time the detectives ask her in for questioning.

They'd watched the eleven o'clock local news before bed. The police haven't released any more information to the public about the investigation. They're still looking for the pickup truck seen near the house the night of the murders. Ted still hopes, but with little conviction, that the truck holds the key – that the driver of that truck is the killer, and only needs to be found.

He doesn't like what his wife has done to protect her younger brother, who, Ted has to admit, is possibly a killer.

'Irena obviously thinks Dan did it,' Catherine said to him, clearly troubled, as she turned out the light. 'Why else would she clean the knife?'

Now Ted stares at the ceiling in the dark. He can't close his eyes, because when he does, he imagines

Catherine finding her mother dead. Her family is clearly a lot more fucked up than he ever knew. He imagines her finally gathering the courage to go into the kitchen and finding her father's mutilated body, the realization dawning that it was probably her younger brother who'd killed them. Even though Ted doesn't agree with it, he can understand her desire to protect Dan. She presumably understands why he might have done it – clearly she thinks he must have his reasons. But whatever they may be, Ted thinks, that's no excuse for murder.

But what he can't understand is how she was able to come home that night and climb into bed beside him and whisper, 'Everything's fine,' before kissing him on the cheek and going to sleep.

Chapter Thirty

EARLY THE NEXT morning, Thursday, Reyes sits back in his chair, deep in thought. It's two days since the bodies were discovered. He taps his pen against the blotter on his desk. There's no sign of the Mertons' credit cards being used, no attempts to take money out at ATMs. No sign of the stolen jewellery or silver anywhere. Overkill on Fred's death. A very careful killer – no shoes, for Christ's sake. Somehow he doesn't think it was a simple home invasion. And they're no further ahead on that mystery truck. They're still going through the auto body paint shops in an attempt to track it down.

What they do know is that Dan Merton and Catherine Merton lied about their alibis.

Reyes calls Dan Merton in for a formal interview. This time he brings his attorney. The two of them show up at 10:00 a.m., and Merton is in a suit. Reyes wonders if his lawyer advised him on what to wear. Is he expecting to be arrested? Dan is looking unrested and unwell.

After being cautioned, and after formal introductions for the tape, they begin. Reyes says, 'We have a witness who swears he saw you go out in your car the night of the murders at around ten o'clock, and another who says she saw you come home later, around one in the morning.' Reyes sees the attorney give his client a sharp glance.

Dan looks even more ill and closes his eyes.

'Maybe we could have a minute?' the attorney says.

'Sure.' Reyes turns off the tape and he and Barr leave the room and walk down the corridor to wait. When the attorney signals for them to return and they resume the interview, Reyes asks, 'Is there something you want to tell us, Dan?'

Dan takes a deep, shaky breath and says, 'I went out for a drive. I had a lot on my mind and driving helps me clear my head. I often go for a drive at night.'

'Three hours is quite a long drive. Where did you go?'

'I don't know, nowhere special. I can't remember.'

Reyes raises his eyebrows at him in disbelief. 'You didn't go back to Brecken Hill to see your parents?'

'No. I went nowhere near their place. I wasn't in Brecken Hill.' There's a vein pulsing visibly under the pale skin of his temple.

'Why did you lie to us, Dan?'

'I didn't want to be a suspect,' he says tightly.

'Did you ask your father for money, perhaps, at Easter dinner?'

Dan gives Reyes a vicious glance.

The attorney interjects. 'I think that's it for questions for now.' Dan looks like he's crumpling inside his suit. 'Unless you've got something else?' Klein asks, turning to Reyes. 'Some kind of direct physical evidence, for instance?' Reyes shakes his head. 'Let's go,' the attorney says and leads his client out.

After they've gone, Barr says, 'If he did it, even if he's managed to dispose of all his bloodied clothes somewhere, there might still be traces of his father's blood somewhere in his car, no matter how well he thinks he's cleaned it.'

Reyes nods and says, 'We'll get a search warrant.' He exhales heavily. 'We need to find those bloody clothes. In the meantime, let's have another chat with Catherine Merton.'

Hungry for information, Audrey shows up at the police station again. This morning, there's a media presence as well, waiting around patiently by the front doors. Audrey decides that this time she'll get out of her car. She blends in with the reporters and cameramen and waits to see what will happen.

She's soon rewarded by Dan coming out the glass doors with a tall man in a good suit – she realizes he must be an attorney. The media swarm in and pepper the two of them with unwelcome questions, as the lawyer tries to fend them off. Audrey is glad she made the effort. She hopes they're really putting the screws to him. She tries to catch Dan's expression, but he's got his head down and his hands up to his face as he scurries away with his protective lawyer.

A short time later, Audrey's patience is rewarded again when she sees Catherine arrive with a woman in a suit, carrying a briefcase. They run the gauntlet of reporters, trying their best to ignore them. Things are getting serious, Audrey thinks. She's beginning to enjoy herself.

Catherine Merton looks much different today than she did the day before, Reyes notes. She's had to pass through the media scrum to get in here, and perhaps it's put her off her game. She doesn't appear to have slept much, and although she's taken pains with her outfit and her makeup, her fatigue still shows. She's brought an attorney with her.

Once he's cautioned her and the tape is running, Reyes says, 'Ms Merton, you told us yesterday that you were home all night on Easter Sunday, after you got home from your parents'.' She doesn't say anything, but she looks as if she's prepared for the worst. 'We have video of you in your car leaving your driveway at eleven oh nine that evening and returning at twelve forty-one in the morning. One of your neighbours has a security camera.' Reyes asks, 'Where did you go?'

She takes a deep breath and glances at her attorney, who gives her a slight nod. 'I went to my parents'. When we were there for dinner, my mother told me there was something important she wanted to talk to me about, but we were interrupted. I never got a chance to talk to her about it and I was worried about what it might be. So I called her cell shortly after eleven, but there was no answer.'

'Yes, we know,' Reyes says. 'We have your parents' phone records.' He asks, 'Why didn't you try the landline?'

She hesitates briefly. 'I thought my dad might already be asleep and I didn't want to wake him.' She continues. 'So I drove over – it's not far. When I got there, I spoke to my mother. She wanted me to intervene with my father about my sister, Jenna. He wanted to cut off her allowance.' She adds, 'This happened from time to time. He never did it.'

'So why the lie?' Reyes asks.

She looks him right in the eye and says, 'Why do you think? I didn't want you to think it was me.'

Reyes stares back at her and wonders if she and her brother were both there, at the same time.

Chapter Thirty-one

LISA WATCHES WITH dismay as the detectives arrive with a search warrant and a forensics team only a couple of hours after Dan returned from the police station. Some of them head inside the house, while Reyes and Barr and the rest of them open the doors of Dan's car, which is sitting in the driveway. They take their time studying it, in full view of the entire street, while a police truck waits to take it away to someplace where they will pull it apart for a clue that her husband is a murderer.

She feels queasy, even though she knows Dan didn't do it. Dan didn't come home that night covered in blood. He couldn't have done it. She remembers what he was wearing when he went out for a drive – the same jeans and shirt, loosened around his neck, that he wore at dinner. And he probably put on his casual windbreaker when he left, the one he always wears in the spring. It's hanging in the hallway closet. She's seen it since and there's not a spot on it. She doesn't remember him coming home, but the next morning, she found those same jeans and shirt, and his socks and underwear, on the floor by the bed and put them in the laundry basket. That was Monday. She did the laundry that day and put everything away. She never saw bloodstains on any of it. She knows she has nothing to worry about. So why is she so tense?

Dan comes up beside her. His lawyer was just here, checking the validity of the search warrant. Then he left, telling Dan privately to keep his chin up, his mouth shut, and to call him if there are any 'developments'.

'This is an outrage,' Dan complains.

'Just keep your cool,' Lisa says. She doesn't want him to become emotional now, with everyone watching. He's been so volatile lately – it worries her. 'They're not going to find anything.'

Jenna's cell phone buzzes and she looks at it. It's Jake again.

'Hey,' she says. She's standing outside Dan and Lisa's house; Dan had called her in a panic when the police arrived. She's standing on the street, a distance from where Dan and Lisa are watching Dan's car being examined.

'How are things going up there?' Jake asks.

She likes the sound of his voice, low and husky. He lied for her yesterday. She wonders if it's just a matter of time before he asks for something in return. He'll probably want money, once she gets some. Now that she thinks of it, Jake is actually quite difficult to read. 'It doesn't look good for Dan. They're searching his house now.'

Audrey had followed the detectives when they left the station – had recognized them, watched them get into a plain, dark sedan – and followed them straight to Dan's house. There, on Dan's quiet, affluent street, they were joined by a forensics van. A team in white suits got out with all their equipment. Two of them started examining the car in the driveway, and the others went inside the house. The detectives stopped to look at the car.

Audrey is delighted. This is getting better and better. Dan is obviously the prime suspect, she thinks. She wants to get out and help them tear Dan's place apart. Instead, she sits in her car on the side of the street and wishes she had a pair of binoculars.

There are neighbours watching from their lawns and driveways, and there are media in the street. She recognizes that reporter, Robin Fontaine, among them. Audrey has her card in her wallet.

She turns her attention back to Dan, who's

standing at the end of his driveway with his wife, Lisa, watching them search his car. As if he feels her eyes on his back, he looks over and spots her. He starts walking rapidly toward her, his face set. Audrey braces herself for a confrontation. To hell with him, Audrey thinks, the street is public property, and she's not the only one here watching what's going on. Dan approaches her window, his face twisted in anger, and Audrey powers it down halfway.

'What the fuck are you doing here?' Dan spits. His face is strikingly pale against his dark hair.

Audrey sees the wildness in his eyes and falters. For a split second he reminds her of Fred when he was younger. Then the illusion is gone, and all she can think is that she might be looking into the eyes of a murderer. She hastily powers the window up again. He glares at her then turns and smashes his fist on the front hood of her car as he strides away, making her jump.

The day wears on and Dan watches coldly while the detectives and the forensic team search his house thoroughly. His heart is racing, but he tries not to show his distress. They have questions that he doesn't know if he should answer. His lawyer has gone, and told him to say nothing. But when they ask him what he was wearing that night he feels he has to tell them. He and Lisa supply the jeans and shirt he wore on Easter, the blazer, and the jacket he wore when he went out later. He doesn't know which underwear and socks he was wearing – they all look the same in the drawer. They take everything.

Outside, they find freshly turned earth in the garden. Detective Reyes is alerted, and they all go out to the backyard, quite secluded, where a technician is indicating the newly disturbed soil, an area of about four feet square, underneath some hydrangea bushes. Reyes looks at him.

'I buried my dog there a few days ago,' he tells them. 'She died of old age.'

To Dan's dismay, they begin to dig. Lisa stands beside him, clutching his hand. Soon they uncover a black plastic garbage bag. They lift it out of the garden carefully while Dan looks on in distress. They open the bag and a foul odour assails them. Inside they discover the decomposing body of a dog. Nothing else.

'Satisfied?' Dan says, barely concealing his fury.

'Keep digging,' Reyes tells them, 'deeper.'

Detective Reyes had been disappointed when he studied the inside of Dan's car. It looked as if it hadn't been cleaned in years. There was dust all over the dash, food wrappers on the floor. Dog hair on the seats. The fact that the car obviously hadn't been cleaned suggested that Dan might not have done the killings after all. There would be blood everywhere after a murder as violent as Fred Merton's. Even if he'd scrubbed himself clean and changed his clothes, he would probably still scrub down the car. But maybe they'll get lucky. Maybe he changed his clothes after the murders and didn't think he had to clean the inside of the car.

As the hours go by and nothing incriminating is found, Reyes's frustration mounts. They've obtained the clothes that Dan claims to have worn the night of the murder – confirmed by his wife, who they know has already lied to them once. They bag the clothes despite their having been laundered, and the windbreaker, which appears to be spotless. Reyes doesn't trust either one of them to tell the truth. If Dan committed the murders, whatever he was wearing at the time is at the bottom of the Hudson River or in a dumpster somewhere. It's not hidden below the dog's grave – Reyes has made sure of that. They take all of his electronics, over his protests. They use luminol in the bathrooms, the laundry room, and the kitchen, but find no traces of blood anywhere.

But then, in the two-car garage, they find something interesting. Inside a large plastic bin, they find an opened package of N95 masks; a package of white, hooded, disposable coveralls; and an opened package of booties. The package of disposable coveralls is open, and there's only one left in the package of three.

Of course, Reyes thinks. A murderer who's canny enough to wear gloves, socks, and no shoes, who leaves no trace evidence – he might have been wearing a protective suit, just like the one he and Barr are staring at. It's very similar in appearance to the ones used by the forensics team. It would explain the complete lack of physical evidence at the scene. The lack of evidence in the car and house. And it would show premeditation. He lifts his eyes to meet Barr's. 'Over here,' he calls to the closest technician.

He turns to Dan, who is hovering at the entrance to the garage with his silent wife, and beckons him over. 'What are these for?'

'I bought them when I was insulating the attic with spray foam, a couple of years ago,' Dan says, flushing. 'You're supposed to wear them. And the mask. The chemicals are dangerous.'

A member of the forensic team photographs the package of disposable coveralls and the package of booties beneath it, then gathers them up carefully. Reyes stares at Dan, who shrinks from his gaze.

Reyes knows they need some physical evidence connecting the killer to the crime scene. The fact that they've found an opened package of disposable coveralls in Dan Merton's garage won't be enough. They need more. They need to find the discarded clothes, or possibly the disposable coveralls.

But so far, they've found no trace of them.

Chapter Thirty-two

IRENA IS ANXIOUS as she arrives at Catherine's house late that afternoon, having been summoned. As Irena greets everyone, she tries to read the room. Catherine looks tense, and so does Ted. Dan is emotional, saying wild things. Jenna watches everything warily. Irena's own nerves are beginning to fray.

She observes Dan closely. There's sweat along his hairline. Lisa looks ill, alternately staring at her husband and then glancing away. Irena remembers them as children, Dan, Jenna, and Catherine, squabbling and crying, and her trying to make everything better. She can't make this better.

Dan says, 'They're going to arrest me – and I didn't do it!' He tells them about the search, how they even dug up his dead dog. Lastly, he tells them about the discovery of the disposable coveralls in his garage.

At this, the room goes very still.

Dan says, 'They think I wore a disposable suit, and that's why they can't find any evidence at the scene, or anywhere else. I told them I got them to spray foam the attic, but they've already made up their minds. They think I'm guilty and *I didn't do it*!'

This is met with an appalled silence.

Then Catherine says, 'It doesn't matter what they *think*, Dan. They need evidence, and they don't seem to have any. The fact that you had a package of disposable coveralls in your garage doesn't matter. You explained why you had them.'

'But they know I went out that night,' Dan says nervously. He glances at Lisa. 'Lisa tried to cover for me, but they have witnesses who saw me go out. I just went for a drive. I go for drives all the time. I didn't go over there and kill them!'

Irena fights a wave of nausea.

'That's not enough,' Catherine says after a moment. 'They know I went out that night too.'

Irena, startled, turns to stare at her.

'What?' Dan says.

'I went out that night too,' Catherine repeats. 'They caught it on camera – the neighbour across the street has a porch cam.'

'You lied to the police?' Dan says, incredulous.

'Yes, I lied to them, just like you,' Catherine says sharply.

'Why?'

Irena sees Catherine hesitate and glance uncertainly at her husband and Jenna. Catherine swallows. 'I went over to Mom and Dad's that night, around eleven thirty. And . . . they were already dead.'

There is another moment of absolute silence, filled only with the clock ticking.

'*You* found them,' Irena finally exclaims, utterly shocked, 'and you didn't say anything? You left it to me to find them?'

Catherine tries to explain herself. Her voice wavers. 'I'm sorry, Irena. I lied about going over there because I didn't want them to suspect me.'

'They're not going to think *you* did it,' Dan protests. 'You're the favourite. Why would *you* kill them?'

Jenna interjects. 'Dad said he was going to sell the house that night, remember?'

Dan turns to face her. 'So what? That's not worth killing them over.' He turns back to Catherine. 'They're never going to suspect you, Catherine.' He pauses. 'That's not like you at all. Why wouldn't you call 911?'

Irena has already figured it out, but now she sees the realization dawn on Dan's face.

'Oh, I get it,' he says slowly. 'You thought *I* did it.' He looks aghast at his older sister.

Irena reads the shock on Lisa's face, the guilty

expressions of Catherine, Ted, and Jenna, and understands. *Poor Dan*, Irena thinks. She briefly closes her eyes and opens them again.

'I didn't know what to think,' Catherine says carefully. 'So I did nothing. I was in shock. I pretended it wasn't happening.'

'Bullshit!' Dan says harshly. 'You thought it was me!' He looks wildly around the room. 'You all think I did it!'

No one speaks, and Dan turns on them. 'Well, I *know* I didn't do it – so maybe it was one of you.'

Irena remembers how they used to turn on each other as children. Relationships and patterns are established early; they don't change. Family dynamics play out again and again.

Dan focuses his attention on his older sister. 'Why should we believe *you*, Catherine?' he asks.

'What do you mean?' Catherine says.

'I mean, maybe they weren't dead when you got there. Maybe *you* went over there and killed them!'

'That's ridiculous,' Catherine says dismissively. 'You just said I had no reason to kill them.'

He looks at her coldly. 'Maybe I was wrong. We all wanted them dead. There's all that money. And you wanted the house. Maybe you got tired of waiting for it and thought you could pin it on me – and then there'd be more for you and Jenna.' He sends a vicious glance Jenna's way. 'Is that what happened?'

Catherine stares back at him, clearly shocked. 'That's absurd, Dan, and you know it.'

Jenna protests, 'If anything, we're trying to *protect* you, Dan. Not throw you under the bus.'

'Protect me?' he cries bitterly. 'When have either of you *ever* protected me? No one ever stepped in.'

Dan turns now to Irena, his face twisted with emotion. 'Except you, Irena. You at least *tried* to protect me, and I'll never forget that.' He adds bitterly, 'But you shouldn't have cleaned that knife.'

Irena looks at them wearily, this fractious brood she raised.

Catherine says, 'We're not trying to hurt you, Dan. I told the police I talked to Mom and I left.' She adds, 'And we're paying for your defence attorney.'

Dan turns to Jenna. 'What about you?'

'What?' she says, startled.

'You have just as much to gain. How do we know *you* didn't kill them? We all know you have a violent temper.'

'Jake was with me all night,' Jenna says coldly.

'Sure he was,' Dan says sarcastically. 'We all know what that's worth. He could be lying for you.'

'Well, he's not.'

'Great. Then you won't mind if I ask him.'

'Don't be such an asshole.'

Irena watches, her nerves splintering, as Dan

looks from Jenna to Catherine, taking his time, as if thinking about something. Then he says, 'It's just that both of you knew about those disposable suits in my garage. And either one of you could easily have taken one.'

Into the pregnant silence, the doorbell rings. And everyone in the room turns to look.

Audrey has deep misgivings regarding what she is about to do. But something had made her point her car in the direction of Catherine's house. And once she got there and recognized everyone else's cars, she knew they were all gathered inside. Somehow she made her way up the driveway to the front door and rang the bell. Now she stands there, waiting, her breath coming fast.

She remembers how much Dan had frightened her earlier that day and thinks: *What the hell am I doing?* She considers turning on her heel and leaving quickly, but then the door opens, and it's too late.

'What do *you* want?' Catherine says, with a note of hostility.

'Can I come in?'

Catherine seems to consider it, then steps back and lets her in. Audrey makes her way into the living room. She meets Dan's eyes and quickly looks away. The atmosphere is thick with tension. She's obviously walked into something, a family argument perhaps. She thinks: *Someone in this room is the killer* . . . She feels fear stirring the fine hairs on the back of her neck.

'I won't stay long,' she says brusquely, to disguise her fear, not even bothering to sit down. 'I spoke to Walter yesterday. I'm sure you know by now that your father did not change his will in my favour.'

'Of course he didn't,' Jenna says with contempt.

She turns on Jenna, incensed by her dismissive tone. 'He didn't have *time*, because one of you murdered him before he could do it!' She lifts her eyes to the others, who regard her with clear animosity, and perhaps fear. Audrey continues with barely contained fury. 'Did your father tell you he was going to change his will? Or maybe it was your mother, going behind Fred's back. *She* knew what your father was going to do, and she didn't like it. So which one of you did she tell, I wonder?' She looks at each of them in turn and says, with a hint of menace, 'I know it was one of you. And I know all your little secrets. Maybe it's time everyone found out what this family is *really* like.'

And then she turns and walks out, both thrilled and frightened at what she's done.

Chapter Thirty-three

ONCE AUDREY HAS made her exit, Dan leaves his sister's house, Lisa hurrying to follow. He gets into his wife's car and slams the door. She climbs in beside him. He backs the car out of the driveway with a squeal and takes off down the street.

'Slow down,' Lisa cries.

He eases his foot off the gas, but his hands clench the steering wheel angrily. 'They think I did it, Lisa, my own sisters,' he says grimly. He negotiates a corner, going too fast. 'And that bitch, Audrey – her and her big mouth.' He thinks of what she knows about him, what she might tell. The expected words of comfort from his wife don't come. He glances at her. Her face is blank.

Lisa is reeling with shock. She sits in the passenger seat, one hand against the dashboard, as Dan drives wildly. Dan is speaking to her, but she's not listening. She's still trying to get to grips with what just happened. Catherine and Jenna think Dan murdered their parents. That much is clear. The question is, what does *she* think?

She has begun to have doubts.

At first, she didn't believe Dan had anything to do with it. She knows what clothes he went out in that night. There was no blood on them. So she didn't mind lying for him to the police.

And then the detectives found the package of disposable coveralls. She'd stood at the opening to the garage, her mind stuttering. If he'd worn the suit and booties, he wouldn't have been covered with blood at all. He could have come home in clean clothes.

And Catherine – how could she find the bodies and say nothing? It's disturbing. That's not like Catherine at all. Surely she wouldn't do that unless she was trying to protect her brother, give him time to get rid of evidence. That's the problem – she believes Catherine over her own husband. Her blood runs cold. He was gone a long time that night.

She believes his sisters want to protect him, even though Dan doesn't see it that way. If they can live with it, maybe she can too. Dan is about to inherit a fortune. Unless he's convicted.

But Catherine and Jenna don't have to actually *live* with him.

And Audrey – why are they all clearly so afraid of her?

Ted watches Dan and Lisa drive away and closes the door behind them. Slowly, he returns to the living room. Ted sits down heavily beside his wife and leans back against the sofa. He's exhausted by all of this. He's grateful that his childhood was relatively simple, as an only child. Catherine's family is a fucking train wreck.

Jenna stands up. 'I'll be going, then. Let me know if anything happens.'

'I'm going too,' Irena says.

They almost seem to have forgotten about Irena, sitting in her corner, Ted thinks. He wonders if she feels mostly irrelevant to them now.

Catherine walks them to the door.

Ted closes his eyes. Soon he hears his wife come back into the living room, feels her sit down on the sofa beside him.

He's thinking about what Dan said. He was lashing out – Dan was against the ropes and he knew it. Catherine and Jenna are trying to help him. Ted has decided he's staying out of it; he'll let the chips fall where they may.

But it's niggling at him, what Dan said. Accusing

Catherine, accusing Jenna. Because the truth is, Catherine was *there* that night. And Ted hasn't come to terms with the fact that Catherine was able to come home and pretend that everything was fine. He's not sure how well he really knows her any more. 'Why did he say that, about the disposable suits?' Ted asks, turning his head to look at her.

'What?'

'That you knew where they were. How would you know?'

She shakes her head dismissively. 'Jenna and I were over there one day for lunch when he was working on the attic, that's all. We laughed at how he looked in his hazmat suit. I think you were golfing that day.'

Ted averts his eyes. 'And what was Audrey talking about?'

Catherine huffs. 'Ignore her. She's just angry that she didn't get the money. She's harmless.'

But Ted can tell she's worried. And it makes him worry too.

Jenna drives home, heading north from her sister's comfortable suburb. She's soon on the outskirts of town, and then onto the dirt roads of the countryside. As she drives, she thinks about how much she hates her aunt Audrey. Audrey has always seemed to like her least. She's not sure why. You would think her ranking of favourites would align with her parents': Catherine first, then Jenna, then Dan. But Audrey seems to have her own preferences, ranking Jenna in last place. It's not like Jenna's ever done anything to her.

It's clear that Audrey is threatening them all. She would never have dared to do that when their father was alive. But she's obviously feeling vindictive and reckless. She thinks she's been robbed of a fortune, and that it's their fault.

Audrey is privy to the family secrets, most of them anyway. She knows things about them, things that might prejudice the police, and the public, against them. Audrey knows, for instance, about Jenna's early violent streak.

When Jenna was six years old, furious at Dan for teasing her, she'd pushed him right off the top of the slide in their backyard. He'd fallen backward with a scream and landed hard on the ground. It could have been much worse – he'd only broken his arm, not his neck. Catherine had seen it happen and gone crying to their parents.

'What kind of child pushes another one off the top of the slide?' Audrey gasped, horrified, making more of it than she should have. Unfortunately, she happened to be there that day. Then she'd stayed behind with their father while their mother took Dan to the hospital to have his arm put in a cast. Jenna sat under the kitchen table playing with her Barbies and listened to Audrey and her father talk about her. 'You'd better keep that temper in check, young lady,' Audrey had said as she left. Jenna has disliked her ever since.

Following that, she'd given Catherine a concussion, and Audrey knew about that, too, because their father told his sister everything about the kids, the worse the better. Jenna had picked up a plastic bat and struck Catherine, who had fallen and banged her head on the pavement, when they were having an argument. Catherine had been rushed to the hospital. Their parents told people that Catherine had fallen while playing.

Jenna had been properly punished for that one.

At home that night, Audrey watches the eleven o'clock news in her pyjamas, sipping a chamomile tea. There's nothing new about the Merton case. She sits in bed, seething at the television set, thinking unhappily about her lost inheritance, which she had so hoped to be able to enjoy. She'd imagined a house of her own in Brecken Hill, fine clothes, and trips to Europe and the Bahamas. There's brief footage of them searching Dan's house earlier that day, but she has no idea if they found anything incriminating. They're not saying. She remembers how frightened she was when Dan came toward her car window, the rage in his fist as it hit her car.

Now that she's had time to think about it, she can hardly believe she crashed the family gathering at Catherine's afterward. Where had she found the courage?

She decides to pay a visit to the detectives in the morning.

Chapter Thirty-four

IT'S FRIDAY MORNING, and Reyes and Barr are reviewing the case. The crime scene has yielded disappointingly little in the way of evidence or clues. They have found no physical evidence left behind by the killer. Reyes is beginning to believe they are dealing with someone rather clever, someone able to plan a double murder and perhaps get away with it. But not if he has anything to do with it.

They know there was possibly another vehicle in the vicinity that night – the one the neighbour, Mrs Sachs, claims to have seen. A pickup truck that could not have been mistaken for Catherine's, Dan's, or Jenna's cars. Or Irena's either. Whoever was driving it may have seen something. It's possible the person in that truck may have killed the Mertons. But his instincts tell him otherwise. Unless one – or more – of the Merton offspring hired someone to kill the parents – possibly the person in the truck. But their police bulletins, the description to the media, the inquiries at shops that do that kind of custom paintwork – nothing has come of any of it.

The sergeant from the front desk knocks lightly on Reyes's open door. 'Sir,' she says.

'Yes, what is it?'

'There's someone here to see you about the Merton case. Audrey Stancik?'

Reyes glances at Barr. 'Fred Merton's sister.' They haven't had her in to talk to yet, but she's on their list. He rises from his desk. 'Let's see why she's here.'

They walk into the waiting area, and Reyes sees a plump woman with shoulder-length blond hair rise from one of the chairs. She's well groomed, wearing bright coral lipstick and dressed in a beige pantsuit, a brightly printed blouse, and sensible heels. He estimates that she's probably around sixty years of age. Fred, he remembers, was sixty-two.

They get Audrey settled in an interview room. Barr offers her coffee, which she gladly accepts. 'Milk and two sugars,' she says.

'What brings you here?' Reyes asks at last.

'I know you've interviewed everyone in the family,' she says, her eyes shrewd, 'except me.' She takes a sip of her coffee and puts it back down.

231

Reyes wonders if she's merely a busybody who feels left out, but what she says next makes his ears prick up.

'I know a lot about that family,' she says. 'And unlike the others, I'm willing to tell you about it.'

Jenna takes the train into New York City on Friday morning and meets Jake for coffee at a place they both like, the Rocket Fuel café. It's a place where artists like to hang out – it's cheap and grungy, with scarred tables and mismatched chairs, and the coffee is strong. She gets there first, watching for him out the window, waiting for him to come through the door. She hasn't known him that long. She doesn't know him that well. She hopes she hasn't made a mistake.

She sees him enter the café, long and lean, and remembers how attracted she is to him. She'd almost forgotten about that. She smiles as he saunters over to her. She stands up and gives him a long kiss, sparking looks from the other patrons.

'Hey,' Jake says, his voice low and sexy. 'I've missed you.'

'I've missed you too,' she says, and realizes that it's true. She loves the smell of paint and turpentine coming off him, mixing with the smell of sweat.

Once he gets his coffee, they sit huddled close together at her small table. 'It's so good to see you,' he says, stroking her hair. 'How are you doing? Are you okay?'

She nods. 'I think so. But Jake –' She looks deep into his eyes and lowers her voice. 'Catherine and I, we think maybe Dan did it.' He looks back at her gravely. She realizes that he's not that surprised. It hits her then that everyone is going to see Dan as the obvious suspect.

She leans in closer, whispering. 'The police obviously think he did it. He told them he was in that night, all night, and Lisa backed him up, but the cops have witnesses – he went out in his car, and he was gone for hours.' She adds, 'He's got an attorney now.'

'Are they going to arrest him?'

'I don't know. I hope not. Catherine says they don't have any evidence. They didn't find anything at his house.' She pauses. 'Except –'

'Except what?' Jake asks.

She tells him about the disposable coveralls in the garage and swears him to secrecy.

Jakes says tentatively, 'I saw him ask your father for money that night, and he shot him down.' He adds, 'I didn't tell the detectives about that.'

She looks down at the scratched table in front of her. 'I don't know what to do.'

'There's nothing you *can* do,' Jake assures her. 'Just sit it out. What's going to happen is going to

233

happen.' He reaches out and takes her hand. 'And I'm here for you. You know that, right?'

She leans in and kisses him softly on the mouth, grateful. She breaks off the kiss.

'Do you want me there tomorrow? At the funeral?' he asks.

'If you don't mind,' she says. She grimaces. 'It's going to be fucking awful. The police will be there, watching everything.'

If Dan tries to talk to Jake at the funeral, she thinks, she'll be there, right beside him, and put a stop to it. Their coffees finished, she says, 'Maybe we should go back to your place and figure out what you're going to wear tomorrow.'

'That's just an excuse to get me into bed, isn't it?' he says.

She smiles.

Chapter Thirty-five

'GO ON,' REYES says to Audrey, interested to hear what she has to say.

'That family had problems,' Audrey begins. 'Sheila wasn't good for my brother. She was weak and frivolous. She didn't bring out the best in him. Fred hated weakness; it made him angry.'

'Then why did he marry a weak woman?' Barr interjects.

She glances at Barr. 'I don't know,' she admits. She sighs and says, 'Maybe it was easier for him than marrying a strong one.' She pauses for a moment. 'Sheila – she was a self-absorbed woman who didn't show much interest in her children. It was a troubled family. They won't tell you that, but I know. They want everyone to think everything was perfect. But the kids hated Fred.'

'Why?' Reyes asks.

'Because he was awful to them. Fred could be cruel, especially to Dan.' She takes a sip of her coffee, then continues. 'Fred had more money than he knew what to do with, and he didn't skimp on his kids, especially in the early years.

'Those kids were brought up accustomed to having wonderful things,' Audrey explains. 'But then Fred started taking things away. His kids had disappointed him, you see. He had such great expectations for them when they were little. He was especially unhappy with Dan. Both girls have more going for them than Dan ever did, if you ask me. Anyway, Fred was a brilliant businessman, and Dan just didn't have what he had. Dan wanted to please his father, but nothing was ever good enough. And Fred belittled him all the time, destroyed his confidence. It's as if once he decided that Dan was never going to measure up, he couldn't resist taking out his anger and dissatisfaction on him at every turn. He sold the company so that Dan couldn't have it. I'm sure that it was probably the right business decision, but I also know that he did it with malice. He wanted to hurt Dan, for disappointing him.' She stops and takes a deep breath. 'He could be petty that way.'

'So you think Dan killed them,' Reyes says.

'I don't know,' she replies. 'But I'm certain one of them did.'

'Why are you so sure?'

'Fred was dying. He had pancreatic cancer, and he knew he didn't have much time. He refused all treatment, except painkillers. Anyway, he felt that he'd been overly generous to his kids, and that perhaps it had ruined them.' She tells them how Fred was going to change his will, and her conviction that at least one of the kids knew, that perhaps Fred, or possibly Sheila, had told them, and paid the ultimate price for it, before he could carry out his intentions.

Which certainly makes it unlikely that Audrey killed them, Reyes thinks. She was going to get the money soon anyway.

Audrey says, 'If you ask me, one of them is a psychopath and had no trouble killing their parents. You just have to figure out which one.'

She sits back in her chair and says, 'Let me tell you a few things about those kids.'

Around lunchtime, Lisa slips out of the house while Dan is puttering around in the garage. She takes her car, telling him she's going to run some errands, though she has a different destination in mind. He's furious at his sisters; he's convinced himself that they have betrayed him, simply by thinking the worst of him. She hadn't liked it either, and she can understand his feelings of hurt and betrayal. And fear. But she also believes his sisters want to protect him. When she told him this, he said, 'You don't know them like I do,' and refused to discuss it any further.

She doesn't want the conflict between Dan and his sisters on display tomorrow at the funeral. She must bring him around somehow. They must present a united front; she can't have it looking like he's estranged from his sisters. And he's so on edge, prone to unexpected outbursts.

The other thing is, she's not entirely sure they're wrong about him. She needs support. She needs comfort. Because she's never been so frightened in her life.

She drives the short distance to Catherine's house, thinking about what she's going to say. She's become quite close to Catherine since she married Dan. Lisa has confided in Catherine more about their financial situation than Dan would strictly approve.

She pulls into the driveway, noticing that the curtains in the living room are drawn. It's hard to believe it's only been three days since Sheila and Fred were discovered; it feels like so much longer. Her whole world has been turned upside down.

Catherine lets her in. As soon as the door is closed behind her, Lisa bursts into unrestrained tears. Catherine pulls her into a hug and Lisa lets it all out.

Finally, they sit down in the living room, and when Lisa is cried out, she apologizes. Ted has come into the room, but wisely leaves again, retreating upstairs. 'I'm not coping very well,' Lisa says miserably.

'You're coping as well as anyone would,' Catherine tells her.

Lisa looks back at her, noticing the tension in Catherine's face, her body. She screws up her courage and asks the question she came to ask. 'You know him. Do you really think Dan could have done it?'

Catherine averts her eyes for a moment and then drags them wearily back to meet hers. 'I don't know what to think.'

'Me neither,' Lisa admits in a whisper. 'Ever since they found those disposable suits.'

After she's finished at the police station, Audrey drives to Ellen's house and pulls into the driveway. She needs to talk to someone, and there's nobody else she can talk to about this other than Ellen.

'Audrey,' Ellen says opening the door, having spotted her car from the window. 'You want some coffee?'

'Sure,' Audrey says, following her into the kitchen.

'What's the latest?' Ellen asks as she busies herself with the coffee maker.

Audrey settles her bulk at the kitchen table,

considering how much she should tell Ellen about where she's been.

'I've just come from the police station,' she admits.

Ellen turns around and stares. 'Why? What's happened?'

'I told them the truth.'

'What truth?' Ellen asks, promptly forgetting about the coffee.

Audrey swallows. 'I told them that I thought one of the kids did it. That Fred or Sheila probably told one of them that Fred was going to change his will in my favour.'

'Oh, Audrey,' Ellen says slowly. 'Are you sure that was a good idea?'

'I don't know,' Audrey admits. 'Maybe not.'

'Are you absolutely certain Fred was going to change his will?' Ellen asks.

'Yes,' Audrey says firmly. She can tell Ellen doesn't quite believe her. What the hell does she know about it? 'I'm positive. He promised me. He wanted to punish his children. And I think he was rewarding me for my silence all of these years.'

'Silence about what?' Ellen asks, curious.

'Nothing you need to know,' Audrey hastily assures her.

Friday night after work, Rose lies down on her bed, still in her skirt and blouse, too drained to think about making something to eat. Instead, eyes closed, she stews about her situation, her thoughts going over and over the same ground. Her nerves are getting the better of her. She regrets, now, what she's done. It was a mistake. *Why did she do it?* But she knows why – because she's greedy, she's impatient, and she took a shortcut. If she could go back in time and undo everything, she would.

After a while, she gets up off her bed and looks through her closet. She must find something to wear to the funeral tomorrow. She decides her black suit will have to do.

Chapter Thirty-six

SATURDAY IS SUNNY and mild – a lovely day for a funeral, Reyes thinks, straightening his tie. He and Barr will attend, as well as some officers in plain clothes, mingling with the mourners, keeping an eye on the family and those close to them. Keeping an eye on everyone.

Reyes drives to St Brigid's Church in Brecken Hill, where the rich people go. It's rather grand, and he's never been inside. He parks in the lot and walks up to the church, taking his time, looking around. He's early, but a steady stream of people in expensive cars are entering the parking lot. He remains outside, watching mourners circulate in front of the church, arriving to pay their respects. They form little clusters, middle-aged women in dresses and hats, men in dark suits, meeting and mingling with people they know, speaking in low voices. There had been no viewing at the funeral home, at the request of the family. Just the funeral, and a private committal service for the family. In Reyes's experience, there's always a viewing and a wake. There will be a gathering at the golf club after the funeral.

He sees Barr arrive. She looks so different in her simple black dress and heels that, for a moment, he hadn't recognized her.

The funeral is scheduled for two o'clock. None of the family is here yet. Then Reyes notices Audrey, with a woman in her mid-thirties. They look alike; it must be her daughter. He wonders if Fred's niece hated him too. She doesn't look particularly happy, and Reyes would bet it's not because she's sad about her aunt and uncle, with whom, he's heard, she's had little contact.

The family arrives together, in two black limousines that stop in front of the church. Catherine, Ted, and Irena alight from the first, followed by Dan, Lisa, Jenna, and Jake Brenner in the second. Reyes studies each of them closely. Dan Merton looks pale and edgy, constantly pulling at his collar; his wife, Lisa, is stiff and seems to be dreading what's to come. Catherine is beautifully turned out in a tailored black dress, straight-backed, composed, and regal. She's rising to the occasion, while Dan and his wife appear to be slightly overwhelmed

243

by it. Ted stands strong and resolute beside Catherine, ready for what's ahead. Jenna has made a small concession to the occasion and is wearing a black skirt and a subdued blouse and looks relatively conventional except for the shock of purple hair.

The family proceeds along the walk and up the steps to the church, eyes lowered, not stopping to talk to anyone. At the front door, the priest greets them and ushers them inside. Slowly, the rest of the attendees make their way into the church.

Barr comes up to stand beside him at the top of the steps.

'You look very nice,' Reyes says.

'Thank you.'

He says, 'You take the left side, I'll take the right.' As she moves away, Reyes locates the plainclothes officers mixing with the mourners, making eye contact with each. They're not expecting anything, but it's always good to have extra pairs of eyes. There's another officer stationed in the parking lot and another along the street for overflow parking; both are specifically looking for a dark pickup truck with flames painted on the sides. If they spot anything, his phone is on vibrate. But he doesn't think the truck will turn up; the driver has to know they're looking for him.

As organ music fills the church, Reyes takes a seat close to the front on the right side, at the end of the pew next to the outer aisle. He figures there are close to three hundred people in the church by the time they are ready to start. He wonders how many of them actually knew the Mertons and how many are here simply because they were murdered.

There are two matching, gleaming mahogany coffins at the front of the church. Surrounding the coffins are plentiful flower arrangements of roses and lilies; the scent filters to where Reyes is sitting, reminding him of other funerals he has attended. But this one isn't personal, it's work. He keeps his eyes on the family in the front row as the service begins.

Catherine realizes she is clenching her entire body tightly as the service proceeds toward its conclusion, and forces herself to physically relax. She's gratified by the number of people in attendance. The flowers are lovely – Jenna chose well, she thinks. She's happy with the coffins they selected. The service is respectful, tasteful. They've done a good job. It's not easy to pull together a large, impressive funeral in a short time under such difficult extenuating circumstances. Now all they have to do is get through this and the reception afterward. By tonight, it will all be over and she can let herself collapse.

They'd had a rocky start this morning, but Lisa was able to get Dan speaking to her and Jenna again, persuading him that it would look bad if he and his sisters seemed estranged. Lisa had convinced him that they must present a united front, a family in mourning, together.

Catherine had spotted the two detectives in the crowd; they're behind her somewhere, she can practically feel their eyes on the back of her neck. She sits at the end of the front pew, closest to the centre aisle. Beside her is Ted. Next to Ted is Jenna, then Jake. She's surprised to find that he actually owns a decent suit. Maybe he rented it. Then Dan and Lisa and Irena. She knows that Audrey is sitting with her daughter – who flew in for the funeral – at the end of the pew, and it upsets her. She wonders if Audrey has said anything to the detectives. Catherine has given her reading, and the priest is finishing up. There has been singing – a beautiful 'Ave Maria'. The service is almost over when she senses a movement to her right. She glances over quickly. No, it can't be. Dan is standing up as the priest drones on. Lisa has her hand on Dan's forearm, tugging at it, her face looking up at him dismayed, then she whispers something. Catherine thinks she's telling him to sit down. Dan is flushed now; he's got that stubborn look on his face that she recognizes from when they were kids. He's had enough hypocrisy – he wants to leave, she thinks. Then, as he stumbles past the knees of his wife, Irena, and Audrey and her daughter and reaches the end of the pew, he turns to the front of the church and Catherine realizes with horror that he is going to speak. She meets Lisa's eyes and they show panic. Lisa is silently begging her to do something, to prevent some catastrophe. But what can she do? Should she try to stop him? Catherine turns her attention to the front of the church and watches in a terrible state of indecision as Dan approaches the lectern. She can hear the rustle of movement in the church as the mourners, half drowsy from the service, are jolted out of their boredom at the sight of Dan at the front of the church. She feels Ted's hand pressing down on hers, steadying her.

Catherine swallows and fights the urge to interfere. Maybe it will be okay. And then the priest is finished and steps away, and Dan begins to speak.

'I wasn't going to speak at Mom and Dad's funeral.' He swallows. The flush on his face is more pronounced now, and he tugs nervously at his collar. 'I'm not much of a public speaker, so this is difficult for me.' He pauses, looks out at the crowd, and seems to lose his nerve. Catherine prays that he does lose his nerve, that he stumbles through something short and harmless like *thank you for coming* and retreats to his seat. But then he seems to find his courage. 'I wasn't going to speak because as many of you might know, my father and I did not get along. But there are some things I want to say.'

Chapter Thirty-seven

CATHERINE LISTENS, HER body rigid. Dan's voice is trembling with nerves, but he seems determined to go through with this.

'Many of you know my father as a good man, a decent man. He was a successful businessman – and he was very proud of his success.' He looks out at the crowd, avoiding the faces of the family in the front row. 'But he was different at home. We saw another side of him that you never saw. He was a difficult man. He was hard to live with. Demanding, hard to please.' He pauses.

Catherine senses people shifting uncomfortably in their seats behind her, but she's frozen, staring at her younger brother, afraid of what's coming next.

Dan continues. 'I was bullied mercilessly – not at school, but by my own father. He was cruel and vindictive. He was especially hard on me, as the only boy, and probably because I disappointed him the most. I was the biggest disappointment of his life – he told me that, often.' He stops, as if to gain control of himself. 'We were taught to keep quiet about these things.' Then he seems to change his tone, and his delivery, as if he's going off script. The words come faster. 'He was abusive. I recognize that now. When I was a kid, I just thought I deserved it, but I know now that no one deserves to be treated that way. He must have suffered, at the end. It was a horrible way to die. You're probably going to hear things about me, but I want all of you to know that I didn't do it. Even after all the terrible things he did to me, I didn't kill him. And I would never kill my mother. I hope she didn't suffer too much. I hope she died quickly.' He's rambling.

Catherine is horrified. He's gone from being flushed to very pale. She can see that he's losing his grip. He's holding on to the lectern as if he might fall if he doesn't. She can see a sheen of sweat on his face. She has to put a stop to this. She lurches to her feet and walks up the centre aisle the short distance to the lectern. He's stopped speaking and watches her approach warily, as a hush falls over the church. She takes his arm gently. He tries to shake it off but then suddenly gives in, as if he's forgotten anything more he wanted to say, and goes with her back to the pew, where they all shift over and he sits down beside her. As Catherine takes her seat, she can hear the low hum of people starting to whisper. People will talk about this; it will be in the news. She's furious at Dan but trying hard not to show it. She tries, once, to meet Lisa's eyes, but Lisa is staring at the floor.

Reyes considers what he's just seen. It makes him wonder if Dan Merton is a rather disturbed young man. Reyes turns around and searches out Barr behind him and to the left. She meets his eyes, raises her eyebrows. The service is over. Reyes checks his phone as he rises. There's been nothing. If they'd seen the pickup truck they would have buzzed him. He swallows his disappointment.

Rose Cutter rises from her seat at the back of the church and thinks about sneaking away quietly without getting in line to speak to the family. Catherine would expect to see her. But there are so many people; it's going to take a long time. She doesn't want to talk to the family. She just wants to get away. She slips out of the church.

Irena hovers nearby, keeping an eye on things as the family gathers at the entrance to the church for people to pay their respects on the way out. She was deeply disturbed by Dan's speech. Now Dan is there, straitjacketed between his two sisters, who've told him to say nothing but *thank you for coming.* They are all worried about what people will think, about what the detectives will think.

Irena longs for this ordeal to be over. The funeral, the gathering afterward, the investigation. It's all so exhausting. She hasn't been sleeping well. She feels like she has vertigo, as if she's standing on the edge of a precipice, about to fall. She watches Dan.

He turns to his right and leans across Jenna to Jake, and says, 'Jenna says you were with her all night the night Mom and Dad were killed. Is that true?'

He hasn't lowered his voice, and Irena can hear him from several feet away, and the people close by glance at him.

Jake looks embarrassed and says something she doesn't catch.

Dan smiles unpleasantly. 'Right. Like you're not lying for her.'

Irena notices then with a sickening jolt that Detective Reyes is standing beside her, observing, listening. She feels uncomfortable with him so close, hearing everything. She watches in dismay as a disaster unfolds in front of them. She's helpless to stop it.

Jenna turns to her brother and hisses something she can't quite hear. Probably telling him to shut up.

'Why?' Dan says angrily. 'What did you ever do for me?'

Irena holds her breath. She's furious at the detective standing beside her, seeing everything. Lisa appears to be coaxing Dan to leave. She's speaking to him quietly, pulling on his sleeve.

But Dan looks in Irena's direction and spies Detective Reyes standing beside her. He calls, 'Detective!' and waves him over. 'There's something you should know.'

Irena sees that everyone in the family except Dan has gone rigid at the sight of the detective. The people in the line fall away awkwardly. Reyes takes a few steps until he's standing near Dan. 'Maybe we could go outside?' the detective says quietly.

Dan waves his suggestion aside and says, loudly, 'My sisters don't have alibis either. You know Ted lied for Catherine. And I bet Jake here is lying for Jenna.'

Reyes looks at Jake, who averts his eyes.

'And Catherine and Jenna both knew about the disposable suits in my garage.' His voice is sly now. 'Either one of them could have taken one; I don't even lock the garage most of the time. You need to know that. I didn't kill them – but maybe one of them did.'

It seems as if everyone still inside the church has stopped moving, riveted to the scene. Irena sees

Audrey and her daughter on the periphery. Audrey is avidly taking it all in, a smirk on her face.

Irena knows this family. They're going to turn on one another. That's what they do, these kids. It's what they've always done. Irena suddenly becomes aware of the sound of photographers furiously taking pictures.

Exhausted from the events of the last week, Reyes collapses into his favourite armchair in the evening, thinking about the funeral earlier that day, while his wife gets the kids ready for bed. He should really give her a hand, but she'd taken one look at him and told him to go put his feet up, he looked worn out.

Is it true, Reyes asks himself, that both sisters knew about the disposable coveralls in Dan Merton's garage and had access, as he claimed? Might one of them have committed the murders, hoping he'd take the fall? And to get a bigger portion?

Catherine lied about going back to the house that night. Did she kill them then? She might have taken one of those suits, rather than risk purchasing one somewhere herself, and possibly to cast suspicion on her brother. Maybe she's only pretending to be the protective sister. Audrey claims that Fred or Sheila must have told one or more of the kids about their father's plan to change his will in

Audrey's favour. If that's true, who knew? Would losing half of the estate to their aunt be enough to drive one of them to murder?

And Jenna ... well, Jake isn't a very good liar. What really happened in that hour while Jenna and Jake were in the house with Fred and Sheila? Did they come back afterward and commit the murders together? Or did Jenna possibly do it on her own? For now, Jake is standing by her alibi.

He must talk to both sisters again. And he wants another crack at the former nanny, who probably knows that family better than anyone.

Chapter Thirty-eight

CATHERINE WAKES UP Sunday morning, still drained from the long and difficult day before. She picks up the newspaper outside her door and sees reporters and TV trucks in the street. Up until now the press had mostly left them alone. They surge toward her and she quickly slams the door. She looks down at the paper in her hands.

The *Aylesford Record* has again run the story about her parents' murders on the front page. But this time it's different. There's a photograph, and it makes her suck in her breath – a candid shot of that awful moment in the church when Dan started spilling his venom to that detective. Catherine studies the photo – she looks cold and angry. Dan is animated, Jenna startled. It's a very unflattering photograph of the family, and it makes her cringe. Catherine walks slowly into the kitchen and sits down at the table, reading the article quickly, with growing distaste. The distance and the respect afforded the Mertons thus far because of their wealth and position has disappeared. The gloves have come off and now the press is out for blood.

Who Killed Wealthy Couple? Family Rift Disrupts Funeral

She skims the article, and as she does, certain key phrases and sentences pop out at her.

. . . speculation that it was a robbery that turned violent . . . Perhaps a new theory of the case is emerging . . . Dan Merton overheard telling police that his two sisters, Catherine Merton and Jenna Merton, should be considered suspects . . . a shocking display of dissension in a family that has always been very private and conscious of its position in the community . . .

Catherine's heart sinks as she continues reading.

Police are focusing their attention on the three adult children . . . each expected to inherit a portion of the Mertons' estate . . . A source, who spoke on condition of anonymity, claims money might not be the only motive for the murders. The family was apparently a troubled one, a claim borne out by what happened at yesterday's funeral . . .

Catherine looks up as she hears Ted enter the kitchen.

'You won't believe this,' Catherine says, feeling sick to her stomach, throwing the newspaper onto the table in front of him as he sits down across from her. Catherine gets up to put the coffee on.

Ted reads silently, his face grim. 'Jesus,' he says.

Catherine says bitterly, 'Why doesn't Dan understand that he should just shut the fuck up?' She adds, 'And we all know who that anonymous source is.'

Lisa stares down at her coffee, which has grown cold. She's read the disturbing article in the *Aylesford Record*.

She's never been so frightened, so alone. Dan has come unglued. He's effectively cut them both off from his sisters through his actions yesterday at the funeral. He expects her to remain loyal to him and have nothing more to do with Catherine and Jenna. It's as if he's lost his mind. They fought about it last night after the disastrous funeral and interminable event at the golf club, but he wouldn't listen to reason. He seems almost to have convinced himself

257

that one of his sisters murdered their parents and set him up to take the fall.

Or is that what he's trying to convince her of?

It's incomprehensible, all of it. Lisa's in an impossible position.

Reyes and Barr interview Irena Dabrowski again early on Sunday morning, while waiting for the search warrant for Catherine Merton. The cleaning lady sits across from them in the interview room for the second time. Reyes believes she might hold the key. He believes that one of the Merton kids killed their parents. He's convinced she thinks so too. She certainly knows more than she's telling.

'We know you're protecting somebody.'

'I'm not protecting anyone. I don't know who did it.' She looks down at the table and says, a little desperately, 'I don't want to know.'

Reyes leans forward intently. 'But you do know, or you have a pretty good idea,' he says. 'It was one of the kids, wasn't it? We know it was one of them – or maybe two of them or all of them together – and so do you.' She raises her head and he sees tears start to form in her eyes. He waits, but all she does is shake her head.

He opens the folder on the desk and takes out photos of the murder scenes and spreads them out on the table. She glances down, then quickly looks away.

'So which one of your former charges is capable of that, do you think?'

Finally, she licks her lips, as if she's going to say something. Reyes waits, trying not to show his impatience.

She says, 'I don't know who did it.' She slumps in defeat, as if the effort to hold it in any longer is too much for her. 'But I think any one of them might be capable of it.'

'Why?' Reyes coaxes, his voice quieter now.

She swallows. Takes a sip from the water glass with a trembling hand. Wipes her tears away with a tissue. 'Because as much as I love each of them, I know what they're like. They're clever, and selfish, and greedy, and they were fathered by a psychopath. I did my best, but I wouldn't put it past any of them.' She wipes away another tear and looks up at him. 'But they would never have done it together. They don't do anything together.'

Audrey rereads the article in the *Aylesford Record*, and while she's pleased at the strife among Fred and Sheila's children, now out in the open for all to see, it doesn't dampen her sense of injustice. There's nothing in the article about Audrey being denied her rightful share of the estate. She hadn't told Robin Fontaine about that. Audrey had been the unnamed source who'd spoken about the problems within the

Merton family, none of the juicy details of which had made it into the article. They're probably afraid of a lawsuit, she thinks. Maybe it's time to take it up a notch. Maybe she needs to call back that reporter and tell her what she told the detectives – that Fred was going to change his will and one of those kids is a murderer. But they probably won't print that either. She doesn't have any proof.

Ellen drops by for their regular Sunday morning walk. They like to hike the various trails around Aylesford in good weather. Each Sunday, they drive together to the head of one of the trails. Now, they each carry water bottles, and as they walk, they talk.

It's quiet out here along the nature trail, with just the occasional jogger or cyclist passing them. Audrey impulsively tells Ellen what she's thinking of doing.

'You're the one who talked to the reporter,' Ellen says.

'Yes. What, do you think I shouldn't have?'

Ellen is slow to answer. As Audrey walks along-side her, she considers Ellen. She has never been one to rock the boat – she's led a rather subdued life. Audrey has always been the colourful one, she thinks, while Ellen is more reserved, a bit mousy, with her brown hair streaked with grey, her simple slacks and cardigans in quiet shades. As if she doesn't want to be noticed.

'I don't know,' Ellen admits finally. 'To accuse someone of murder –'

'I just can't stand by and do nothing,' Audrey insists. 'At least I can try to get justice for Fred.'

'Maybe you should leave it to the police,' Ellen suggests. 'You don't actually *know* that one of them did it.'

Audrey snorts derisively.

'How can you be so sure?' Ellen persists.

Audrey stops walking and looks at her, as if coming to a decision. 'I'm going to tell you something. Something awful. But you must swear you'll never repeat it. To *anyone*.'

Chapter Thirty-nine

AS AUDREY TELLS her story, Ellen walking beside her, she slips back into the past. She thought she would never tell anyone, but now Fred is dead and she doesn't have to protect him any more. She knows she can trust Ellen not to say anything. As she speaks, long-buried memories and emotions take over. It's a relief to finally tell someone after keeping it locked inside for a lifetime.

She tells her about the house they grew up in, a ramshackle rural property in Vermont that had seen better days. Audrey was eleven and Fred was thirteen that summer. Their father had been on a downward trajectory for years. He'd lost one job after another because of his drinking, and Audrey wasn't sure how her parents were putting food on the table. She thought that sometimes a cheque would come in the mail from her mother's parents.

But there was always a new bottle of whiskey on the kitchen counter every evening, empty by morning when she got up to get herself ready for school. And somehow another one would appear the next evening. She often wondered, embarrassed and bitter when some of the kids on the school bus made fun of her threadbare clothes, where the money for the booze came from.

There was a woodstove in the grubby kitchen. In the living room, on the mantel of the fireplace, was an old, framed photograph of their paternal great-grandfather – whose sole claim to fame was that he'd been hanged for murder. A narrow wooden staircase led upstairs to three bedrooms and a bathroom. Audrey remembers the sound of her parents' bedroom door slamming. The sound of weeping coming from her mother down the hall.

She never brought friends home from school. Sometimes she would be invited to other girls' houses, on the school bus route, but she never returned the offer. Somehow the kids understood. People knew her dad was an alcoholic.

But it was worse than that. Their dad was an ugly, angry alcoholic. And the more he drank, the nastier he got. He'd take it out on Fred, if Fred was mouthy, and he was mouthy that summer. He'd slap Fred across the face. Fred never cried. But he got tall and strong that year and finally he slugged his father back, making him crash against the kitchen table and onto the floor as Audrey and her mother watched in disbelief. He never hit Fred again.

Instead he occasionally slapped around their mother. But he was mostly verbally abusive, calling Audrey names, telling her that she was fat and stupid, like her mother. Fred didn't stick up for his sister, but she worshipped him anyway. She thought of him as the functioning head of the family. She thought that, somehow, he'd get them out of this.

Audrey was desperate to be normal, to pretend that they were like other families. So she cleaned the empties out of her dad's car – sometimes beer cans but mostly whiskey and vodka bottles – and put them in the trash. She cleaned the house. She made an effort. Her mother soon came to depend on her more and more. Audrey worked hard at school because the one thing she knew was that she didn't want to end up like her mom and dad; she wanted to get the hell away from home. Sometimes she felt like she and Fred were the grown-ups, taking care of their parents.

Fred was brilliant. Everyone said so. He sailed through school effortlessly, with top grades. Audrey thought her brother was the smartest person she knew. He excelled at sports, attracted friends easily. He was good-looking and all the girls had crushes on him. Audrey made friends easily too, and was good in school, but she was chubby and plain and not good at anything in particular, other than doing what she was told. But Fred was different. He had confidence. He knew he was going places.

Sometimes when things were bad in the house, they'd sit out in the empty barn and talk.

'I wish he was dead,' Fred said one day.

Audrey knew who he was talking about. She felt the same way. Sometimes she'd fantasize about her Dad driving drunk and crashing the car, killing himself instantly. In these fantasies, no one else was ever hurt. Maybe there was even insurance money that they didn't know about. A lot of young Audrey's daydreams were about coming into a lot of money, since they had so little of it. An unexpected inheritance. A lottery win. Buried treasure.

'If he was dead, we could go back to the city and live with Mom's sister,' Fred said, as if he'd given it some thought.

Fred liked his Aunt Mary, who'd doted on him when he was little, but whom they hadn't seen in years.

'I thought Mom wasn't talking to Aunt Mary any more,' Audrey said.

'You have no clue, do you?' Fred said. 'Aunt Mary hates Dad. That's why she won't visit.'

'Then why don't we visit her without him?' Audrey asked.

He gave her a look that told her how dumb she was. 'Because we have no money. Dad drinks it all,' he said.

Audrey fell silent. Maybe Aunt Mary was the one sending money. It gave her hope. 'Maybe Mom will decide to leave Dad and then we can go live with Aunt Mary.'

He gave her a look of frustration. 'She won't.'

'Why not?'

'Because she's too stupid and too scared.' He sat thinking, silent for a minute. 'But I've had just about enough of that asshole.'

Things got increasingly tense that summer. Without school, Audrey was at loose ends. Fred 'found' an old ten-speed bike and used it to visit his friends, leaving Audrey at home by herself. Her mother had managed to get a part-time job at the grocery store in town. Her father slept all morning, then woke up hungover and nasty. She avoided him as much as she could.

Then one day in August, she was coming back from a walk in the fields in the middle of the afternoon. Fred had gone off on his bike to join his friends at the lake, saying he wouldn't be back until late. Her mom was working her shift at the grocery store.

As she came past the barn, the door opened and Fred stepped out. He looked flushed and his hair

266

and clothes were rumpled, but he was smiling as if he were pleased with himself. She was surprised to see him there and wondered if there was a girl in the hayloft. She was about to turn away and pretend she hadn't seen him when he spotted her. He went completely still and stared at her, the smile disappearing.

'What are you doing here?' he said sharply.

'Nothing,' she said quickly.

'Have you been watching me?' he asked.

'No. I've been out in the fields.'

He seemed to make a decision, then looked back toward the barn door he'd just come out of. 'I think our problem is solved,' he said.

'What do you mean?' Audrey asked, not understanding.

He gestured with his head for her to follow him. She walked closer and then stepped into the barn behind him, inhaling the familiar, musty smell of hay. Then her eyes adjusted to the dim light, and she screamed.

Her father was hanging from a centre beam, a thick rope coiled around his neck. His eyes bulged and his tongue hung out, his neck bent at an unnatural angle. He was grotesque. He hung completely still, clearly dead.

She was still screaming.

'Shut the fuck up,' Fred said, giving her a shake.

She fell silent and looked at her brother. For the first time, he seemed unsure of himself, as if he couldn't predict what she was going to do. She was only eleven, but she put it together. She looked back at her father and tried to swallow, but her throat was dry. There was an old oil barrel kicked to the side on the earthen floor. It looked like suicide, but she knew better.

'It had to be done,' he said.

She was shocked into silence. She'd never imagined that Fred would do such a thing. She thought he might persuade their mother to leave. She never thought – it had never occurred to her – that he'd do something like this.

'I've got to go,' he said. 'I'll be back later.'

'What am I supposed to do?' Audrey asked, panicked. She didn't want to be left alone with a dead body in the barn.

'Go look for him around suppertime. You can find him. And then call the police. They won't suspect anything. He was a total loser. No one will be surprised that he killed himself.'

'But . . .'

'But what?' he said coldly.

'How . . .' She was going to say *how could you do it?* but she couldn't get the words out.

He misunderstood. 'I told him I had something I wanted to show him in the barn. Once I got him in

here, I came up behind him and choked him uncon-
scious with the rope. Then I strung him up. That
was the hard part. He's heavier than he looks.' He
added, 'You weren't supposed to see me here.'

She turned to him. 'Would you have told me the
truth, if I hadn't seen you?'

He tilted his head at her. 'No. But now that you
know, you're going to keep it to yourself.' He
wasn't asking. He was telling her. 'I did it for us.'

Chapter Forty

ELLEN DRIVES HOME in a fog of disbelief. She'd had to pretend it didn't disturb her as much as it did, what Audrey told her. But it was awful, truly awful. She doesn't know if she'll ever be able to look at Audrey the same way ever again. Audrey had gone along with it. She covered up the murder of her father. Ellen reminds herself that Audrey was only eleven years old, a child.

Ellen realizes she's been sitting in her car in her driveway, staring straight ahead, without moving. She gets out of the car, enters the house, and kicks off her walking shoes. Then she goes into the kitchen and leans against the counter, trying to process what she now knows.

She tries to reconcile what Audrey has told her with the Fred she knew. According to Audrey, Fred was a cold-blooded killer. Why would she lie about it? She has nothing to gain by making the story up. And there had always been a coldness, a selfishness, about Fred. Ellen had thought him a narcissist. She'd never known him to be violent, even when angry, but he was relentless in pursuit of his own interests. And after what Audrey told her – now she knows he was almost certainly a psychopath.

Audrey is convinced this *taint of psychopathy*, as she calls it, is present in one of Fred's children. Is it an inheritable trait? She must Google it. Audrey says it is. She said her and Fred's great-grandfather had been a murderer too.

Ellen remembers clearly the first day she met Fred Merton, because it was the day that changed her life. Fresh out of school, she'd been intimidated by the manner in which he'd conducted her interview. He shot her a few questions, then said he liked the look of her. She hadn't been sure how to take that – was he being inappropriate? In those days, it was just a passing question, not thought about too deeply. And she needed the job. He offered it to her and she accepted. Over the ten years that she'd worked for him, she'd come to know him well. Fred was all about himself – other people were simply a means to an end. He had great charm, even charisma, but she knew what that charm was – something he used to get what he wanted. So when he tried it on her, she resisted. She resisted him for

271

years. When she finally gave in, it was on her terms, and for her own ends, although she didn't let him know it. Not then.

But what Audrey told her has unnerved Ellen. Only now does she realize the risk she took. She pours herself a glass of wine, although it's barely noon.

It's a warm spring day and after her long walk with Ellen, Audrey goes straight to the kitchen and opens the refrigerator. She pulls out a plastic jug of pre-mixed iced tea, pours herself a tall glass, and gulps half of it down, still thinking about what she'd revealed to Ellen, after all these years. Ellen had seemed shocked. Well, it *was* shocking. Ellen has lived a rather sheltered life, compared to Audrey. She tops up her glass and carries it into the living room. She sits down and pulls her laptop off the coffee table onto her lap.

As she scans her email, and then reviews the online news, she begins to feel a bit light-headed. She gets up, goes to the bathroom, and splashes cold water on her face. She returns to her computer, still feeling a bit off. She tries to ignore it, until she starts to feel unwell. She has a headache now and is nauseated. She wonders if she's caught something. But then she notices that she's clumsy as she tries to use her mouse, and as she reaches for her glass of iced tea. Something is very wrong. Her vision is blurred. Alarmed, she uses her cell phone to call 911, then vomits all down the side of the sofa.

It's around noon on Sunday when Catherine answers the door and registers the people assembled on her doorstep. Detectives Reyes and Barr are there with a search warrant and an entire team behind them. Ted comes to stand beside her.

She wants to protest but tells herself she has nothing to worry about. She lets them in. What else can she do? There's nothing for them to find.

As the search proceeds, she and Ted remain in the background. She grows increasingly uncomfortable as they go through her personal things. She blushes as they rummage through her underwear drawer, the dirty laundry hamper. They carefully photograph everything, including the contents of her jewellery box. They take her electronics, even her cell phone.

She's beginning to understand what Dan must have felt when they searched his place. She's unnerved and furious, but there's nothing she can do.

Ellen puts the wine glass in the sink and leaves the kitchen. The alcohol has steadied her a bit. She's about to go upstairs to lie down when the doorbell rings. She turns back to answer it.

It's her daughter, Rose. She looks worse every time she sees her, and Ellen's anxiety increases at the sight of her. 'Rose, honey, come in. Is everything all right?'

'Everything's fine,' Rose says, clearly lying. She looks like she hasn't slept. Or eaten much either lately. Her clothes look big on her.

'You don't seem fine,' Ellen says, worried. 'You look tired. And you're getting so thin. Why won't you tell me what's wrong?'

'There's nothing wrong! It's just work, Mom. It's stressful, that's all. I just came over for a visit. I don't need the third degree.'

Ellen throws up her hands in a peace gesture. 'Sorry. Are you hungry? Can I make you something to eat? A sandwich?'

'Sure. Thanks.'

Rose follows her into the kitchen, where she starts making a couple of tuna sandwiches.

'It's too bad you missed the funeral yesterday,' her daughter says.

'I'd promised your Aunt Barbara that I would visit.'

'I know. But you should have seen it. Dan – it was pretty upsetting, what he said. I felt so bad for Catherine.'

Ellen turns around and looks at her daughter, the awful things Audrey had told her on their walk still clear in her mind. 'I read about it in the paper this morning.'

Rose looks troubled and tells her the details the newspaper left out. 'I've always known from Catherine that things weren't great in that family, but I didn't realize they were that bad.'

Ellen shakes her head. 'Have you talked to Catherine? You guys are such good friends.'

'I went over to see her,' Rose says. 'She's a mess.' She concentrates on her sandwich.

'You should try to see more of her,' Ellen says. 'She's one of your best friends, and I'm sure she could use your support.'

Catherine watches as they spray her house with chemicals, focusing on the kitchen and bathroom sinks and the basement laundry room, looking, she assumes, for signs of blood, like they did in Dan's house. They don't find any.

They search the grounds outside, front and back, which Catherine finds mortifying. Neighbours are watching from the street and from behind windows. The press is there. She hides inside.

It takes several hours, but at last they're finished. The detectives and their team have taken away Catherine's car. She's furious about that too. At least they still have Ted's car, but it's a two-seater, and not the most practical. She asks one of the technicians how long it will be before she gets her car back, but he doesn't answer her.

When they're finally gone, she shuts the door firmly after them, feeling like she wants to break something.

'At least that's over with,' Ted says. He seems relieved. 'Now maybe they'll leave us alone.'

She looks back at him with narrowed eyes. Why is he so relieved? Surely he didn't expect them to find anything. She forces a tight smile. He can't be doubting her. Everything's just getting to her. It's getting to all of them.

Chapter Forty-one

THE NEXT MORNING, Monday, Catherine realizes the date. Not that it's six days since her parents were found murdered. But that it's April 29. With everything that's happened, she's lost track of time. She's late.

Ted has already left for work, but Catherine has taken more time off. She's glad he's not here. She slips into the upstairs bathroom, nervous. The police had been there the day before, and she remembers how they had rifled through all the things in the bathroom cupboard. Now she takes out a pregnancy test. She removes it from its package and prepares to pee on the test strip. She tries not to get her hopes up. She's only four days late. And all this stress – it could easily throw her off. She's probably not pregnant at all. But she could really use some good news.

She pees on the strip and waits.

She can hardly bring herself to look. When she does, she bursts into tears.

She's pregnant. At last.

At nine o'clock, Reyes has Jenna back in the interview room. She assures him that she doesn't need an attorney. Once they're settled in, the tape running, Reyes says, 'Easter Sunday, when you stayed an hour longer than anyone else after dinner, did your father or your mother mention anything about your father planning to change his will to leave half of his estate to his sister?'

She frowns, shakes her head. 'No. There's nothing to that – it's just what Audrey's saying. It's bullshit.'

'Maybe not. Your father had pancreatic cancer. He was dying, putting his affairs in order.'

She seems surprised. 'We didn't know that.'

He looks at her steadily. 'Your brother, Dan, said some things at the funeral,' Reyes says.

'Yeah, well, that's Dan.'

'Did you know about those disposable coveralls in his garage?'

'Yes, we all knew about them, Irena too. We'd all seen him in one of those suits, when he was working on the attic.'

'Did you know he left his garage unlocked?'

'I suppose we all did. He never locked it, for some reason. Just the house.'

'He's suggesting it was you or your sister who murdered your parents.'

She raises her eyebrows at him. 'You're not taking him seriously, are you? He's always had a chip on his shoulder. He thinks he got it the worst of all of us, that Catherine and I had it so much better.' She sighs deeply. 'We don't get too upset about it, because he's right.'

Audrey wakes in a hospital bed, wearing a hospital gown, surrounded by machines, and with an IV in her arm. For a moment she can't make sense of it. What is she doing here? Was she in an accident? And then it comes back to her – the illness, the vomiting – dialling 911 just before collapsing on the floor. Thinking that she might be dying, slipping into unconsciousness. She doesn't remember anything after that.

But before that, she'd been drinking iced tea, from her fridge.

She's absolutely parched, and reaches for the paper cup of water on the table beside her and drinks all of it. She presses the call button and waits for someone to come.

Catherine Merton arrives, with her attorney.

'Good morning,' Reyes says to her politely as the

four of them get settled in the interview room. He starts the tape, makes the necessary introductions, and begins.

'Did you know that your father intended to leave half his estate to his sister, Audrey?'

She snorts. 'That's what she says. None of us believe her.'

'This wasn't discussed at dinner that night?'

'No, of course not. Because she's making it up. He would never have done that.'

'I'm not so sure,' Reyes says. 'He tried to make an appointment, but his lawyer was away. He made an appointment for the following week, but by then he was dead.' She holds his gaze without wavering. 'Your father was dying,' he says. He sees a twitch of surprise in her eyes. 'Perhaps that's why he was reorganizing his affairs.'

'I didn't know,' she says. 'What was wrong with him?'

'Advanced pancreatic cancer. He probably had only a few months.' He lets her digest that for a moment. Then he says, 'We found something interesting when we were searching your house.'

She focuses her eyes on him, suddenly wary. 'What are you talking about?'

'A pair of earrings.'

'You'll have to be more specific,' she says sharply. 'I have a lot of earrings.'

'But this was a pair of earrings that went missing from your mother's jewellery box on the night she died.'

'What?' She looks on her guard now.

'A pair of diamond earrings. Square cut and a carat each. Quite valuable.' He opens the folder in front of him and hands her a picture of the earrings. She stares down at the photograph, her face colouring. Reyes says, 'This is from an inventory of what was missing from your parents' home – from the insurers.'

'I borrowed these. A couple of weeks ago.'

'Can anyone confirm that?'

She looks up at him angrily. 'What are you suggesting? That I murdered my parents and kept these earrings?'

'They're the only pieces missing from your parents' home that we've found, and we found them in your jewellery box.'

'Because I *borrowed* them!'

'I'll ask you again, can anyone confirm that you borrowed them?'

'No, of course not. It was between me and my mother. But I occasionally borrowed things from her.'

'Did anyone see you wear them, in the week or two before your parents were murdered?'

Here, the attorney intervenes. 'She said she borrowed them. Let's move on.'

He can't tell if Catherine is telling him the truth. She's a hard one to read. Her attorney, however, is looking increasingly concerned.

'Why did you leave your cell phone at home that night, when you went back to your parents?'

She looks startled. She swallows nervously. 'I forgot it. I left it behind on the hall table when I picked up my keys. I-I often forget things when I have a lot on my mind.'

Reyes gives her a disbelieving look. He leans forward. 'Here's the thing, Catherine. You and your siblings stand to gain millions from your parents' deaths. Your brother says you knew about the protective suits in his garage and that you knew he doesn't keep the side door to the garage locked, something confirmed by your sister, Jenna. The only recovered pieces of the missing jewellery were found in *your* house. We know you were there again later that night – you admitted it. But first you lied about it, and had your husband lie about it too. And you left your cell phone at home that night, perhaps so your movements couldn't be traced.'

'This is ridiculous,' Catherine exclaims hotly. 'I didn't kill them – they were already dead when I got there!' She stares back at him in the sudden silence; she seems shocked at what she's just said.

Her attorney looks stunned.

After a long moment, Reyes says, 'But that doesn't make sense. If that's true, why didn't you call 911?'

She says miserably, 'I think you know why.'

He simply sits there and waits.

At last she says it, her voice breaking. 'Because I thought Dan did it.'

Chapter Forty-two

CATHERINE HAS MADE an appointment for that afternoon at one o'clock at the lawyer's office to discuss the wills. She'd arranged it with Walter Temple and let her siblings know. This is what they've all been waiting for.

Ted had left work and picked up Catherine at home. She'd had to Uber it to and from her interview with the detectives that morning, because they'd taken her car away. Now, as they walk into the building in downtown Aylesford that houses the law firm, Catherine finds herself feeling slightly sick. She's still reeling from the interview with the detectives this morning, and a combination of anticipation and fear is making her stomach churn. Or maybe it's the beginning of morning sickness. She hugs her secret to herself, her little spark of private joy. She will wait to tell Ted at the right moment. She reminds herself they have nothing to worry about. Their father hadn't changed his will, despite what Audrey said. Walter had told Dan as much.

She and Ted are the first to arrive. As they're sitting in the waiting room, Dan and Lisa come in. Catherine rises and Lisa automatically goes to her for a brief hug, while Dan stands a few feet away. When Jenna arrives, the women manage some small talk while Ted and Dan remain mostly silent.

Walter comes out to the waiting room promptly at one o'clock and ushers them all into a boardroom, around a long rectangular table. He's holding a file, which he places on the table.

'I'm glad you're all here,' he says, looking at each of them, 'although I never dreamed it would be in such tragic circumstances.'

Catherine can feel the tension in the room. Their father might have changed his will years ago and never told them. She imagines him laughing at them from beyond the grave. She imagines him sitting in that empty chair, preparing to enjoy himself. Catherine glances furtively at each of her siblings, suspecting similar thoughts are running through their minds. Dan is pale and fidgety, and Lisa grabs one of his hands to still it.

'Your mother's will is quite straightforward. Years ago, she'd signed documents agreeing to leave her out of your father's will, in return for the house and a sum of her own. She didn't want to stand in the way of you children receiving the bulk of your inheritance should your father die first. Her estate is to be divided among the three of you equally. Your father's will is of greater significance. I'll begin with his specific bequests, then talk about the remainder of the estate,' Walter says. 'There are some minor bequests to various organizations –' He names a local hospital and a few other small charities her parents were involved with. Catherine shifts in her seat with impatience and nerves. Finally he gets to the crux of it.

'To Irena Dabrowski, one million dollars.'

That's a substantial sum. She glances around the table at the others. They're mildly surprised, too, but they seem pleased for their old nanny.

'To Audrey Stancik, one million dollars.'

Catherine allows herself to relax. It's true then. He hadn't changed his will to give her half.

Walter continues. 'The remainder of the estate, after tax, expenses, and so on – I'll spare you the legal language.' He looks up at them. 'The remainder of your father's estate is to be divided equally among his children.' He looks around the table at them.

Catherine can feel the relief in the room, like an exhalation. She realizes now it's not just her and her brother and sister who have been tense. Ted beside her visibly relaxes, and she can see a calmness come over Lisa's face too. They've all been on tenterhooks these last few harrowing days. She glances at Ted and squeezes his hand.

Dan actually sits back in his chair and closes his eyes, the very picture of relief. Catherine catches Walter looking at him with distaste. She wonders what he's thinking. Walter was at the funeral, and he was one of their father's closest friends.

Catherine speaks up. 'And can you tell us what the estate is worth, roughly?' She watches Dan's eyes snap open as he sits up and directs his attention back to the attorney.

'Just a moment,' Walter says heavily.

They all look back at him expectantly.

'This may come as a bit of a surprise, but the three of you are not Fred's only children.'

Reyes reviews Dan Merton's finances again, taking a closer look. They know that about six months ago, just before his father sold his company, Dan withdrew the majority of his money from his investment firm to loan half a million dollars to one Amir Ghorbani, secured by a first mortgage on his home in Brecken Hill. This is why Dan has no ready money. But what jumps out to Reyes this time is the name of the attorney on the document. Rose Cutter. He stares at the name. Rose Cutter is the illegitimate half-sibling of the Mertons, who is inheriting an equal share under Fred's will. The one that the legitimate siblings don't know about. He says to Barr, 'Take a look at this.'

Catherine gapes at Walter and then looks around the table; there is dismay on all their faces. 'What?' Catherine says. 'We don't know about any other children.'

'I don't believe it! Dad had some bastard child, is that it?' Dan says. 'And now they get a share? No fucking way.'

'Who is it?' Catherine asks.

'A young woman,' the attorney says, 'by the name of Rose Cutter.'

Catherine immediately turns to Dan and he stares back at her, in shock. Lisa, beside him, has also gone suddenly still.

'Do you know her?' Walter asks, clearly surprised.

'She's a close friend of mine,' Catherine says in disbelief. She feels like the breath has been sucked out of her.

After a moment, Dan says, 'She persuaded me to make an investment with her and tied up most of my savings. She's the reason I needed money.' Now everyone stares at Dan. For long seconds, the room is quiet. Then Dan says, raising his voice, 'It's because of her that the police think I killed our parents.' He turns to Catherine. 'This is your fault. You're the one who suggested she talk to me.'

At first Catherine has no response. But then she snaps back, 'I didn't realize you were going to commit almost all your money to her. And I didn't know Dad would sell the business and you'd be out of a job.'

'Yeah, well, neither did I,' Dan says.

Walter clears his throat. 'I didn't realize you were acquainted with her. No one knew that Rose Cutter was in the will except your father. Not even your mother knew. Certainly Rose Cutter does not know.'

'I guess he wanted it to be a surprise,' Jenna says sarcastically.

'But does she know that we have the same father?' Catherine asks. She wonders if Rose has known all along. All these years they've been friends, and Catherine had no idea. But maybe Rose did.

'That I don't know,' Walter says. 'Her mother might have told her. But her mother would not have known about the will, I'm certain of that.'

If Rose *has* known all along, Catherine thinks, she can't help feeling betrayed, used, even spied upon. 'Can we fight it?' Catherine asks.

'I wouldn't advise it,' Walter says. 'Fred acknowledged to me long ago that she was his daughter. Her mother, Ellen Cutter, worked for your father at one time. He paid her for Rose's upkeep for over twenty years. And then there's DNA testing.' He adds, 'It would be expensive to fight it and you would lose.'

Catherine thinks bitterly, *Maybe Rose knows exactly who she is.* And maybe she expects Catherine and the others to welcome her into the family as a sister and happily share their money.

She doesn't know them very well.

'How much is the estate worth?' Dan asks now.

'After tax, about twenty-six million,' Walter says. 'Your mother's property adds about another six.' His face takes on a look of thinly veiled disgust. 'Congratulations. Even with your half-sibling, you are all now very wealthy.'

Catherine stares at the attorney, reading his expression. She realizes that he thinks one of them is a murderer. Maybe, Catherine thinks, when this is all over, they should find a new lawyer.

They leave the attorney's office and stop to talk in the parking lot afterward. The ice seems to have broken between Dan and the rest of them. They are united now against a common enemy, a usurper.

'I don't fucking believe it,' Jenna says.

'I don't know why we didn't see this coming,' Dan says. 'He was so shitty to Mom.' He grimaces. 'I suppose we're lucky there aren't more.'

'As executor, I have to call Audrey and tell her she's getting a million dollars,' Catherine says. 'But I'm not going to be the one to tell her about us having to split the rest with Rose – I don't want to give her the satisfaction. I'm happy for Irena, though.' The others nod their heads in agreement.

They talk for a little while longer. Before they disperse to their various cars, Catherine says to Dan and Jenna, 'We have to stick together. Don't tell the police anything. This is all going to blow over, and we'll all be rich.'

Chapter Forty-three

NUMBER 22 BRECKEN Hill Drive is a massive property – complete with a lavish Italian fountain in front.

'Jeez,' Barr says as they approach. 'A bit much, don't you think?'

Reyes doesn't give an opinion. The owner, Amir Ghorbani, is expecting them. Reyes rings the doorbell, and an elaborate trilling can be heard echoing from inside. Barr rolls her eyes.

The door opens and a man about forty years of age greets them. He looks closely at their identification. 'Please, come in,' he says and directs them into a large living room, where they sit down beneath an ornate crystal chandelier.

The house feels empty, quiet; Reyes doesn't think there's anyone else there.

As if reading his mind, Ghorbani says, 'My wife and children are visiting family in Dubai.'

'As I mentioned on the phone,' Reyes begins, 'we're investigating the murders of Fred and Sheila Merton.'

The man nods. 'It's terrible. Everyone in Brecken Hill is upset about it. I'm fairly new here, but as far as I understand, nothing like this has ever happened here.'

'We understand you have some business with their son, Dan Merton,' Reyes says.

The man goes still. 'Business? No, I don't have any business with him.'

Reyes pulls out a folder and hands him the document that shows Dan Merton advancing five hundred thousand dollars to Amir Ghorbani, secured by a first mortgage on the house they're sitting in. The other man reads it, clearly astonished.

'I've never seen this before in my life,' he says. 'I have never borrowed money from Dan Merton. The only mortgage on this house is with the bank. That can't have been registered. The bank would never allow this to happen.' Ghorbani looks at the paper again. 'I've never heard of Rose Cutter. She is not my lawyer.' He sits back. 'But I'll tell you something else. I've seen Dan Merton sitting outside this house, at night, on several occasions. He'd sit out there in his car, watching the house.'

Reyes is surprised to hear this. It's rather strange behaviour. 'So you'd met him?' Reyes asks.

'No. I hired a private detective to find out who he was.' He adds, 'It worried me; I didn't know what he was doing there.' He shakes his head, looking nervous now. 'Someone got his money, but it wasn't me.'

Reyes shares a glance with Barr. Rose Cutter has pulled a fast one on her half-brother, Dan.

Ghorbani says, 'Do you think he murdered his parents? He was here that night, Easter Sunday. Outside my house.'

'What time?' Reyes asks.

'I noticed him probably around ten thirty, maybe a bit earlier. He usually stayed for an hour or so, but he was gone that night after only ten or fifteen minutes. I remember looking out the window and noticing he'd left, because I would never go to bed until he was gone.'

Even with the surprise sibling, Ted thinks, as he drives them home, Catherine's share of the estate will still be roughly eight million. Worth celebrating. But Catherine seems to be deeply distressed at finding out that Rose Cutter, who she's always considered a close friend, is her half-sister. He has to admit, it startled him too. It will change things between them, and he can tell Catherine doesn't like it.

'Well,' Catherine says, leaning back in her seat, 'now we know.'

Ted doesn't want to bring it up, but he has to know. He asks, 'What happened at the police station this morning?'

She turns to him. 'They found a pair of my mother's earrings in my jewellery box.'

'So?' But his mind is already racing ahead.

'So – they're saying it's a pair that went missing from Mom's the night of the murder. They have some kind of inventory from the insurance company. But I borrowed those earrings a couple of weeks earlier. And after what Dan said at the funeral . . .'

'You can't mean they seriously suspect you?' Ted asks in dismay, glancing at her.

'I honestly don't know, but it feels that way.'

Ted stares at the road ahead of him, his hands gripping the steering wheel tightly. He feels like he's in some surreal movie, driving down a familiar road while his life reels around him.

They drive the rest of the way in silence. Ted is thinking about the earrings. He doesn't remember her borrowing any jewellery from her mother. But why would he?

Just before they pull into the driveway, Catherine

says, 'Ted, maybe you could back me up on the earrings? Say you knew I borrowed them?'

He parks the car and looks at her, worried. He'd decided he wasn't going to lie to the police any more. How can he be in this position? But Catherine didn't murder her parents. It's simply impossible. And Catherine just inherited eight million dollars. More, if Dan is convicted, because he'd forfeit his share.

'Sure,' he says.

Lisa was surprised by the revelation about Rose Cutter. She doesn't know her. But she doesn't see the problem. Eight million is plenty. They can share. But her satisfaction with the contents of the wills is marred by the way the attorney had looked at her husband. He obviously thinks Dan did it; he could barely hide his revulsion. She is overwhelmed with shame. She can't bear for people to think of them that way. But the worst is the fear.

Dan sulks in the passenger seat beside her as she drives them home in her car.

'It's okay,' Lisa says. 'It's still a lot of money.'

Dan snorts and says, 'Too bad we can't enjoy it.' She remains silent. 'We should be popping champagne, planning a trip to Italy. Buying a new house. But we can't. How would it look? People are already saying I killed them.'

'It will take time to settle the estate anyway,' Lisa says. 'And once they find out who did it, then we *will* be able to enjoy it,' she says, trying to soothe him. Or maybe she's trying to soothe herself.

He stares out the window, nervously gnawing on a thumbnail.

Jenna drives home from Walter's office, thinking about the wills. She should be happy – she *is* happy. She's going to be rich. But an unknown half-sibling being treated equally with them – that rankles. She doesn't really know Rose Cutter, although she met her at her sister's wedding years ago.

She's a bit uneasy about Jake. Jake has lied for her. Their fling – or whatever this is – is fun for now, but what if they get tired of each other? What if one of them wants to break it off? Could she trust him then?

It would be nice if they arrested someone, and she almost doesn't care who, as long as it isn't her.

Chapter Forty-four

BARR POPS HER head in Reyes's office door, slightly breathless.

'What is it?' Reyes asks.

'I just got a call from the hospital. Audrey Stancik was admitted yesterday, and they think she was poisoned.'

Reyes and Barr get to the hospital as fast as they can. They finally track down Audrey Stancik's doctor, Dr Wang. 'She was poisoned?' Reyes asks. 'Are you sure?'

The doctor nods briskly and says, 'No doubt about it. Ethylene glycol. If she hadn't called us as quickly as she did, she might well be in a coma by now. We've treated her with fomepizole – it reverses the effects of the poison and prevents organ damage.' He turns as if to be on his way. 'She's going to be fine. She'll be released later today.'

'Wait,' Reyes says. The doctor stops for a moment. 'Where would ethylene glycol come from?' Reyes asks.

'Antifreeze, probably. That's your department, not mine. You can see her. She's eager to talk to you. Room 712.'

They locate Audrey's room, and Reyes knocks gently on the partly opened door and they enter. It's a semi-private room; there's another woman in the bed across from her. Reyes pulls the curtain around Audrey's bed for privacy and he and Barr stand by her bedside. 'How are you feeling?' he begins.

She frowns weakly at them both. 'I've felt better,' she admits, 'but they tell me I'm going to be fine. No lasting damage.'

'What happened?' Reyes asks.

'It was the iced tea,' Audrey says firmly, 'I'm sure of it. I keep a plastic jug of iced tea in my refrigerator. When I got home from a walk on Sunday morning, I had a glass of it. It was after that I started to feel sick.'

Reyes glances at Barr.

'Someone tried to kill me,' Audrey insists. 'Someone broke into my house and tried to poison me.' She adds, 'It has to be one of those kids.'

'Why would any of them want to kill you?' Reyes asks.

299

'Because I know one of them is a murderer. And whoever it is probably knows that I'm talking to you – and to the press. I was the anonymous source in the newspaper yesterday.'

Once inside the house, Catherine tells Ted she's going upstairs to lie down. She has a pounding headache, tight across her sinuses, probably from the stress of everything – the police interview this morning, the will, the news about Rose this afternoon.

Catherine needs to think about Rose, what to do about her. She doesn't feel like she's gained a sister, but that she's lost a friend.

She gets underneath the covers and pulls them up to her chin. She tries to empty her mind so that she can sleep and get rid of her headache. Summoning happy thoughts, she thinks about the money she will get, and about the baby she's going to have, and how she will tell Ted. She's hoping for a girl. She imagines decorating the nursery in her parents' house – it and everything in it will be hers now. Dan and Jenna don't care. They will have the house and contents valued and that will come out of her share of the inheritance. When she said that's what she wanted, in the parking lot after the meeting with Walter, Dan and Jenna were not surprised, but Ted had been. When she mentioned that it was her intention to move into the house, he had been taken aback. She wasn't immediately sure why – he knew she'd always wanted that house.

'But—' Ted protested.

'But what?' Catherine replied.

Ted swallowed and said, 'Your parents were *murdered* in that house – do you still want to live in it?'

She didn't want him to think her cold. 'It's where I grew up,' she said stubbornly, plaintively, letting her eyes fill up. She wanted to say, I can live with it, can you? But she wasn't sure she was going to like his answer. This is something else she will have to deal with, her husband's squeamishness.

And the earrings – her mind races on. Why don't the detectives believe she borrowed those earrings? And now there is no way she will fall asleep because she's thinking about Audrey. Had she already spoken to the detectives? She remembers catching sight of Audrey in her car in the parking lot of the police station, watching as she came out, how she threatened Catherine and her siblings when she found out she wasn't going to be rich.

Audrey knows her history. When Catherine was young, she wasn't always the perfect daughter. When she was twelve, she stole a necklace. She was over at a friend's house, and the girl's parents weren't home. Catherine went upstairs to the bathroom, and, curious, slipped into the parents' bedroom. She didn't want to snoop in general, she only wanted to look in

Mrs Gibson's jewellery box. She had lots of lovely things. There was a sweet little necklace at the bottom that Catherine picked up and held up to the light. A delicate gold chain with a single small diamond. Catherine slipped it into the pocket of her jeans. She thought Mrs Gibson wouldn't notice it missing right away, and she wouldn't be able to connect its disappearance to Catherine's visit.

But it was her own mother who found out about the necklace, after Irena discovered it hidden under Catherine's mattress when she was changing the bed. Irena told her mother, who confronted her about it and forced the truth out of her. Then she marched her over to the Gibsons' and made her return the necklace and apologize, her face flushed with shame. She was full of resentment at her mother, because Catherine was right – Mrs Gibson hadn't noticed the necklace was missing at all. It had ended her friendship with the Gibsons' daughter. Catherine's mother was mortified. She told Catherine's father when he got home and he berated her and made her feel so ashamed and angry that she wanted to run away from home.

Of course her father told Audrey. He told her everything, as if he liked to display his children's failings. And there was the time after that, when she'd tried to shoplift a diamond bracelet from a jewellery shop when she was sixteen. Police had been called, but her father got her out of it. She really had a hard time staying away from sparkly things.

Reyes and Barr are met at Audrey's house by technicians from the forensic team. A study of her home shows no evidence of a recent break-in. But a large window has been left open at the back of the house, and someone could have entered that way. Audrey will be coming home from the hospital later that day. Reyes carefully closes and locks all the windows.

They take away the jug of iced tea for analysis, and the glass left on the coffee table. Reyes wrinkles his nose at the vomit streaking the sofa and pooled on the living-room floor.

Barr comes up beside him. 'Are you thinking what I'm thinking?' she asks.

'You think she might have poisoned herself?'

Barr shrugs. 'She strikes me as the histrionic type. It wouldn't surprise me.'

'No sign of a break-in,' Reyes says, 'but that doesn't necessarily mean anything.'

Barr nods. 'The window was open.'

'And she called 911 just in time,' Reyes says. The technicians begin dusting for the possible intruder's fingerprints, but Reyes already suspects that they won't find any. The detectives have to get back to the station to deal with Rose Cutter, so they leave the technicians to it.

Chapter Forty-five

ROSE CUTTER CAN feel her heart beating in her chest.

She sits at her desk in her law office on Water Street. She's a sole practitioner, dealing mostly in real estate. She pulls down the blinds on her store-front office and turns the sign on the door around to read CLOSED. She's sent her assistant home early. It's shortly before five. She just wants to go home.

She was too ambitious, and it's gotten her into trouble. She's always wanted more than she had, and she's always been jealous, even resentful, of her better-off friends and acquaintances who have family money. Starting your own practice is difficult – and expensive. Office space, equipment, insurance, law fees, an assistant's salary – it's been harder than she expected to make a living. She's still renting a place to live, and she has student loans to pay.

Rose thinks about the Mertons. She knows how

rich they are. After all, Catherine has given her a taste of what her life is like. And Catherine always insists on paying – whether it's for a day's sailing, with champagne and lobster, or for an expensive dinner – and Rose lets her, because they both know she can easily afford it and Rose can't.

Back before Fred Merton sold his company and cut Dan loose, Rose knew Dan had to be sitting on a pile of money. She saw an opportunity. She was able to persuade Catherine to get Dan to talk to her about an investment opportunity he might be interested in.

She persuaded him to take his money out of where he had it and invest as a private lender to the owners of 22 Brecken Hill Drive, with the property as security. It offered a significantly higher rate of return than what he was getting elsewhere, for a twelve-month term, and it was risk-free. But then he lost his job and wanted to get the money back early. She couldn't help him; she told him he'd have to wait. There was nothing she could do.

In fact, there is no mortgage on that property. She forged the documents to get Dan's half million to invest in what was supposed to be a sure thing. She had a hot tip on a stock. She thought she'd make a killing on it and get some fast money. She was greedy, but she fully intended to return his money when it came due, with no one the wiser.

305

But it hasn't turned out that way. The sure thing failed. Dan doesn't know what she's done. But if she can't come up with the money in the next few months, he will find out.

When she got the call a few minutes ago from a Detective Barr, Rose had swivelled her chair to turn her back to her assistant and closed her eyes. The detective asked her to come down to the police station. She hung up the phone, sent Kelly home, and sat perfectly still, wondering how much the police knew, what they might accuse her of.

Now, as she arrives at the station, she walks in with her head high and her back straight. She puts on her confident lawyer persona and greets the two detectives with a smile.

'What can I do for you?' she asks, sitting down in the interview room.

'As you probably know, we're investigating the murders of Fred and Sheila Merton,' Detective Reyes says. 'I understand you know Catherine Merton quite well.'

'That's right. Catherine and I have been friends for years. We were at school together.'

'We understand that you were handling an investment for her brother, Dan.'

She must keep her composure. Everything depends on how she handles this. 'Yes, that's right.'

'Can you tell us about that?'

'I was looking for a private lender for a client, and Catherine mentioned to me that her brother might have some money to invest. Dan and I met, and he went ahead with the investment, taking a first mortgage on the property.'

Reyes is nodding along. Then he says, 'I'm afraid I must caution you,' and proceeds to do so.

She feels her face go hot as a wave of panic rolls over her. The detectives are watching her closely. She feels as if she can't breathe.

'Would you like some water?' Reyes asks.

She nods without answering, and Detective Barr pours her some water. She's grateful for the interruption; she needs to think. But she can't think. Barr hands her the water and she drinks greedily, her hand trembling.

Audrey, just home from the hospital, doesn't manage to reach the phone in the kitchen before it goes to message. She freezes at the doorway to the kitchen, her heart pounding when she recognizes Catherine's voice on the speaker. She doesn't pick up; she doesn't want to talk to her. The message is short. Catherine says that Fred left her and Irena each a million dollars in his will. Then she hangs up abruptly, leaving Audrey staring at the phone. She doesn't know how to feel.

Of course she's glad to have one million; she'd

almost resigned herself to getting nothing. But Audrey had expected so much more. She has no grounds on which to challenge Fred's will. But she's not going to give up the fight for justice for her brother. And now she's convinced that one of them just tried to kill her too. She's not just curious any more. She's in danger.

Would Catherine call if she'd poisoned Audrey and thought she might be lying dead on the floor? Yes, she would. She would cover her tracks, leave a message fulfilling her executor duties. If she *was* the killer, and her poisoner, imagine her surprise if Audrey had answered the phone. Now she wishes she had.

This is all because she spoke to that reporter, Robin Fontaine.

Audrey feels a sudden need to talk to someone she can trust. She picks up the phone and calls Ellen.

Reyes studies Rose Cutter, sweating in the chair across from him and Barr. She puts the water down on the table.

'I want an attorney.'

'Fine,' Reyes says and leaves the room for her to call her lawyer. A short time later her attorney arrives and is closeted with her client. Then the lawyer opens the door and tells the detectives that they are ready. They resume their places and record the interview on tape.

Reyes says, 'What you told us is all bullshit, isn't it? There is no mortgage on Twenty-Two Brecken Hill Drive. We've already spoken to the owner.'

She says nothing, as if she's frozen in fear.

Reyes asks, 'What did you do with Dan Merton's money?'

'No comment,' Rose says finally, her voice strained.

'We know that the mortgage you prepared was fraudulent and was never registered.'

'No comment.'

'All right,' Reyes says, changing direction. 'Where were you the night of April twenty-first?'

'I'm sorry?' Rose says, as if she doesn't understand the question.

'You heard me. Where were you on the night of Easter Sunday?'

'What's this about?' Rose's attorney asks sharply.

'Fred and Sheila Merton were murdered that night. And Ms Cutter here is a significant beneficiary under Fred Merton's will.' He watches Rose suck in a breath; she looks as if she might faint.

'What are you talking about?' Rose asks, her voice shrill.

'You're Fred Merton's illegitimate daughter. Don't pretend you didn't know.'

She turns to her attorney, her mouth dropping

309

open. Then she turns back to the detectives. 'I don't know what you're talking about.'

Reyes says, 'You are going to inherit a fortune.'

The attorney is clearly taken aback at what she's walked into.

'You're making this up,' Rose says. 'You must be.'

Reyes studies her closely. 'I assure you I'm not. So – where were you on the night of April twenty-first?'

Rose stutters, 'I-I had Easter dinner at my mom's, with my Aunt Barbara. Then I went home.'

'And you were alone all night?'

'Yes.'

'You can't be serious about these insinuations,' the attorney pipes up, finding her voice at last.

'Well, we already know she's motivated by money,' Reyes says. Rose shoots him an angry, nervous look. 'She defrauded Dan Merton out of half a million dollars. Who's to say she'd stop short at murder?' He turns back to Rose and says, 'You can go, for now. But you'll be hearing from us about the fraud charge.'

As she stands up, he says, 'You'd better go see Walter Temple in the morning. He'll be expecting you.'

Chapter Forty-six

DAN CAN'T SLEEP. He tosses and turns until well past midnight. Lisa, beside him, has finally fallen into a deep slumber, exhausted from the emotional strain of the last few days.

He gets quietly out of bed and pulls on socks and underwear, jeans and a sweater. He needs to drive somewhere. Anywhere. It's a compulsion he has sometimes.

He lets himself out of the house and gets into Lisa's car. He resents that he no longer has his own car. He'll buy another one, he decides, when this is all over, something sporty and powerful and impressive. He turns off his cell phone and drives into the dark spring night.

Dan remembers how, when he was seventeen, he developed a crush on a girl at school, Tina Metheney. He was obsessed with her. He followed her around at school, stared at her in class, brushed up against her in the hall. He was just a kid, painfully awkward, and he didn't know how to deal with his overwhelming feelings of sexual desire. He thought he was in love. She didn't like it. She told him to leave her alone, to *stop looking at her like that*. It was more than mere rejection. She left him feeling like he revolted her, that he frightened her.

His father had given him his first car not long before that, and Dan loved to take it out. He would go on long drives in those days to escape from the pressure cooker of the house. It was the closest he could get to freedom. Dan drove past Tina's place many times, and one day soon after she'd told him to leave her alone, he parked outside her house waiting for her to come home. He wanted to talk to her, to make her understand. But when she saw him there, waiting for her, she wouldn't speak to him. She went inside the house and told her father, and that night her father had come to the Mertons' house and complained to Dan's father. Fred was embarrassed and angry. He hauled Dan into his study and gave him an excruciating dressing-down in front of the other man. Tina's father said he wouldn't press charges if he left his daughter alone. Dan sat in a chair staring at the carpet, frightened, bereft, and utterly ashamed. Press charges? For what?

After that, he was swamped with shame and lone-
liness and confusion, convinced for a long while that
he would never have a girlfriend. He was humiliated
by Tina and by his father, who told everyone in the
family what he'd done. *He stalked a girl. He freaked
her out. She almost called the police.* His dad harped
on it for months.

Dan didn't dare look at Tina after that. He stayed
away from her. He stayed away from all girls, terrified of what might happen. He worried that she'd
told other girls at school about him, that he was
some kind of weirdo. It felt so unfair. And sometimes, late at night, after everyone was asleep, he
would have to drive past her house. Sometimes he
had to stop and park outside. But the feelings of
desire and adoration he'd had for Tina hadn't sur-
vived the rejection and humiliation. He felt a
meanness toward her now, and toward everyone
involved in his disgrace. It gave him some small
feeling of power to sit outside her house like this,
without anyone knowing, doing what he was for-
bidden to do.

Now, as he drives – a form of self-soothing,
really – he finds himself thinking about Audrey. She
knows all about what happened with Tina. Audrey
thinks he's strange, because his father blew the whole
thing out of proportion, made it out to be something
it was not. Since that night she threatened them at

Catherine's house, Dan worried she might say something about it to the detectives, or to the press. He knows she was the anonymous source in that newspaper article. He doesn't think Tina's family will come forward and say anything about him. The Metheneys are like the Mertons, rich and very private. You don't let people know about your personal business. But he wonders what they're saying about him now around the Metheneys' dinner table. *He was so creepy. I knew there was something off about him. Maybe he killed his parents.*

He tightens his hands on the steering wheel and somehow finds himself outside Audrey's. The house is completely dark, there are no lights on at all. There is no one here to see him. He parks the car, and watches.

Audrey has too much on her mind to sleep.

She gets out of bed and goes to the kitchen for a glass of water. She can trust the tap water. Everything else in the house that was already open or unsealed she's thrown down the drain. The clock on the kitchen stove tells her it's 1:22 in the morning. She stands at the sink, letting the water run until it's cold, and then fills a glass and carries it into the living room. Moonlight spills in through the living-room window and she can see perfectly well. No need to turn on any lights. She walks over to the window

314

and looks out. There's a car on the street, right in front of her house. A man is sitting in the car, just a shadow in the dark, and he seems to be watching the house. She takes a startled, involuntary step back. She must have spooked him because she sees his face turn away and his arm move to turn on the ignition. He pulls into the street and passes under a streetlight briefly as he speeds away.

She didn't get a good look at him. But she recognized the car – it was Lisa's. It gives her a jolt. She stands at the window, her heart pounding.

It must have been Dan, sitting outside her house in the middle of the night. Did *he* poison her? Was he sitting out there trying to get up the nerve to break in and see if she was dead? Well, now he knows.

Or maybe he's just up to his old tricks.

Ellen Cutter squirms restlessly in bed. At length she pushes back the covers and goes to the kitchen to make herself a cup of decaf tea. She looks at the clock on the wall. It's just past three in the morning. It's so quiet. It reminds her of when she used to get up in the middle of the night to breastfeed her daughter when she was an infant, so long ago. Just the two of them, alone on the sofa in the dark.

She thinks about her daughter now, how troubled she seems, how stressed and overworked. She wasn't always like that. Rose had sailed through law school after spending a few years working at different jobs. But now Rose is struggling. If only she could help her.

She thinks about Audrey's visit earlier that evening. Her friend is getting a million dollars from her brother in his will. And she's complaining. She obviously feels she's owed much more for keeping quiet about what Fred did all those years ago. She feels loyalty should be repaid.

And this bit about being poisoned. Ellen doesn't know what to think. She believes Audrey ingested poison. She still looked ill. She'd been in the hospital – although she hadn't called Ellen while she was there. The detectives had visited her, examined her house as a crime scene. You don't lie about that. It's too easy to be caught out. But it does occur to her that Audrey might have poisoned herself. These murders seem to have sent her over the edge. She's so angry about being cheated out of what she thinks she deserves, so certain that one of the kids is a murderer, that perhaps she's making things up . . .

Ellen remembers the night Audrey first told her that Fred was going to change his will to give her half. She remembers how elated Audrey was, and how secretly jealous she felt.

She and Audrey pretend they tell each other everything, but it's not true. Nobody tells anybody everything.

316

Ellen has never told Audrey that Rose is her brother's child. She's never told anyone but Fred. And now Fred's other children are each inheriting a fortune. Audrey feels short-changed, but that's nothing to what Ellen feels.

When Ellen couldn't get pregnant with her husband, she finally gave in to Fred's advances and slept with him. She got pregnant quite quickly then. Fred had been furious when he found out. But he'd gotten over it when he realized she was never going to tell anyone. Her husband never knew Rose wasn't his biological daughter.

When her husband died unexpectedly of a heart attack when Rose wasn't even a year old, Ellen had gone to Fred and asked for money. She didn't have to say it; he knew she could prove Rose was his child. He paid her regularly for years. Not a lot, but enough.

Ellen tries not to think about how Fred cold-bloodedly murdered his own father, but she's been imagining it in her mind's eye over and over, ever since Audrey told her. She'd Googled psychopathy and now she knows it's partly genetic.

But her Rose isn't like that. Rose is lovely.

Chapter Forty-seven

THE FOLLOWING MORNING, Tuesday, Dan calls his attorney, Richard Klein. 'They want to question me again,' he says. 'What should I do?' He can hear the anxiety in his own reedy voice.

'Hang on. Calm down,' Klein says. 'What's happened?'

'That fucking detective just called and asked me to come down to the station again for more questions. I don't have to go, do I?'

'No, you don't. But maybe you should. I'll be there with you. We need to find out where they're going with this. I'll meet you there in half an hour, okay?'

'Okay.'

'And Dan, I'll be right beside you. Don't say anything until I get there. And if I don't think you should answer a question, I'll tell you.'

When Dan arrives at the police station – Lisa stayed home, her face white as he left – he waits inside until his attorney shows up minutes later. Seeing the other man, in his good suit, with his confident manner, reassures Dan a little.

'Why are they coming after me like this?' he asks his attorney. 'This borders on harassment! They don't have any evidence, do they? They couldn't have. They'd have to tell you, wouldn't they?'

'They'd have to tell me sooner or later. Not yet, though. You're not under arrest, Dan. So let's see what they have to say.'

Once they're settled in the interview room, the tape running, Reyes begins bluntly. 'We have a witness who saw you in your car in Brecken Hill on the night of the murders, at about ten thirty.'

Dan feels his insides turn to liquid and shoots a frightened look at his lawyer.

Klein says, 'No comment.'

Reyes leans in closer and looks him in the eye, and Dan feels faint.

'Your father sold his business out from under you. You couldn't find a job. You'd tied up most of your savings – half a million dollars – in an investment in a mortgage on a house in Brecken Hill and couldn't get the money back when you needed it. You sat outside that house – not far from your parents' house, by the way – staring at it, night after night,' Reyes says. 'The owner of that house saw you there on Easter night. That's pretty strange behaviour, Dan. Did you know you would never see that money again? What were you thinking, Dan? Were you angry? Desperate? You'd been ripped off once too often?'

Dan feels as if all the blood has drained from his head. 'What do you mean I'll never see that money again? What are you talking about?' he asks, his voice strident.

'That money is gone, Dan. There *is* no mortgage on Twenty-Two Brecken Hill Drive. The owner has never heard of you, or your money. It was all a fraud, perpetrated by Rose Cutter, the attorney.' He adds, 'But perhaps you already knew that.'

Dan stares at the detective in shock. No mortgage on . . . that can't be. He signed the papers. He trusted her. She lied to him. 'I didn't know!' he almost shouts back at the detective who is tormenting him.

'Did your father refuse to give you the money you badly needed at Easter dinner? You told us you were nowhere near Brecken Hill that night, but we now know that was a lie. You had the disposable suit—'

'This interview is over,' Klein says, standing up. 'Unless you're going to arrest my client, we're leaving.'

'We're not arresting him – yet,' Reyes says. 'One last thing,' he adds, as they turn to go. 'Someone tried to poison your aunt Audrey. What do you know about that?'

'Nothing,' Dan says, and they leave without another word.

Rose sips her morning coffee, staring out the window of her small kitchen. She hasn't gone into the office today – what's the point? The police know about the fraud, and they are going to charge her. There's no way out of it. She's going to go to jail, at least for a short time.

It was never supposed to come to the attention of the police, of anybody. Dan was never going to know. It was to be a victimless crime – he was going to get his money back. But it hasn't turned out that way. And now they think she's a criminal, and they're accusing her of murder.

Will they find out everything? She feels fear creep along her spine. Because there's more. She dresses carefully in her best navy suit, a crisp white blouse. She takes care with her makeup. She keeps her back straight and holds her head high as she walks out of the house on her way to see Walter Temple, of the firm Temple Black. She will hold her head high for as long as she possibly can.

*

Ted is scrubbing his hands at one of the sinks when his receptionist approaches him and says, 'There are two detectives here to see you.'

He turns to her and says, 'What?' His immediate reaction is alarm. He doesn't want to talk to the detectives here. He doesn't want to talk to them at all. 'I have patients to see. Tell them I can't talk to them now.'

She goes away and he finishes scrubbing his hands, his heart beating furiously now. This must be about the earrings. He must support his wife – he has no choice. The thought of lying to the police again makes him nervous. They already know he's a liar.

His receptionist reappears, her brow wrinkled. 'They insist on seeing you now. They won't leave.'

He averts his face so she can't see how rattled he is. 'Fine. Send them into my office.'

He takes a couple of minutes to compose himself and then enters his office briskly, to show that he's in a hurry and can't give them much time. Also, he wants to disguise his nervousness. He knows there are sweat stains starting to appear beneath the arms of his blue scrubs. Detectives Reyes and Barr are seated in the two chairs in front of his cluttered desk. 'What can I do for you?' Ted asks before he even sits down.

'We just have a couple more questions,' Reyes says.

'Sure, but I don't have a lot of time, so –'

'As you know, there were some items that went missing from the Mertons' home the night of the murders. Some of Sheila's jewellery. We have an inventory. When we searched your house, we found a pair of earrings in your wife's jewellery box that were part of that inventory.'

'Oh, yes, I know all about that,' Ted says, trying to sound casual, as he sits down. 'Catherine borrowed those earrings from her mother a couple of weeks ago.'

'Did she tell you that?' Reyes asks. 'Or do you actually *know* it?'

Ted can feel himself colouring; he can't think of how to answer.

Detective Barr says, 'It's simple. Did you see her wearing the earrings before the murders?'

'Yes, she wore them.'

'Good. Then you can describe them for us,' Reyes says.

But he can't. He stares back at them blankly. Catherine should have told him what the fucking earrings looked like. How stupid. 'I can't remember,' he says finally, feeling himself flush an ugly red. 'But I know she borrowed them.'

'I see,' Reyes says, rising from his chair. 'We won't take up any more of your time.'

As the two detectives turn to leave, Ted says

rather strongly, 'Catherine had no reason at all to harm her parents. We're financially comfortable. Catherine would hate me for saying this, but I'm afraid it's Dan you should be looking at.'

Reyes turns back around to face him. 'Fred Merton had decided to change his will to give his sister, Audrey, half, substantially cutting into your wife's inheritance.'

'Audrey's saying that,' Ted says, 'but no one believes it.'

'I believe it,' Reyes says. 'Fred was dying. Perhaps he said something to your wife. And if Sheila knew what he was going to do, she may have told her – or one of her other children. That's motive enough for me.' The two detectives exit the office.

Ted waits until he hears them leave the dental practice and then he gets up from his desk and closes his office door. He wants to slam it, but he restrains himself. He paces the small area of his office, thinking of the smug look on the detective's face as he was leaving. They don't believe him about the earrings. They're acting like they think Catherine killed her parents. It's insane. It must have been Dan. He's the one with the most obvious motive. It *must* have been him. So why are they looking so closely at his wife?

Ted slumps down in his chair, suddenly exhausted, ignoring the patients he has waiting. He thinks about that night, Easter Sunday, at Catherine's parents'. Sheila had said she had something to tell them, but they'd been interrupted by Dan's arrival. Was it about Audrey and the will? But later Catherine had told him it was Jenna's allowance her mother had wanted to talk to her about – that's what she told him the next morning. Only then she said her parents were dead when she got there.

His stomach is churning, and he feels dizzy.

Now he remembers something else about that night, something he'd forgotten. When he was sitting on the sofa with Jake, and Dan was standing in the corner of the living room, talking to his father, Catherine and her mother had come down the stairs together. He'd barely registered it because he was eavesdropping on Dan and his father. Maybe Sheila told her about Audrey and the will when they were upstairs. Maybe Catherine knew.

He thinks about how much Catherine wanted that house. How attached she gets to material things. Like houses, and earrings. She left her cell phone at home that night.

He sits at his desk and tries to pull himself together.

Chapter Forty-eight

ROSE WALKS INTO Temple Black through the heavy glass doors to reception, summoning all the poise she can muster. It's the kind of law office she has always aspired to work at – one that oozes money, and power, and success. Not like her shitty little storefront, with its 'walk-ins welcome' sign. She should have joined a large, prestigious firm like this one, rather than setting out on her own, but the truth is, she didn't have any offers. Maybe she wouldn't have gotten herself into trouble if she'd had someone watching over her. They always warn sole practitioners about that. But it's too late to think these things now.

As she follows the receptionist down the corridor to Walter Temple's office, she happens to glance through the glass into one of the boardrooms and recognizes a law school friend, Janet Shewcuk. Janet sees her and turns quickly away.

Rose has never met Walter Temple. He welcomes her warmly. He must not know yet, she thinks, about what she did with Dan's money.

'Ms Cutter,' he says, 'thank you for coming.'

She gives him a tentative smile. 'The police told me yesterday – about the will,' she says, sitting down opposite him, crossing her legs at the ankles.

The older attorney nods. 'It's good news for you, although I imagine it may be a little upsetting, too.'

She looks back at him. 'So it's true?'

'Yes. You have been named as a beneficiary in Fred Merton's will.' He clears his throat. 'I'm not sure if you knew he was your biological father.'

She shakes her head. 'No.' She sits completely still as he goes over what she will inherit. When he's finished, she takes a deep breath and says, her eyes fixed on the surface of his desk, 'I had no idea about any of this. I didn't know he was my father. This is – unimaginable.'

As she gets up to leave, Walter says, with a warning in his voice, 'You should prepare yourself – the others don't like it.'

Rose drives directly to her mother's house. Her mother is surprised to see her.

'We need to talk, Mom,' she says, walking briskly through the front door.

They sit down across from each other in the small

327

living room. Her mother looks at her expectantly. 'What is it?' she asks.

'Dad wasn't my real father, was he?' Rose says. It sounds accusatory. Her mother's face takes on a pained, almost frightened expression as Rose stares at her. Her mother looks down into her lap and says, 'No, he wasn't.' She hesitates for a moment. 'Your father couldn't have children,' she explains. 'So I found someone else.'

When her mother doesn't fill the silence, Rose says, 'You had an affair.'

Her mother looks at her, almost pleading. 'I wanted a child so badly, Rose. It was the only way.'

Rose stares at her mother. She'd never known the man she'd believed was her father; he'd died when she was about a year old. Still, it's a strange thing to know about your parents. About yourself. 'I just found out that Fred Merton was my father.'

Her mother asks, clearly surprised, 'How?'

'Fred Merton made me a beneficiary in his will,' she says, and watches her mother's face transform. Astonishment first – and then pleasure.

'He did? How much did he leave you?'

'About six million,' Rose says, hardly believing it, even now. 'The same as the other kids.'

'The same – oh my God,' her mother says, with an expression of utter amazement. 'I had no idea you were in the will at all!' Her mother leans forward and takes one of her hands and clasps it in her own. 'This is wonderful, Rose! Because you're his flesh and blood just as much as those other kids are. You *deserve* an equal share of his wealth.' Her mother continues excitedly. 'He always knew you were his. And he gave me money for your care, every month, from when you were little until you graduated law school.' She becomes more serious and adds, 'I'm sorry I kept it from you. Perhaps I should have told you. But he didn't want that, and I didn't want to rock the boat. At first I was afraid he might stop sending money, and I needed it. And then, after that – I guess I was just a coward.'

Rose feels a fluttering in her stomach. This really is the sort of thing you dream of, if you're raised by a single mom and your friends are wealthy. It's like a fairy tale. But all fairy tales are tinged with darkness.

Her mother says, 'They might not accept you as a sister right away, even though Catherine's your friend. But I'm sure they'll come around. Oh, honey – this will change your life!'

But Rose is only half listening now.

Lisa walks around the house, numb, disoriented. It's a week exactly since the bodies were discovered. She tries to act normally, but it's hard. When Dan arrived home earlier from his police interview, he was angry and upset. He didn't want to tell her why. But she finally got it out of him. He admitted they had a witness who saw him in Brecken Hill the night of the murders.

They were sitting in the living room, across from each other. He was on the sofa, and she was in the armchair. That's when she realized that she'd been keeping herself at a distance from her husband lately. When, exactly, had she stopped sitting beside him, her hand on his shoulder, looking up into his face, commiserating with him? Instead she sat coldly opposite, watching him while he had his head down, staring at the floor.

She sat rigid in her chair. 'Is it true?' she asked, a quiet horror and bitterness in her voice. The disposable coveralls had been concerning, but she knew why they were there; he'd used them for the work in the attic. He'd told her that he'd been driving around that night, trying to calm down, that he hadn't been anywhere near Brecken Hill. She'd believed him.

'Yes,' he admitted. 'But I can explain.'

She sat there reviewing her options, as he tried to beg his way back into her heart.

'I never went to my parents' again that night, I swear,' he said. He told her then how Rose Cutter had swindled him. The money was gone. It was the owner of the house who had seen him.

She sat there thinking what a fool her husband was, to be taken in by Rose Cutter, to lose half a million dollars like that. Maybe his father had been right about him all along. Still, if he wasn't convicted and inherited all that money, they'd be rich. She didn't necessarily have to stay married to him forever.

'I drove to that house in Brecken Hill and just sat there, thinking,' Dan said, speaking quickly. 'I was so angry at myself for tying up our money for so long – I didn't know we'd need it. The police think I knew what she'd done and that I'd never get the money back, and it makes it look like I killed Mom and Dad.' He stood up, in a rage. 'That fucking bitch – this is all her fault! If she hadn't pushed that deal on me we wouldn't be in this mess!'

Lisa could see his point. They'd had half a million dollars in investments. The house was fully mortgaged because interest rates were so low. But Dan had taken that money out without telling her at first, and been duped. That money could have kept them nicely for a long time, until he got himself sorted out. And now the money is gone. It struck her that because of Rose Cutter, her husband might have been driven to murder.

Now, she thinks about it all again. Dan is out in the garage, trying to take his increasingly unhinged mind off things. She's inside the house, tidying aimlessly, thinking about how one thing leads to another.

Chapter Forty-nine

IRENA PULLS HER cat up onto her lap and listens to it purr as night falls.

She was grateful when Catherine called her last night about the will, but it would have been nice if she'd come in person with the news. Irena knows she's peripheral to their lives now. It smarts a little, after all she's done for them. But she pushes the wounded feelings aside.

Irena has just returned from going to Catherine's herself this evening. She wanted to know what was going on, how everyone was holding up, and Catherine was the one most likely to know. When Catherine told her that Lisa had called to tell her the police had a witness putting Dan in Brecken Hill the night of the murder, Irena had felt a chill roll up her spine.

She remembers her last interview with the

detectives, her reluctant admission that any one of those kids might be capable of murder.

She remembers how Fred used to delight in pitting them against one another. He believed in a zero-sum game, Fred did. There could only ever be one winner in any situation. He would set them up in competition, and it was never fair.

Things look bad for Dan, Irena thinks. She's not so sure Catherine cares, despite her protestations. Or Jenna either. Dan, as always, has been left hung out to dry.

The next morning, Wednesday, Ellen is bracing herself for a difficult conversation. Audrey is on her way over for coffee, and she doesn't think Audrey is going to like what she has to say. She's not going to like hearing that Ellen's daughter, Rose, is her brother's daughter. And that Rose will get more from Fred Merton's estate than Audrey will. But she will undoubtedly hear it sooner or later, and it's better that it come from her.

She tells herself that, on the other hand, Audrey might be pleased that those spoiled kids are going to have to share their fortune with an outsider. They don't like to share. And Audrey has always been fond of Rose. Perhaps she will be pleased, after all, that she is Rose's aunt, and that Rose is her niece.

Ellen thinks it might get a little ugly with the Merton kids – maybe not with Catherine, who's so fond of Rose, but with the other two – and she's hoping Audrey will be on her side.

But Audrey has been so different lately, a more extreme version of herself; Ellen is quite nervous.

Rose doesn't bother going to the office, for the second day in a row. She calls her assistant, Kelly, and tells her again to hold the fort and cancel any appointments. She tells her she has a cold.

She's hiding. She doesn't want to face anyone, knowing that she will soon be prosecuted for fraud. Her law career will be over anyway, and the practice will fold. She hopes she can avoid prison. With her inheritance money she can make restitution, throw herself on the mercy of the court.

She's going to have more money than she's ever dreamed of, so she really doesn't need to go into her shitty little practice ever again.

Her mind turns uneasily to those detectives, to her meeting yesterday with Walter Temple. She tells herself that everything is going to be fine.

Later in the morning, Reyes is notified that Audrey Stancik is at the front desk and wants to speak to the detectives.

She looks better than the last time they'd seen her

in the hospital, Reyes thinks. There's more colour in her cheeks.

Audrey barely waits until they're seated before she says, 'Have you made any progress on who tried to kill me?'

'There was definitely antifreeze in the iced tea,' Reyes says, 'but no evidence of who was in your home and might have put it there.'

She sighs dramatically, clearly disappointed. 'Last night, Dan Merton was sitting in his wife's car, watching my house.'

'You're certain it was him?' Reyes asks.

'Yes.' She adds, 'He does that, you know, I told you that.' She leans forward. 'I have some other information that I think will be of interest to you. I imagine you already know that Rose Cutter is Fred's natural daughter, and that she's named in his will.'

'Yes.'

She gives a little snort. 'Well, I just found out.' She takes a moment to smooth her ruffled feathers. 'Her mother, Ellen Cutter, is a friend of mine. I've known her for almost forty years. She worked for my brother as his secretary a long time ago – that's where we met. We both worked for Fred's company then.'

She continues. 'It's just that – Ellen knew that Fred was going to change his will to give me half right before he died. Because I told her – the same night he told me.' She adds, 'And I don't believe for a second, no matter how much she pretends otherwise, that Ellen and Rose didn't know Rose was in the will. Fred would have told Ellen, and Ellen would have told Rose.'

'Why do you think that?'

'Because Fred liked to let people know when he was doing them a favour. Just like he enjoyed letting people know when he was doing something to hurt them. He liked the feeling of having power over people, of being able to give things and take things away. If you'd known him, you'd understand what I mean.'

Chapter Fifty

ROSE CUTTER IS at home, trying to enjoy her day of playing hooky from work. She needs to think. There's so much going through her mind. A sudden, sharp knocking on her door makes her jump.

Her entire body tenses. Maybe she should pretend she's not home.

But the knock comes again, persistent. She hears a shout through the door. 'I know you're in there, Rose.' She recognizes Catherine's voice. 'I've already been to your office and I can see your car in the driveway.'

Reluctantly, Rose gets up and opens the door. She has to face her sometime. She steps back and Catherine enters the house. Rose tries to gauge her expression. But Catherine, as usual, is hard to read.

'Can we sit down?' Catherine asks.

'Sure,' Rose says, moving into the living room,

where two small couches face each other over a low table.

'So,' Catherine begins once they're settled, because Rose can't bring herself to speak. 'I'm supposed to believe you're my half-sister.'

'Catherine, I know this must be upsetting,' Rose begins. 'I had no idea. My mother only admitted it to me yesterday, after I learned about the will.'

Catherine looks away in disdain.

Rose now sees how this is going to go. Catherine isn't happy about having a half-sister. She'd hoped she would be – that their relationship might develop from one of friendship into one of sisterhood. But Walter had warned her. Rose's misgivings escalate; she feels almost like she's suffocating. She speaks, rushing her words. 'I'm sorry, Catherine. It must be upsetting for all of you. I don't mean to cause any harm. You're my friend.'

'Your *friend*?' Catherine says. 'You stole Dan's money! Oh yes, I know all about it. What kind of *friend* does that?' She leans forward. 'How could you?'

'It wasn't like that, Catherine,' Rose protests desperately. 'I was just – *borrowing* the money. I was going to pay it all back. No one was ever supposed to know.'

'Well, we all know now, don't we?' Catherine looks back at her with contempt. 'So you can pay him back.'

'I can't,' Rose whispers, looking down. 'I don't have the money to pay him back. Not yet.'

'What?'

'I invested it and lost most of it.'

'How could you do something like this?' Catherine repeats angrily.

'How? I'll tell you how,' Rose says, finding her mettle. 'I didn't have what you had, growing up. I wasn't rich and connected. I've had to work for everything I have. And I got greedy and impatient. You wouldn't understand.' But then she tilts her head and lowers her voice and says, looking at Catherine intently, 'Or maybe you would. Maybe *you* got greedy and impatient and murdered your own parents. Is that what happened, Catherine? Or was it Dan?'

Catherine glares at her with cold eyes. She stands up quickly and looks down at Rose, still seated. 'We'll sue you if we have to, to get back what you owe my brother. And I will make it my personal mission to make sure you are prosecuted to the fullest extent of the law. And you will *never* be accepted as part of this family.'

Audrey arrives home from the police station, her mind racing. She believes what she told the detectives – Fred would have told Ellen about the will. And Ellen would have told Rose. And Rose has the same troubling genes from Fred that the others do. It might have been any one of those four kids who killed him and Sheila. Audrey feels utterly betrayed by Ellen, who has always been her best friend. Ellen had never revealed anything of this to her.

She wonders if Rose is capable of murder. Ellen might soon have to ask herself the same question. If so, she'll be all alone in her own private hell.

Audrey is grateful that she's never had any cause to worry about her own daughter.

Jenna rolls out of Jake's bed and starts pulling on her clothes. It's late afternoon, but she'd come into the city to see him, and as usual, they ended up in bed before they did much of anything else. He's gotten little marks of paint all over the sheets. He's going to need new bedding.

She's pouring herself some juice from the fridge when he enters the tiny kitchen, doing up his jeans. She looks at him for a moment – admiring him.

'There's something I have to talk to you about,' Jake says.

She tenses; there's a hint of something in his voice that she doesn't like. What is it, nervousness? 'What?' she says, smiling over her shoulder at him to cover her own uncertainty.

'I'm a bit short.'

She pretends not to understand, to buy time. 'What do you mean?'

'My rent went up, and I don't have enough to cover it.'

Jesus, she thinks. That didn't take long. What's it been, a little over a week since her parents were murdered? And he's already asking her for money. She takes her time putting the juice back in the fridge, her back to him. Then she closes the refrigerator door and turns to face him, still not sure how she should handle it. 'Can they do that?' she asks, playing for time. 'Just raise it without notice?'

'I'm talking about my studio space. They can do whatever the hell they want.'

She knows he's right. She's seen his studio space, and it's all under the table.

'I can't lose my studio,' he says, with a bit more flint in his voice.

He doesn't like it that she's stalling, that she's not just throwing money at him, she thinks. But it's a delicate dance they're doing here, something that will likely set the tone for the future. They don't know how they're going to do as a couple, long term, or if there's even going to be a long term. He knows she has money or will eventually. *A lot* of money. And he's lied to the cops for her. He witnessed that awful fight with her parents the night they died, and he told the police he was with her all night. She owes him, but still, she doesn't like it that he's asked.

'How much do you need?' she says, trying to sound like she really doesn't mind, that this is something a new lover would do. She's thinking a few hundred will be enough to help him out.

'Could you manage five thousand?' he asks.

She turns to him in surprise. 'How much is your rent?'

He looks back at her, meeting her eyes. 'It's just that I want to have some in reserve, so that I don't have to worry. You know I'm doing a big installation piece right now – I can't be thinking about having to move.'

And there it is. She knows. He's asking for more than he needs. He's asking for what he *wants*. And his wants are going to get bigger and bigger.

'I don't have money like that lying around,' she says.

'I know. But you can get it now, right?'

She notices the *now*. 'I suppose I can try to ask Walter for an advance,' she admits.

He nods. 'Great. I have to get going – I want to get some more work done. Stay as long as you like.'

He approaches her and gives her a long, intimate kiss. She pretends she's enjoying it as much as she usually does. But when he leaves, she stares at the closed door after him for a long time.

Chapter Fifty-one

AS REYES AND Barr approach Ellen Cutter's modest but well-kept bungalow, Reyes muses about what kind of woman she is. She's certainly able to keep a secret.

The door is opened by a woman in her early sixties. They produce their badges and introduce themselves. 'May we come in?' Reyes asks.

She lets them in and they all sit down in the living room.

'We're investigating the murders of Fred and Sheila Merton,' Reyes says. 'We understand that your daughter, Rose, is the biological child of Fred Merton.'

'Yes, she is,' she answers a trifle sharply.

'We're not here to dispute that,' Reyes says. 'She shares equally in Fred Merton's will with his other children.'

'Yes. It was quite a shock to learn that,' she says. 'I just found out yesterday. Rose told me.'

'You had no idea that your daughter was a beneficiary?'

'Absolutely not.'

'Where were you on the night of April twenty-first, Easter Sunday?'

She seems taken aback. 'What? Why?' He simply waits. 'I was at home. My sister came, and my daughter, for Easter dinner. Rose left, but my sister stayed over and went home in the morning. She lives in Albany. Why are you asking me this?' He looks at her steadily. She gives a short laugh, uncertain. 'You're wondering if I killed them? That's ridiculous.' She looks nervously now from Reyes to Barr, as if unsure of her footing.

Reyes explains. 'Fred Merton had decided to change his will, cutting his children out of half of his considerable fortune.'

'How would I know that?' Ellen says.

'Because your friend Audrey Stancik told you.'

He notices her surprise, watches as she loses some of her assurance. 'Maybe she did, I don't remember,' she says, trying to be offhand about it. 'But I had no idea Rose was in the will at all. I had nothing to do with this.'

He lets a silence fall, waiting to see if she'll fill it. She does. 'My sister stayed over that night, as I

344

said. She didn't go home until the next morning. You can ask her.'

'What about Rose? When did she leave?'

'About eight o'clock.' She reads their faces and says, 'Rose didn't even know Fred was her father till after he was already dead.' Reyes says nothing. 'My daughter has nothing to do with this,' Ellen says dismissively. 'Maybe you should look at the other children, the ones who *knew* they were going to inherit.'

Reyes isn't going to tell her that her daughter is about to be arrested for fraud. He'll leave that to Rose. But he can't resist saying, as they leave, 'Maybe you don't know your daughter as well as you think you do.'

Ellen watches the detectives as they leave. Audrey's behind this, she thinks, she must be. Audrey must have told them she'd told Ellen about the expected change to the will. And now Audrey's turned on her – pointed the police at her and Rose, because she's angry about Rose's inheritance. That's just crazy. Audrey is one of her oldest friends. She thinks bitterly, *you really can't trust anyone, can you?*

She tries to call Rose, but there's no answer.

Walter Temple looks up from his desk and watches Janet Shewcuk scurry down the hall past his office with her head down. He stares after her, and it strikes him suddenly that she's been avoiding him these last few days. The feeling of uneasiness that's been tapping him on his shoulder lately now circles around and stares him in the face. He's felt concerned ever since he met Rose Cutter. He turns to his computer and looks up where Rose Cutter went to law school, and when. He does the same for Janet Shewcuk, his junior associate.

Then he sits back anxiously in his big leather chair, dreading what he must do. He closes his eyes for a long moment and asks himself if he can just do nothing. Then he opens his eyes, pulls out the card from the top drawer of his desk, and calls Detective Reyes.

The receptionist at Temple Black directs Reyes and Barr to Walter's office as soon as they arrive. Walter looks as if he has something heavy weighing on his mind, Reyes thinks.

'What is it?' Reyes asks, as he and Barr seat themselves across from the attorney.

Walter sighs wearily and says, 'Two or three months ago, I asked my junior associate, Janet Shewcuk, to do a wills review for Fred and Sheila Merton. It was coming up to five years since they'd looked at their wills and we usually do a review around that time.'

'Go on,' Reyes says.

'Yesterday, Rose Cutter was here to talk about the will. And something didn't seem right.'

'Like what?'

Walter shakes his head. 'I don't know. Something was off. I just didn't believe her – that she didn't know about any of this.' He bites his lip pensively. 'It's been bothering me ever since. Then I did some digging and discovered that Janet and Rose had gone to the same law school at the same time.'

'And you thought they might know each other,' Reyes says, 'and that she might have told Rose what was in the will?'

Walter nods miserably. 'I thought maybe it would be better if you asked her.'

Reyes says, his pulse quickening, 'Let's talk to her.'

'I'll get her for you,' Walter says and leaves his desk.

A couple of minutes later he returns to his office with a young woman in a grey suit, her blond hair pulled back in a neat ponytail. He pulls out a chair for her as she sits down nervously, then he introduces the detectives. When Janet Shewcuk realizes they're detectives, she is clearly frightened. When Reyes tells her they're investigating the Merton homicides, she begins to tremble.

Reyes says, 'We understand you're familiar with

347

the Merton wills.' The young attorney flushes a guilty red. He waits.

'I reviewed them,' she admits, going redder still.

'You don't happen to know Rose Cutter, do you?' Reyes asks.

She swallows, her eyes blink rapidly. 'We went to law school together.'

'I see,' Reyes says. The woman attorney glances furtively at her boss and looks like she's about to cry. 'And you told her that she was a beneficiary under Fred Merton's will.'

Then she does begin to cry, messily. Walter hands her a tissue from a box on his desk. They wait it out. At last she manages to say, 'I know it was a breach of confidentiality. I should never have said anything.' Her face is a portrait in misery. 'But Rose is a lawyer too – she wasn't going to say anything. I didn't think it would hurt anyone.' She looks at them, distraught. 'How was I to know that they would be *murdered*?'

'And when did you tell Rose about this potential windfall?' Reyes asks.

'It was maybe two months ago? It was such a surprise when I saw her name right there in the will. I didn't tell her when I first found out. I didn't mean to tell her at all. But we were out one night and I had a bit too much wine.'

Reyes steals a look at Walter and his face is like

348

thunder. Reyes asks, 'After the murders, did Rose ask you not to admit you'd told her?'

'No. She didn't have to,' Janet answers miserably. 'We both knew if it got out it would ruin my career.' She looks up at them and says, 'Surely you don't think *she* did it?'

Chapter Fifty-two

ROSE IS STANDING outside her mom's front door. Her mother has been calling her, but Rose hasn't answered. She really doesn't want to talk to her, but she knows she must. She rings the bell.

Her mother opens the door, visibly upset. 'I'm glad you're here. I've been trying to reach you.'

'I know, I was tied up,' Rose lies.

'The police were here,' her mother tells her.

'What?'

'About Fred and Sheila's murders.'

'What the hell are you talking about?' Rose asks, thrown off balance, following her into the living room, where she sees her mother has a glass of wine poured. As her mother explains, Rose feels her anxiety escalate.

'Just because I knew that Fred was going to change his will, giving half to Audrey, they had the gall to suggest *I* did it – to protect your interest. I didn't even know you were in the will! They asked me if I had an alibi.'

'They can't be serious,' Rose protests as she sits down beside her.

'Fortunately, Barbara was here all night.' Her mother turns to her and says, 'They were asking about you too. But I told them you didn't even know Fred was your father till after he was dead. You didn't know about the will either.'

Rose remembers with a sickening feeling how the detectives questioned her about the murder. 'I went home to bed after Easter dinner with you,' Rose says. 'I don't have an alibi.' She feels light-headed.

Her mother tries to reassure her. 'Well, I wouldn't worry. There's no way they can suspect you. You didn't know anything.' Her mother asks, 'Have you spoken to Catherine yet?'

But Rose isn't listening. Her insides are clenched in a knot.

'Rose?' her mother says sharply.

She looks up at her mother and says, 'There's something I have to tell you.'

Back at the police station, Reyes and Barr are approached by an officer who has something to show them. He seems excited. He and Barr follow the officer to a computer monitor and they all look at the screen.

'I'll be damned,' Reyes says. He claps the officer on the back. 'Good work.'

Once her daughter has left, Ellen paces the living room, horrified about Rose and the terrible thing she's done. When Rose told her about the mess she'd gotten herself into with Dan's money she simply couldn't believe it. She'd been struck dumb, literally unable to speak for a long moment.

Ellen hadn't been as supportive as she might have been. But – how could Rose be so selfish? So reckless? So stupid? It was completely unlike her. This wasn't the Rose she knew. She finally understood why her daughter had been so stressed, why she had lost weight. She's so angry at her. And she told her how disappointed she was.

Ellen has always taken a great deal of pride in Rose, in being her mother. But people are going to find out about this. Rose will probably go to jail – not for too long – but the thought of visiting her daughter in jail makes Ellen feel utterly humiliated. Everyone will know what she did. She won't be able to practise law any more, after she worked so hard. And Ellen will forever be ashamed of her. She won't be able to say that her daughter is an attorney. Her daughter is a criminal, and she won't be able to say anything at all.

Now, as Ellen cries, tears running down her face, a small part of her wishes she hadn't been so harsh with Rose, wishes that she'd hugged her daughter before she left, the way she always does. But she hadn't. This is going to be hard to forgive. She needs time.

She continues to pace, with a detour into the kitchen to refill her wine glass. At least Rose will get her inheritance. She'll be able to start over, once she gets out of jail. They will probably have to move away – how could either of them hold their heads up after this? It would have been so lovely if Rose hadn't broken the law, and she inherited all that money. She could have had everything she wanted. Ellen could have been so proud of her.

She knows, too, now, that they have already questioned Rose about the murders – Rose admitted it. She is going to be charged with fraud. But those detectives can't seriously think Rose had anything to do with the murders; it won't matter that she doesn't have an alibi. Rose didn't know she was in the will.

She never thought Rose could be remotely capable of stealing someone else's money. She remembers that awful detective's last words to her: *Maybe you don't know your daughter as well as you think you do.*

Ellen can't stop thinking about what she read online about psychopathy, and how it can run in families. She thinks about the Mertons. Her Rose is now part of that family. What if one of them *is* the murderer? She knows Audrey has always thought so.

Audrey may never speak to her again, and this pains her. She had hoped their long friendship could weather the revelation of Rose's parentage.

Then it crosses her mind that if one of the other Merton children is convicted of the murders, they will forfeit their share, and there will be more for Rose.

It was inevitable, Rose thinks, sitting once again in the hard chair in the same interview room, her attorney beside her, concerned. As evening approaches, the two detectives question her aggressively. She'd hoped Janet wouldn't say anything, that no one would find the connection. But here she is, and the detectives have already spoken to Janet.

'You knew you were in the will, Janet Shewcuk told you,' Reyes repeats. 'You lied to us.'

'Yes, I knew,' Rose admits finally, exhausted. 'But I didn't kill them.'

'You don't have an alibi,' Reyes points out. 'You

354

needed money to pay Dan back so that you wouldn't go to jail for fraud. Is that what you were thinking? That if Fred and Sheila were dead, and everybody got their inheritance, you could pay him back, and no one would be any the wiser? Or, more likely, if the money didn't come through from the estate in time, and they found out what you'd done with Dan's money, they would just keep it quiet and let you pay him back and forgive you, because you're family?'

'I didn't kill them,' Rose repeats stubbornly. But fear has crept down her throat and settled in her gut.

Chapter Fifty-three

THAT EVENING, CATHERINE carefully sets the scene. Despite everything that's going on, she wants the moment she and Ted have waited for to be perfect. She's bought flowers for the table. She's ordered a gourmet meal from their favourite French restaurant, which she's keeping warm in the oven.

When Ted arrives home from work, she takes his jacket and tells him she has a surprise for him. He turns and looks at her and she smiles. 'It's not a bad surprise,' she says.

'Oh, good. Because we've had a lot of those, lately,' Ted says.

'Put all that out of your mind,' she tells him. 'Come with me.'

He follows her into the dining room, where she has set a lovely table. 'Smell that?' she asks. 'I've ordered in, from Scaramouche.'

'What's the occasion?' Ted asks.

'I'll tell you, but first, sit down.'

She brings the food to the table, and they sit across from one another. She lights the candles.

She's put a bottle of red wine on the table, which he automatically opens. He reaches over to pour for her but she places her fingers across the top of her wine glass and smiles at him. He glances up at her in surprise.

'None for me,' she says. He doesn't seem to get it. She tells him, 'It's not good for the baby.'

'You're pregnant?' He gets up and comes around to her side of the table. She stands and he embraces her. She can't see his face.

It is, she thinks, a perfect moment.

Later that evening, Ted slips out of the house. He tells Catherine he's going to pick up a few things. She seems happy, chattering on about how she'll have to switch from wine to tonic and lime – without the gin – so no one will suspect she's pregnant. At least for a while. Until they're past the three-month point. He urges her to relax, have a bath and pamper herself while he's out. He tells her how happy he is about the baby and that he'll be home soon to take care of her. Then he leaves the house, closing the door behind him.

He wants a child, of course he does. He's just not

sure he wants one with her. He imagines the two of them, with a baby, living in the murder house, and has to suppress a shudder.

He drives to the arranged meeting place. He's going to see his sister-in-law, Lisa. He has a terrible need to confide in someone, and there's no one else he can talk to about this. He hopes he's not making a mistake in trusting Lisa. But if he doesn't do something, he's going to explode. He and Catherine have been worrying out loud that Dan may be a murderer and agreeing that they must do what they can to protect him.

But maybe Dan isn't the murderer.

After the detectives visited him at his office yesterday, Ted told Catherine what they'd said. How stupid she'd been for not telling him what the earrings looked like. She'd gone very still and said, *Shit*. She described them then, but the truth is, he can't remember her ever wearing them. On the other hand, he never notices her jewellery.

He has no idea what Catherine is really thinking. Does she know he suspects her? And now this – she's pregnant. He could do without this good news.

He stands against his car in the falling dusk in the parking lot of a Home Depot and speculates about what's been going on over at Dan's house. He hopes to find out.

He watches Lisa drive up in her little car and stop. She gets out and approaches him, looking worried. Unexpectedly, she throws herself against him for a hug. He remembers how she always hugs Catherine. She hugs everyone. She's a woman who thrives on comfort – both giving and receiving.

She pulls away and says, 'Sorry, I'm a mess.'

'That's okay, I'm a mess too,' he says.

'Where's Catherine? Why are we meeting here?' she asks.

'I wanted to talk, just you and me,' he says. Is he imagining it, or is her back going up? She's closer to Catherine than she is to him.

'Why?'

He hastens to reassure her. 'I'm just finding this hard. I thought you might be too. I thought we could give each other moral support.'

She leans against his car then, beside him. 'I know Catherine is trying to protect Dan.' Her voice trembles. 'But – I keep imagining what might have happened . . .' She stops speaking and stares straight ahead of her across the parking lot, as if seeing the murders in her mind's eye. Finally, she says, her voice bleak, 'I know Catherine wants to protect him – but I'm not sure I can.'

'What do you mean?' Ted says, turning toward her. *Does she know something? Something they don't?*

359

She swallows. 'If he did it . . . could *you* live with him?'

Ted looks away. So there's nothing definitive, nothing she can say to help him. He's living with the same horror. He met with Lisa hoping she would tell him something to confirm Dan's guilt, that he'd confessed to her or something. Then Ted could stop doubting. But she doesn't know any more than he does. They're both in the dark. They stand in silence for a while.

She speaks slowly. 'I try to tell myself that he couldn't have done it, not the Dan I know – but what if there's a Dan I *don't* know? They have a witness putting him in Brecken Hill that night. He lied to me about it. But I keep telling myself he didn't do it, because part of me can't believe it, and doesn't want to believe it.'

Ted looks at her and feels a terrible need to unburden himself. He swallows and says, 'I know what you mean.'

She shakes her head. 'I don't think you do.'

'Listen,' Ted says, his voice low and strained. 'I don't know if Dan did it or not. But if he didn't, then it was probably Catherine.'

She looks at him, obviously shocked. 'Why would you think that?'

'She was *there*, Lisa.'

'*After* they were dead.'

360

'That's what she says, but she came home that night and acted like everything was fine. She made up an entire conversation she had with her mother, who was already dead. And said nothing for two days. Who does that?'

'She thought she was protecting Dan.'

He nods. He hesitates, on the brink of betrayal. Should he confide in Lisa or not? He exhales. 'That's what we all thought. But the police came to my office – they found a pair of Sheila's earrings in Catherine's jewellery box when they searched our place. They say they're one of the items that went missing from the house that night.'

'What? I haven't heard anything about that.'

'Catherine says she borrowed them a couple of weeks before, but I don't remember seeing them.'

'Maybe she did borrow them.'

'Maybe,' Ted says. 'She swore to me she did.' After a pause, Ted says, 'That detective seems convinced that Fred was going to change his will to give Audrey half, and that one of them knew.'

'That's bullshit, isn't it?'

Ted shrugs. 'They don't seem to think so, because Fred was dying, and they seem to believe he was putting his affairs in order.' She nods thoughtfully. He continues. 'I know Sheila had something she wanted to tell Catherine that night. Maybe that was it.' He hesitates, but he can't help himself, he

361

needs to tell someone. 'Catherine was upstairs alone with her mother that night, just before dinner. Maybe Sheila told her about the will then.' Lisa stares at him, her eyes big. After another silence, Ted asks, 'Is Dan saying anything to you – about Catherine?'

'Just that she knew about the disposable suits in our garage, and that he never locks the door.' She averts her eyes. 'He claims she's trying to set him up, but I never believed it . . .' She trails off.

'I don't know what to believe,' Ted says.

'It could have been either one of them,' Lisa says slowly, obviously shaken. 'What are we going to do?'

'I don't know. But don't tell Dan about the earrings, okay?'

Chapter Fifty-four

THE NEXT MORNING, Thursday, the detectives interview Jake Brenner again. He has taken the train up to Aylesford. He's more wary this time.

'Jake,' Reyes says, 'we're going to give you the opportunity to come clean with us.'

'What do you mean?'

'We know you didn't spend the night at Jenna's place here in Aylesford on Easter Sunday. You've been lying to us.' Jake blinks rapidly. Reyes says, 'You were caught on the security camera at the Aylesford train station. You took the eight forty back to New York.'

Jake's eyes dart back and forth between the two of them. 'Okay, yes, I went back to the city that night,' he admits at last.

'And you didn't have a problem with lying for her?' Reyes asks. He watches the other man swallow.

'No.' He explains. 'She came into the city the next day, Monday, and spent the night. Everything was good. On Tuesday morning, I left for work, and she called me to tell me her parents had been robbed and murdered and asked me to say I was with her all night on Easter Sunday. She said it would just be easier.' He adds, 'I agreed because I didn't think she had anything to do with it.'

Reyes pushes photos of the crime scene across the table in front of Jake's face. He glances down, his face blanching. He suddenly looks like he might be sick.

'You don't honestly think she could have done this,' Jake says.

Reyes doesn't answer that. Instead he says, 'Obstruction of justice is a serious charge.'

'I never thought – I mean, she was perfectly normal on Monday. It never occurred to me that she could have killed them. I mean, why would it? I knew they fought that night, but fuck –'

'What did they fight about?' Reyes asks.

He's willing to tell them everything now. 'The father was mean to everyone at dinner. Insulting everybody. The others all left really pissed off, even the cleaning lady. We were about to leave and then Jenna got into it with her dad.' He pauses, as if he doesn't want to say what he has to say next. 'Her father started complaining about how useless they

364

all were and said that he'd decided to change his will and leave half of everything to his sister, and that he'd already made an appointment to do it. Jenna was furious. I wanted to go but Jenna wouldn't leave. It was ugly.'

'Did it get physical?'

'No, but they were both shouting.' He adds, 'She told me afterward that she's the only one who ever stands up to their father. The others are too afraid of him.'

Well, well, well, Reyes thinks, when they've finished with Jake. Jenna Merton, at least, knew for certain that her father was going to change his will. And Jake wasn't with her that night. Reyes taps his pencil on his blotter, deep in thought.

Each of those four kids stands to gain millions. All of them are roughly the same height, right-handed, and physically capable of committing the murders.

Perhaps, he thinks, the kids are in on it together, and this is all part of a grand plan. Perhaps they are playing him. He has no evidence of conspiracy, but any conspiring could easily have been done in person, without leaving any trail. They are sowing enough confusion among them to create reasonable doubt – they're all behaving as though they might have done it. Getting people to lie for them. The earrings in Catherine's jewellery box. Dan being sighted in Brecken Hill. Jenna lying about what happened that night after the others left and saying Jake had been with her. Even Irena's behaviour with the knife. And Rose – maybe they're all in this together somehow.

Is he being manipulated by all of them? He remembers how Irena said that they would never work together.

Is he not going to be able to solve this case? Reyes rubs his eyes tiredly. He refuses to acknowledge the possibility. The truth is there. He just has to find out exactly what happened.

And then he has to be able to prove it.

They have to talk to Jenna again.

Jenna's cell buzzes and she sees that it's Jake calling. Maybe he could tell she wasn't very happy about him asking her for money.

'Hey,' Jenna says. 'What's up?' she asks lightly.

'I've been in Aylesford, talking to the police,' Jake says, his voice tight.

'What the fuck are you talking about?'

'They *know*, Jenna,' Jake says.

'They know what?'

'They caught me on the security camera at the Aylesford train station going back to the city that night. I told them the truth – that I wasn't with you.

And I told them about the argument with your parents.'

She's stunned. And furious. 'What, *exactly*, did you tell them?' she asks, her voice cold.

'That your dad said he'd decided to change his will and give half to his sister.'

She doesn't speak for a moment. Then she demands, 'Why the fuck did you tell them that?'

'Just stay away from me. I don't want anything to do with you,' Jake says, and disconnects the call.

Chapter Fifty-five

THAT EVENING, JENNA visits her sister.

Catherine lets her in and they settle once again in the living room, curtains drawn. 'You want anything?' Catherine asks. 'Wine? Gin and tonic?'

'Sure,' Jenna says, sitting down in one of the armchairs. She sees Catherine's already got a gin and tonic on the coffee table. 'Wine, please.' Ted is hovering in the background the way he does, as if he's not certain he's welcome. But he obviously wants to be there – he wants to hear what she has to say.

Jenna has noticed a change in Ted. He's lost some of his assurance. You'd expect him to be basking in the glow of all the money coming from Catherine's inheritance, Jenna thinks. She studies him silently while Catherine is in the kitchen getting her drink. Ted doesn't give a shit about Dan, or care about the

368

family reputation the way Catherine does – why, then, is he looking so distressed? It strikes her, like a revelation; maybe he doesn't believe Dan did it at all. Maybe he thinks Catherine did it.

'You okay, Ted?' she asks.

Ted says, clearly on edge, 'They found some earrings of your mother's here, in Catherine's jewellery box. Catherine borrowed them, but the detectives don't want to believe her.'

'What earrings?' Jenna asks.

Catherine comes back in from the kitchen and says, 'The antique diamond studs, with the screw backing. You remember those? I borrowed them a while ago, and now they're giving me a hard time about it.' She hands her a glass of red and then sits on the sofa, folding her legs underneath her. 'So, what's happening?' she asks.

Jenna gives her sister a long, contemplative look. Then she says, 'The detectives want to interview me again tomorrow morning. I wanted to talk to you first.'

Catherine leans forward a little, reaching for her glass. 'Why?'

Jenna hesitates for a moment, then says, 'Jake changed his story and told them he wasn't with me that night.'

Catherine goes still, her glass interrupted on its way to her lips, and says, 'Was he or not?'

'No,' Jenna admits. 'I asked him to lie for me.'

There's a long silence. 'What a bunch of liars we all are,' Catherine says finally, and takes a sip of her drink.

'I was home all night. I didn't kill them,' Jenna insists. 'I just don't need the grief.'

'That makes two of us,' Catherine says.

'I'm taking an attorney with me.'

'And what will you tell them?' Catherine asks, looking into her glass.

'Nothing.'

Catherine nods. 'Look,' she says carefully. 'We all know Dan probably did it. But they don't seem to have any hard evidence. Even the witness that puts Dan in Brecken Hill that night – so what? It's not enough. It's nothing. It's not like he was seen at Mom and Dad's. We should all just try to relax. We need to hold our nerve.'

Jenna looks up from her wine glass. 'I had an argument with Dad that night, after the rest of you left. He said he was going to change his will, give Audrey half. He was fed up with all of us. Jake heard all that – and he told the detectives.'

'He was really going to do that? Are you sure?' Catherine asks.

'That's what he said.' She looks hard at Catherine and asks, 'Did you know?'

'What? No, of course not.' There's a taut silence.

'Jesus,' Catherine says, and finishes the rest of her drink in one go. Then she says, 'That doesn't look good for you, does it?'

Later that night, after Jenna is gone, Catherine sits up in bed, pretending to read a novel, while Ted does the same beside her. It's a good thing he can't read her mind. Because as the page blurs in front of her, she's seeing something else – her mother's pale face, her eyes open and staring. She's remembering kneeling down, bending closer, as if to kiss her cheek. But instead, she reaches for the diamond earring in her mother's earlobe. Sheila is wearing the antique diamond studs that Catherine has long coveted. She must have them. Her mother had been wearing a different pair at Easter dinner. Catherine can say she borrowed these. No one will know.

Dan and Lisa sit on the sofa in the den, watching television. They have been awkward and tense with each other. That ease they'd always shared is long gone. Dan isn't sure what Lisa thinks about the murders. Maybe she thinks he did it, he doesn't know. But he's pretty sure she doesn't love him any more.

Unable to concentrate on the show, he finds himself thinking about how it's all gone to shit so fast. And none of it's even his fault. It's everybody else's fault. His father's, for selling the business and ruining his career. Rose Cutter's, for pushing that investment on him and defrauding him. His sister Catherine's, for suggesting Rose talk to him in the first place. He fidgets as his mind runs away with him, his leg jumping up and down on the couch. He can tell he's annoying Lisa.

He gets up. 'I'm going out for a drive.'

She looks up at him. 'Why? Where are you going?' As if she's suspicious of him.

He doesn't like her tone, so he doesn't answer. He leaves the den, half expecting her to get up and follow him to the door, ask him to stay home. But she doesn't. She stays in the den, as if she no longer cares what he does. He grabs a denim jacket – not his usual windbreaker, the police have that – and leaves the house. He has to get out. He can't sit still another minute with all this tension coursing through him. He needs to drive.

He climbs into Lisa's car. It pisses him off that he hasn't got his car back yet and no one can tell him when he will. Everything seems to be getting taken away from him. He turns off his cell phone and backs out of the driveway. He drives aimlessly at first, along familiar roads. Driving helps him think. It usually calms him. But lately it hasn't, and it's not working tonight either. His anger is festering, growing.

His mind settles on Rose, whom he blames for

everything. She stole from him and now she's getting an equal share of the family inheritance – money that was supposed to go to him and his siblings.

He knows where she lives. He's looked it up. It was inevitable – he finds himself driving to her house. When he gets to her street of modest starter homes, he parks across from her house and stares. The lights are all out, except for one over the front door. There's no car in the driveway.

He's so angry at her. He clenches the steering wheel so hard that his hands begin to ache. But still he sits there, watching.

Rose arrives home shortly after 11:00 p.m., having had dinner with friends. She hadn't enjoyed it. She'd been quiet and distracted throughout, enough that her friends noticed. She denied that anything was wrong. They'll find out soon enough. She hasn't told anyone about the will, and it looks like the Mertons haven't either. It hasn't yet made the news. But it's all going to come out any day now.

The street is dark as she pulls into her driveway. She's glad she left the light on over the front door. As she parks her car and gets out, she notices the small car across the street. There's a man inside, and she thinks he's watching her. Instantly, her heart begins to race. She can't tell who it is – it's too dark. She doesn't want to stop and get a good look.

She has to get inside. She rushes up the steps to the door and fumbles with the key, listening for the sound of a car door opening behind her, footsteps on the pavement. Once inside, she locks the door and throws the deadbolt. Then she leans against the door in the dark, breathing fast.

She desperately wants to turn on all the lights, but she doesn't. She doesn't want him to be able to see her inside the house. She sits in the kitchen in the pitch dark with her cell phone in her hand, poised to hit 911.

Finally, around one in the morning, she gets up the nerve to creep out to the living room and look outside from behind the curtain. The car is gone.

Chapter Fifty-six

DESPITE HAVING HER attorney beside her as she enters the police station the next morning, Jenna is uncharacteristically nervous. She's furious at Jake for betraying her. He's nothing but a coward. At least she won't have to pay him anything to keep him quiet. He has nothing to hold over her now; he's told them everything he knows. Perhaps he will come to regret his decision when he can't make his rent. That gives her some small satisfaction. Maybe it's all for the best. It's not like she really has anything to worry about.

They settle in the interview room, Jenna and her lawyer beside her on one side of the table, and Reyes and Barr on the other. Jenna composes herself while the introductions are going on for the tape, before the questions start.

Reyes begins. 'Your boyfriend has sold you out.'

'He's not my boyfriend *any more*,' she says, with a small, tight smile.

'He says he wasn't with you the night of the murders, that you asked him to lie for you,' the detective says.

She glances at her lawyer, and then looks back at Reyes. 'That's true. I did ask him to cover for me. But I didn't kill my parents. I drove him to the train station after dinner, then went back to my place alone.'

'Why did you lie?'

'Why do you think? So you wouldn't think it was me. Same reason my brother and sister lied.'

'You're all going to be millionaires,' Reyes says.

'Exactly. We all knew we'd be suspects.'

'Jake told us about the argument you had with your father that night. I understand it was very heated. He told you he was planning to leave half of his wealth to his sister, Audrey.'

'We had an argument,' Jenna admits. 'He might have said that. But my father always said things like that when he was angry. I didn't take it seriously. It probably looked worse to Jake than it was.'

'Right now, you're the only one we know for certain knew about your father's intention.'

She shrugs. 'I wouldn't be so sure. If he really meant to do that, Mom must have told Catherine. She would have told her if she knew.'

'Why Catherine, particularly?'

'She told Catherine everything. She was the favourite. Our mother never told me and Dan anything.'

'Are you aware that your aunt Audrey has been poisoned?' Reyes asks.

'I heard. I wonder who she pissed off this time.'

'She's fine, by the way,' Reyes says.

Ellen Cutter is downtown running a few errands when she spots Janet Shewcuk on the sidewalk heading toward her. She's walking with her head down and doesn't see her. But Ellen recognizes her daughter's friend from law school, the one who got a job at a fancy law firm in Aylesford when her daughter didn't. She decides to give her a wide berth, keenly aware that it will soon be known far and wide that Rose has defrauded a client and broken the law. She's about to veer around her when Janet happens to look up and stops dead, her face frozen as she recognizes Ellen. Ellen moves to go around her, but Janet reaches out and puts her hand on her arm. 'Mrs Cutter.'

She's stuck now; she can't pretend she doesn't know her.

And then it gets worse. Janet looks at her, eyes filling up with tears, and whispers, 'I'm so sorry.'

Ellen looks back at her in confusion. Does she already know what Rose has done? Has Rose told

377

her? She doesn't want her pity. Before she can wrench her arm away and walk on, Janet speaks again.

'I know Rose is in trouble, and it's all my fault. I never should have told her she was in Fred Merton's will.'

Ellen feels her knees start to buckle, but she has to hear it all.

Later that day, Reyes and Barr and the forensics team, armed with a search warrant, head to the small house Jenna Merton rents on the outskirts of Aylesford. It's a rural property, a wood-frame house that needs painting. It's out in the middle of nowhere. No immediate neighbours. No one to notice her come and go. She's not surprised to see them.

Reyes isn't sure what he was expecting – a mess inside with ashtrays and bongs and detritus from a dissolute artist's life – but what he sees surprises him. Inside, the rooms are bright and well kept. The walls have been freshly painted white, and there are bright canvases on the walls – he wonders if they are from her boyfriend, Jake. But then he thinks, if they were they'd probably have been taken down and shredded by now. They're modern, abstract, but somehow pleasing. Behind the living room is a sunny back room she has turned into a studio that looks out onto the fields. There are various pieces of sculpture in the studio, and he studies them with interest. He sees an entire row of female torsos without heads, just breasts of all shapes and sizes.

'My busts,' she says sardonically.

Some of the pieces are recognizable as female genitalia but others are more conventional. Perhaps she's branching out. They are certainly experimental. One appears to be the head and shoulders of a man that she's been working on in clay. It's unfinished. Or maybe it is finished – he can't tell. He has no understanding of modern art.

'Do you like art?' Jenna asks him, as if reading his mind. She doesn't seem perturbed by them being there.

'I don't know. I've never really thought about it,' he admits.

She shakes her head at him as if he is a philistine. Perhaps he is. But she may be a killer, and she's in no position to judge him, Reyes thinks. He focuses on the task at hand.

He knows she's smart. If she killed her parents, they're not likely to find anything. They go through the entire house. No sign of blood anywhere. None of her mother's jewellery is there. But then, Jenna has entirely different taste.

Her Mini Cooper has been taken away for examination; a rental car is already parked to the left of the house. As they go outside, Reyes recognizes a familiar figure sitting in a car on the dirt road in front of the house. It's Audrey Stancik. Jenna steps out from behind Reyes when she sees her father's sister. She strides over angrily. 'What the fuck are you doing here?' Jenna asks.

'It's a free country,' Audrey replies, smiling nastily at her niece.

'Fuck off,' Jenna snaps. She turns back to Reyes and calls, 'Can't you get rid of her?'

'Never mind,' Audrey says. 'I'm leaving.' She starts her car and drives off.

Reyes and Barr follow the tech team to the backyard. There, they immediately become interested in the fire pit.

The detectives come closer and watch as the team collects every last bit of ash and debris from the fire pit to take back for study at the lab. Reyes feels Jenna come up beside him and turns to look at her.

'It's a fire pit,' she says. 'So what?' He turns his attention back to the blackened circle at his feet. 'You're not going to find anything there,' Jenna says.

The next day is Saturday, and Audrey is at home, feeling lonely and frustrated. She misses Ellen.

What's wrong with those detectives? she thinks. Obviously one of the kids murdered her brother and his wife, but they can't seem to figure out which one. And one of them has tried to kill her, as well – who's to say they won't try again?

She wishes she still had Ellen to talk to. Ellen is so steady, so calming. But Audrey is still angry at her – how could Ellen not tell her, all these years, that Rose is Fred's daughter? Audrey has trusted Ellen with her darkest secret. Perhaps that was a mistake. And Ellen's own daughter may be the murderer.

She's not going to let her brother's killer get away with this. She's obsessed with finding the answer. As she broods, she realizes that, besides the killer, there's one person who might know the truth.

Ellen sits at her kitchen table and stares into space. She knows everything now, and it isn't her daughter who's told her. Ellen has been practically catatonic since she ran into Janet the day before and learned the awful truth. She can't bring herself to call Rose.

She puts her face in her hands and weeps as if she is broken, her heart seizing in fear. Rose had lied to her repeatedly, and she'd had no idea. She couldn't tell. That either makes her daughter an extremely good liar or makes Ellen extremely stupid. She'd always thought her daughter was honest and open-hearted. She never would have thought her capable of stealing that much money. She didn't know her at all. And Rose had lied to her face when she said she didn't know she was in Fred's will, when the truth is, she'd known for months. What else does she not know about her daughter?

Audrey has put a terrible fear into Ellen's heart, with her stories about Fred and what he did. She is afraid there is an unknowable darkness at the centre of her daughter. She doesn't know if she will ever be able to look at her in the same way again.

Chapter Fifty-seven

AUDREY PULLS INTO Irena's driveway. The house looks quiet. She sees a flit of the curtain in the front window as Irena peeps out to see who is there. Audrey wonders if she'll let her in.

Audrey and Irena know each other, of course, but not particularly well. Both are strong women and were willing to stand up to Fred Merton if necessary. Audrey had always admired Irena, while she despised Sheila. Irena did her best for those kids, no one could deny that. She stepped in and did the mothering that Sheila wouldn't, or couldn't, do. As the kids got older and were less interested in their aunt and more interested in their friends, and as Sheila made it clearer that she didn't like Audrey coming to the house, she saw less of the family, and less of Irena. She doesn't know how Irena will react to her now.

She has always been protective of the kids. And Audrey's here to try to find out which one of them is a murderer.

She steps out of the car and makes her way to the front door. Before she can knock, the door opens and Irena's pale face looks out warily at her.

'What do you want, Audrey?' Irena says.

'I just want to talk.'

Irena stares at her for a long moment. 'Okay,' she says and lets her in.

Audrey breathes an inward sigh of relief. At least she got in the door. She hadn't counted on even that much. 'How are you holding up?' Audrey asks sympathetically. Irena, when she sees her up close, looks awful, with dark rings under her eyes, the greying ponytail too severe for her lined face. She looks older, but of course, Irena must be thinking the same thing about her.

Irena says, 'I'm okay. Would you like coffee?'

'Yes, that would be lovely, thanks.' She follows Irena into her tidy kitchen. As Irena prepares the coffee, Audrey takes a seat at the kitchen table and says tentatively, 'I was so glad to hear you got a bequest. It's only right that Fred and Sheila recognize you for all your years of service.' It sounds awkward, and she feels awkward saying it. 'You did so much for the kids.'

'Thank you,' Irena says.

'Will you retire now?' Audrey asks, for lack of any other way to keep the conversation going.

'I don't know. I've told my clients I'm taking some time off while . . . you know. They understand.'

Audrey nods. At least Irena has turned and is facing her now, while she waits for the coffee to brew. Audrey has to broach the elephant in the room somehow. 'It's so awful, what happened,' she says. 'I can't stop thinking about it.' Her own voice sounds hollow.

Irena nods and says, 'I know.' She confesses, 'I've been having nightmares.'

A large tabby cat comes into the kitchen and jumps up on the table. 'Oh, he's gorgeous,' Audrey says, reaching out to pat the friendly cat.

Irena smiles for the first time. 'Isn't he? But he's not supposed to be on the table.' She lifts him down to the floor, where he rubs against their legs in turns.

Audrey wonders if she and Irena can be allies. 'You found them – it's no wonder you're having nightmares,' she says. Irena nods. 'Anybody would,' Audrey assures her, seeking to build rapport with the one person who knows those kids best. She looks around the small kitchen, her mind working on how best to coax Irena into revealing her secrets.

*

Late in the afternoon, an officer approaches Reyes with an excited expression. 'Sir, we may have a lead on that truck we've been looking for.'

Reyes perks up.

'A woman just called. Said her neighbour has a truck matching the description we put out to the media. She says she noticed he hasn't been driving it the last couple of weeks.' He hands Reyes an address as Reyes grabs his jacket. 'She wouldn't give her own name or address.'

Reyes fetches Barr and explains on the way to the car. They drive to an area of run-down homes with garages and unkempt yards, where money goes for necessities rather than niceties. Why would someone who lives here be driving around in Brecken Hill?

They pull up outside the address they're looking for and park on the street. 'I don't see a truck,' Barr says. 'Maybe it's in the garage.'

Reyes nods. The garage door is closed. He feels a beat of excitement. They need a break in the case so badly – perhaps this is it. They exit the car and approach the front door.

A woman in her fifties answers the door, looking dismissively at them. 'Not interested,' she says.

Reyes and Barr hold up their badges. 'Aylesford Police,' Reyes says. 'May we come in?'

She looks nervous now and steps back, opening the door. 'Carl!' she calls over her shoulder.

A man in his early twenties, needing a shave, comes up behind her. 'Who are you?' he asks.

Reyes makes the introductions again, and the man shifts his eyes to their badges apprehensively.

'What's this about?' the woman asks, but she's looking at Carl, rather than at the detectives.

'I don't know, Mom,' Carl says. 'I swear.'

Reyes says, 'We're investigating the murders of Fred and Sheila Merton.' The woman freezes. Her son looks worried. Reyes addresses Carl. 'Are you the owner of a dark pickup, with flames painted on the sides?' Carl hesitates, as if considering his options, then nods. 'We'd like to see it,' Reyes says.

'It's not his truck you're looking for,' the mother says.

'It's in the garage,' Carl says. He puts a pair of sneakers on his bare feet and leads them through the kitchen and out the door into the garage, his anxious mother following. Carl flicks a switch, and the garage fills with light.

Reyes walks toward the truck, looking it over. It's a dark-coloured pickup, with orange and yellow flames painted along the sides. Just like Hot Wheels. Reyes doesn't touch it, but looks in the windows. It's messy and dirty and doesn't look like it's been cleaned in a long time.

'Do you mind telling us where you were on the night of April twenty-first?' Reyes asks.

Carl answers nervously. 'I don't remember. I don't remember what I was doing on whatever day.'

'It was Easter Sunday,' Reyes says.

'Oh. I imagine I was home, right, Mom?'

Now his mother looks scared. 'I-I'm not sure,' she says. 'I can't remember exactly.' She fumbles. 'We had dinner at my sister's. Then we came home.' She turns to her son, a wobble in her voice. 'Did you go out after?'

She knows he went out, Reyes thinks, but she's leaving the lying up to him. She doesn't know what he might have done. She looks at her son as if she's used to being disappointed, he's just levelled up, and she's preparing herself.

'No, I'm pretty sure I stayed in that night.'

'Let's go down to the station and have a chat,' Reyes says.

'Do I have to?' Carl asks.

'No, we just want to talk to you. But if you don't, I might arrest you and read you your rights and take you downtown anyway. And then we'll come back with a search warrant. Which would you prefer?'

'Fine,' he says, sullen.

Chapter Fifty-eight

'HERE'S THE THING,' Reyes begins, when they're all seated in the interview room. 'Your truck matches the description of the vehicle seen driving away from the Merton house on the night of Easter Sunday, the night that Fred and Sheila Merton were murdered. We know you've been keeping that truck in the garage since the description of it went out to the media after the bodies were discovered. So – what were you doing in Brecken Hill that night?'

He shakes his head. 'It wasn't me.'

'It was your truck.'

'I didn't kill anybody.'

'What were you doing there, then?' Reyes asks.

'Fuck,' Carl says. Reyes waits. 'I want a lawyer.'

Now it's Reyes's turn to say *fuck*, but he says it to himself.

'I got somebody,' he says. 'Can I call him?'

'Of course,' Reyes says, and he and Barr leave the room.

An hour later, Carl Brink's attorney arrives and they begin the interview again after Carl has spoken privately with him.

Carl looks nervously at his lawyer, who nods reassuringly. Carl says, 'I was out there that night. I took a wrong turn and went past that house. I went to the next house – it was a dead end – and turned around and went back past it again.'

'What time was this?' Reyes asks.

Carl shakes his head. 'I don't know. Eleven? Twelve?'

'Can you not pin it down a little better than that?' Reyes asks.

Carl looks furtively at his attorney, as if for help. But the attorney has nothing to say. 'That's the best I can do. I may have been a little high.' The attorney gives him a little shake of the head. 'I had nothing to do with what happened there,' Carl insists. He licks his lips nervously.

'Bullshit,' Reyes says. 'Then why didn't you come forward when we put out the description of your truck? You obviously knew we were looking for it – you haven't driven it since.'

Carl hangs his head and says, 'My licence was suspended. I wasn't supposed to be driving that night. And I've kept it in the garage ever since because I knew you were looking for it and I didn't want to get stopped.'

For fuck's sake, Reyes thinks. 'What were you doing out there?'

'I was meeting a friend,' Carl says, averting his eyes.

'You have friends in Brecken Hill? Really?' Reyes allows his disbelief to come through loud and clear. 'Or maybe you were doing some dealing?'

The lawyer clears his throat and says, 'My client has some information that might be useful. Perhaps we could focus on that and not get too caught up in what he was doing there that night?'

Reyes sighs heavily and asks, 'What kind of information?' The attorney nods once at his client.

'I saw something,' Carl says, 'in the driveway where that couple was killed.'

'What did you see?' Reyes asks intently.

'There was a car parked at the end of the driveway, like near the road, not near the house. I thought that was weird.'

'Did you see anybody?'

He shakes his head. 'No. Just the car. It looked empty. The lights were off.'

'What kind of car was it?'

'I don't know. Just a car. But it had a vanity plate. IRENA D.'

*

Reyes and Barr are on their way to Irena Dabrowski's place. 'She gets a million under the will,' Reyes says. 'That's a lot of money for a cleaning lady. We never even searched her car.'

'Well, we can search it now,' Barr says.

'She knew about the suits in Dan's garage, too,' Reyes remembers.

They arrive at Irena's and park on the street. When Irena opens the door, she seems dismayed to see them.

'May we come in?' Reyes asks.

She steps aside and lets them in, suddenly pale, as if she might faint.

'Maybe you should sit down,' Barr suggests and guides her to an armchair just inside the living room.

'We have a new witness,' Reyes tells her. 'Someone who saw something the night of the murders.'

She looks back at them in apparent dread. 'Which one was it?' she whispers.

Reyes is impressed. She's been acting all along. He's annoyed at himself for missing it. 'It was you, Irena. You killed them.'

She stares back at them, aghast. 'Me? What? No. *I* didn't kill them.'

'Someone saw your car at the end of the Mertons' driveway that night.'

She shakes her head in disbelief. 'I didn't kill them. You're making a mistake!'

392

Reyes says, as Barr cuffs her, 'Irena Dabrowski, you are under arrest for the murders of Fred and Sheila Merton. You have the right to remain silent. Anything you say can and will be used against you in a court of law. You have the right to an attorney . . .'

Irena has requested an attorney and it is evening when they begin formal questioning. Irena appears to be very shaken, almost in shock.

Reyes watches her without sympathy. She has played them all along. Cleaning the knife when she went back to 'discover' the bodies, to make them think she was protecting one of the children. Her reluctant admission that it might have been any one of the Merton kids, when it was her all the time. She'd thrown them all under the bus.

The attorney asks, looking worriedly at his distressed client, 'What makes you think my client murdered her employers in cold blood? She was their cleaning lady, for Christ's sake.'

'We have a new witness who saw her car – with her very identifiable licence plate, IRENA D – parked at the end of the Mertons' drive on the night of the murders, sometime between eleven o'clock and midnight.'

Irena shakes her head and mumbles, 'I wasn't there.'

'You receive one million dollars under Fred Merton's will,' Reyes says. 'Correct?'

'Yes,' she admits.

The attorney says, 'A reasonable enough bequest, considering the wealth of her employers and the length of her service.'

'And motive enough for murder,' Reyes counters. 'People have killed for far less.'

'I didn't do it,' she says again, with fear in her voice. 'I didn't even know they'd left me anything. Why would I kill them?'

'Interfering with the murder scene – you did that to direct attention toward the kids, away from yourself.' She's gone ashen. 'You knew about those disposable coveralls in Dan's garage, and that he left the door unlocked.'

The lawyer breaks in. 'I think we're done here. You're going to need more evidence than one questionable eyewitness. Unless you've got more –'

'We'll get more,' Reyes says.

Chapter Fifty-nine

DAN LEARNS OF the arrest when a breaking news report comes on TV that night. He can't believe it. He yells for his wife.

She comes running in from the kitchen.

He turns to her, queasy with a strange mixture of horror and relief. 'They've arrested Irena.' Lisa looks from him to the television, stunned. '*Now* do you believe me?' he says bitterly, but with a note of triumph. He fumbles for the cell phone in his pocket. 'I have to call Catherine.'

Catherine is still up when Dan calls, reading in bed with Ted. They find it hard to sleep these days, often reading late into the night, until they turn off the light and their fear keeps them awake.

She sees that it's Dan, and reluctantly accepts the

call. She's surprised Dan is calling her – he's been doing his best to avoid her.

'Catherine – have you heard? They've arrested Irena.'

'For what?' she says stupidly.

'For the *murders*.'

She sucks in a breath. 'Irena?' She feels Ted moving beside her.

'It's on the news. Look online.'

She taps the app for local news on her phone and sees the headline, *Former Nanny Arrested in Murder of Merton Couple.* Ted is now looking over her shoulder at the phone.

She glances at her husband as the reality of it sinks in. Then she puts the phone back to her mouth and says, 'You'd better come over. I'll call Jenna. We need to decide what to do.' Her mind is racing. What now? Do they stand behind Irena? Say nothing? Or vilify her to the press? She disconnects the call and looks up. Ted is staring at her.

'I can't believe it,' she says, her voice a whisper. 'I honestly thought Dan had done it, all this time.'

Ted holds his wife in his arms for a moment, hugging her tightly. He can't quite believe it either. *Irena?* If they've arrested her for the murders, they must have good reason. They must have evidence. He's been wrong about his wife, whom he had begun to deeply distrust. He's been wrong about her – and she's been carrying this awful burden, all this time, thinking her brother murdered her parents. He kisses the top of her head and feels the terrible tension that he's been carrying around the last couple of weeks begin to release. Of course she's not a monster. She will make a wonderful mother. Now they can move forward, focus on the baby. His thoughts turn to Lisa, how she must be feeling the same way right now. He thinks of their furtive meeting in the Home Depot parking lot. Maybe they can both relax now, and they will never speak to each other of their doubts ever again.

Catherine pulls away from his embrace to call Jenna. Then they both hurriedly get dressed.

It's another strange family meeting. They're all here, back in Catherine and Ted's living room – only Irena is missing.

Lisa feels as if she's holding her breath. She wants so much for this to be true, for the police to be right. She desperately wants Irena to be guilty. She wants her husband exonerated, and Catherine too, whom she loves like a sister. She wants her family back and she wants the money and she doesn't care about Irena – she barely knows her.

When she and Dan arrived, she caught Ted's eye, and they immediately looked away from each other, as if ashamed. Catherine had been on her laptop looking for any information she could find on the arrest. There isn't much, only that new evidence has emerged putting Irena at the scene of the crime at the relevant time. That's all they know.

'I can't believe it,' Jenna says again, voicing what they all feel.

'I wonder what the evidence is,' Dan says. It's what they're all thinking.

'We have to decide how we're going to handle this,' Catherine says. The three siblings look at one another, uncertain. At length Catherine says, 'I think we say nothing, to the police or the press. Don't we owe her that?'

Slowly, Dan begins to nod, and then Jenna does too.

Lisa knows what they're thinking. They're all thinking the same thing: *Thanks to Irena, we're all going to be rich.*

The next morning is Sunday, and Reyes and Barr are at Irena's house bright and early with a warrant and the forensics team. Irena was held overnight and remains in custody. They take a quick look at the car before it is taken away. There are no obvious signs of recent cleaning, or of staining. It will take time to have a more thorough look. Then they go into the house.

The cat is hungry. Reyes finds the cat food and fills its bowls with food and water and watches as it begins to eat. Irena had requested that someone put it in its carrier and take it to Audrey's house to be cared for. Reyes assigns the task to a young officer.

They impatiently watch the crime team do its meticulous work. But they find nothing at all.

Later that day, Irena has something to say. They all reconvene in the interview room, the detectives and Irena and her attorney. Reyes and Barr resume the interview.

'I've remembered something important,' she tells them. 'I had a phone call late that night – from a friend of mine, wishing me a Happy Easter. I don't know when, exactly, but it must have been after eleven. We're both night people, and we often call each other late. We talked for a while, on my land-line. If you get my phone records, that will prove I was home that night, won't it?'

They've already ordered those records. Reyes turns to Barr. 'Check on how much longer till we get them, can you?' She leaves the room. They wait for her return.

She comes back shaking her head and says, 'I've asked them to hurry them up.'

'I wasn't there,' Irena insists.

'We have a witness who identified your car. With *your* vanity plate.'

Irena, pale, but with a new firmness in her voice, says, 'I think I know what might have happened. I think someone else must have used my car that night.'

'One of the Merton kids?' Reyes says. She nods. 'That's a convenient idea, isn't it? Were any of them in the habit of using your car?'

'No. But if any of them wanted to, they could have taken it. I always left a spare copy of my keys in the back, on the patio, under the planter. A full set of house keys and car keys. They all knew. I started doing that because I'd lost my keys twice.'

'Does anyone else know about those spare keys?'

She shakes her head. 'No. It was just Fred and Sheila and the kids.'

'And where do you keep your car?'

'On the street.'

'So you're suggesting that one of them took your spare keys from the backyard on Easter Sunday, after you were at home, and drove your car to the Mertons' house, committed the murders, and returned your car?'

'I'm saying it's possible. I can't think of any other explanation. *I* didn't drive the car out there that night.'

'Did you ever let Catherine or Dan or Jenna borrow your car, ever drive them anywhere?' Reyes asks.

She shakes her head. 'No, they all have much nicer cars than mine.'

Audrey had been astonished when a police officer brought Irena's cat and all its supplies to her door that morning. Now she sits with the big tabby on her lap, listening to it purr as she pets it gently. The traitorous cat doesn't seem to miss his owner at all. Its bowls and its litter box are on the floor in the kitchen. Audrey looks at them and wonders how long the cat will be here.

She can't believe Irena killed Fred and Sheila. Irena seems so grounded, so sensible. The police must have it wrong. When she and Irena spoke, they were in perfect accord – one of the Merton children must have done it. But Irena, like Audrey, didn't know which one.

She wants to know why the police have arrested Irena. There are no details on the news – just that they have new evidence implicating her.

This is all such a surprise; she was so sure it was one of the kids.

The phone records confirm that Irena was at home, on the phone, from 11:11 p.m. until 11:43 p.m. on Easter Sunday. She could not have committed the murders if Carl saw her car there sometime between eleven and midnight, as he claims. She would not

401

have had time. Reyes has to let her go. He doesn't have enough to prosecute her for double murder. He doesn't have enough to prosecute anyone. Now, he stares moodily into space, tiredly trying to make sense of it all.

If Carl Brink is telling the truth, *someone* drove that car to the Mertons' that night. Rose would not have known about Irena's hidden car keys. But he knows that all the legitimate Merton offspring did, and they are all liars. He has three suspects. None of them have alibis. All had motive. He stares at the grisly pictures of the crime scene up on his wall, of Fred and Sheila, murdered in cold blood, and asks himself for the hundredth time – *Who did this?*

Chapter Sixty

THE FOLLOWING MORNING is Monday, and there's a crowd of press outside the police station wanting answers. Reyes has no answers to give them. He brushes past them with a terse 'no comment' and makes his way inside. It's been frustrating, this entire case.

And then finally, mid-morning, a break. Some actual physical evidence has been discovered.

Reyes and Barr lock eyes when they get the news.

Reyes says, 'Let's get all of them – Dan, Catherine, and Jenna – in here to give DNA samples. See if we get a match.'

Ted sits at the kitchen table with a cup of coffee, staring at the newspaper. He's not going in to work today. He feels like something dark and heavy is crouching on his chest. Two nights ago Irena had been arrested, and he thought this nightmare was over. Then yesterday they let her go. No explanation as to why either of those things happened, from the detectives or in the news. Catherine has tried to call Irena repeatedly, but she isn't answering, and they know she has caller ID. Irena doesn't want to talk to her. They need to know what the fuck is going on. Ted feels like going over there and pounding on her door himself.

Catherine wanders into the kitchen, her hand resting protectively on her entirely flat stomach. He feels a twinge of anger. She wants sympathy and support, but he's not sure he can give her that, baby or not.

The phone rings, piercing the silence. Neither one of them has said much to the other yet this morning. He gets up and grabs the phone on the wall. His heart plummets when he recognizes Detective Reyes's voice.

'May I speak to Ms Merton?' Reyes asks.

'Just a sec,' Ted says, and hands the phone to his wife.

He watches her as she listens, his heart rate escalating painfully. What might Irena have told them, he wonders, for them to let her go? Catherine's face is very still as she listens, and the fingers of the hand not holding the phone grip the kitchen counter.

'Now?' she says. Then, 'Fine.' She hangs up the phone.

'What does he want?' Ted asks.

She looks at him, then quickly averts her eyes. 'He says they've found some physical evidence. They want me and Dan and Jenna to come in to provide DNA samples.' She swallows and whispers, 'Ted, what if they found the disposable suit, and Dan's DNA is all over it?'

The dark thing crouching on Ted's chest shifts and settles, heavier than before.

Lisa knows it will all soon be over, one way or another. The detectives have found physical evidence related to the crime. They must have found the bloody clothes, or the suit. They have called Dan to come in to provide a DNA sample.

Once Dan leaves to go to the station, pale but strangely calm, she calls Catherine.

But it's Ted who picks up the phone. 'Hello?'

'Ted. Is Catherine there?'

'No. She's at the police station.' She can hear the panic in his voice. 'She has to give a DNA sample.'

'Dan too.'

'And Jenna. They're doing all of them.'

'What did they find, do you know?' she asks anxiously.

'No idea.'

They share a long, uncomfortable silence over

the line, but neither one reaches out to the other; they are both too frightened.

'Goodbye, Ted,' Lisa says, and hangs up the phone. She suddenly has to sit and put her head down between her knees to keep from fainting.

Easter Sunday, 11:02 p.m.

Sheila sits up in bed, trying to read, but the book isn't holding her attention. Her mind keeps returning fretfully to earlier that evening. Fred has already fallen asleep beside her, snoring irregularly, in fits and starts. She looks over at him, annoyed. She watches him with loathing. It's hard to feel anything else for him, even though he's dying. He's been such a bastard. Why did she ever marry him? He's made everyone's life a misery.

He means to change his will in his sister's favour – he's getting his affairs in order. He always wants to hurt the kids. And she's never had the power to stop it. She hasn't been a very good mother.

She's been so anxious these last few weeks, knowing what Fred is going to do. She's worried about how the kids will react when Fred dies soon and they find out. They'll be so angry. And there's nothing she can do about it.

She hears the doorbell ring downstairs. She looks

407

*at the clock radio on her bedside table. It's late –
11:03. She freezes and waits. Who would come at
this time of night? But the doorbell rings again.
And again. She can't just ignore it. She pushes back
the covers and slides her feet into her slippers, grabbing her housecoat and pulling it on as she leaves
the room, Fred still sputtering behind her. She turns
on the light switch at the top of the stairs, and it
lights up the staircase and the front hall. She holds
the smooth handrail as she makes her way down
the carpeted steps. The doorbell rings again.*

*She opens the door and stares, confused by what
she sees. There's someone in a hazmat suit standing
on her doorstep. She's so surprised she doesn't recognize who it is at first. She notices the cord in the
person's right hand. It happens almost too fast for
conscious thought – the recognition, the horror of
suddenly understanding. And then she turns and
tries to get away. She's not fast enough and is
yanked backward by her neck. As she feels the cord
squeezing tightly around her throat, Sheila tries to
grab her cell phone on the end table, but it gets
knocked away . . .*

Chapter Sixty-one

TWO DAYS LATER, Jenna sits in the now-familiar interview room, her lawyer straight-backed and alert beside her. She's not going to say anything. She has no intention of confessing. She doesn't feel guilty. They had it coming.

Detective Reyes is staring at her as if he knows everything, as if he can get right inside her head and read her thoughts. Good luck to him. It's dark in here, inside her head. But she knows they don't have any physical evidence, despite what they've said. They can't have found the bloodied disposable suit and gloves and everything else. She knows they haven't. They're bluffing.

'Have you ever driven Irena's car before?' Reyes asks.

So they know about the car. She figured that's why they arrested Irena. But why have they let her go? Irena doesn't have an alibi for that night. Jenna knows that. She was going to go home after Easter dinner at the Mertons' and go to bed with a good book. That's what she said.

Have they figured out that somebody else might have used her car? Irena would have told them about the spare keys, trying to save herself. But they all knew that Irena kept a spare set of keys in the backyard.

'Have you ever driven Irena's car before?' Reyes repeats.

Her lawyer has told her to deny everything. 'No.'

'That's interesting,' Reyes says, 'because we have DNA evidence putting you in the driver's seat of her car. We found a hair from your head.'

'That's impossible,' Jenna says quickly, thinking *so that's what they found, that's their physical evidence*. She's fucked up, she realizes now, her heart pounding, saying she'd never been in Irena's car. It's hard to think clearly, in this small, hot room, with everyone staring at her. She can feel herself starting to perspire and she brushes her hair back nervously.

'What is the relevance of this?' the attorney asks.

Reyes answers. 'We have a witness who saw Irena's car – he remembered her vanity plate – parked at the end of the Mertons' driveway on the night of the murders.'

Now the attorney gives her a quick glance and

looks away. 'We're done, no more questions,' the attorney says. 'Unless you have something else?'

Reyes shakes his head. The lawyer rises. 'Come on, Jenna, we can go.'

But Jenna takes her time, her confidence rebounding. She says, 'It's perfectly understandable how a hair from me got in Irena's car. I always hug her when I see her, and usually she gets into her car right afterward. That must be how the hair got there.' She rises to her feet to leave.

'The thing is,' Reyes says, his frustration showing, 'we know Irena was at home that night. She was on the phone, talking to a friend, at the relevant time. We know someone else must have used her car that night. And we haven't found DNA from anybody else in her car, just yours. And we know you found out earlier that night that your father was going to change his will.'

'That's never going to be enough, and you know it,' the attorney says. 'As my client has pointed out, that hair could have been a transfer from a hug.'

Jenna smirks at the detective and follows her attorney out of the room without another word.

Chapter Sixty-two

EVER SINCE THEY released Irena, Catherine has been on edge. They'd never found out why they arrested her, or why they let her go. Irena isn't answering her calls, or her front door, which is unnerving. And they had taken DNA from all of them, two days ago.

Catherine hears the doorbell ring and rises quickly, startled. She feels dizzy, suddenly. Are they here to arrest her now? They can't be. She hasn't done anything. But she feels the panic rising in her chest. Fear for her unborn child.

She reaches to open the door, a deep dread in the pit of her stomach. 'Audrey,' she says in surprise. Her voice turns icy. 'What are you doing here?'

'May I come in?' Audrey asks.

Catherine hesitates, then steps back and opens the door wide. Ted has joined them now, and he's got that expression on his face that she has come to hate – a look of fear. It makes her want to shake him. They make their way into the living room and sit down.

'I've been talking to Irena,' Audrey says.

Catherine stares back at her, her heart in her throat, and steels herself. Why would Irena talk to *Audrey*, when she won't talk to them? She's afraid to look at her husband. 'Why would Irena talk to *you*?'

Audrey says, 'Irena and I have known each other for a long time. We understand one another. I took care of her cat while she was arrested.'

Catherine looks back at her in dismay.

Audrey explains about Irena's car being seen. She adds, 'Irena says that someone else must have used her car that night.'

Catherine tries to speak, but her mouth is dry.

Then Ted says, his voice flat, 'That's – that's ridiculous, surely?'

Audrey replies, 'Actually, they know someone else must have used her car that night, because she was at home, on the phone. They have records.' She pauses, clearly delighting in passing on this information. 'She says that all of you kids knew that she kept a spare set of keys in the backyard.'

Catherine doesn't respond, but she glances quickly at Ted and registers that he has gone a shade paler.

'And I know something else. They found DNA

evidence – a hair – from someone else in the driver's seat of that car, even though Irena says none of you have ever been in her car, as far as she knows.'

'How do you know that?' Ted asks, his voice accusatory, as if he thinks she's making all this up.

'I know a newspaper reporter who's friendly with someone in the lab. She told me, hoping I would give her a story.'

'Whose DNA was it?' Catherine asks, her mouth dry. She can barely get the words out.

'Jenna's.'

Catherine sinks against the back of the sofa, a tumult inside her. *Jenna*. She takes a deep breath. Jenna knew that night that their father was going to change his will. Jake told the detectives. Catherine had been troubled when Irena was arrested; it seemed to turn the world upside down. She'd thought all along that Dan had done it, that he was the one most like their father. She'd always worried about his strange, stalking behaviour; she knows about his habit of driving around alone at night. He inherited their father's worst impulses, she thought, but not his genius for business. 'So they think *Jenna* did it?' she says finally. 'Are they going to arrest her?'

Audrey shakes her head, clearly frustrated now. 'My reporter friend says it won't be enough to arrest her for murder. Apparently they interviewed her and let her go.'

Catherine doesn't want the family name dragged through the mud. She wants it all to go away. She realizes, almost with a feeling of surprise, that it's going to be okay. Nothing terrible is going to happen. Jenna won't go to prison; she won't even be arrested. And neither will Dan. Everything is going to be fine. They can breathe again, now that they know. Life will go on. The scandal will recede, eventually. And they'll all be rich. The only one going to jail is Rose.

She suddenly feels as if a terrible burden has been lifted from her shoulders. She has to stifle the impulse to smile. Instead, she looks appropriately grim and says, 'Thank you, Audrey, for letting us know.'

'I thought I should tell you. I wasn't sure anyone else would.'

Catherine narrows her eyes at Audrey. 'You're enjoying this, aren't you? You've always disliked Jenna the most.'

Audrey gets up to leave. 'Fred should never have been murdered at all. I should have got my rightful share whenever he died of cancer, which would have been soon enough.' She strides to the front door and turns around for a final comment. 'You know what I'd really enjoy? Seeing Jenna convicted.'

*

Dan is at home when he gets a call from Catherine. He feels his body flood with adrenaline as Catherine explains everything. He closes his eyes in relief for a moment. The detectives will back off him now. And it's good to finally know. It's good to know which of your siblings you have to keep an eye on. How odd that he has Audrey to thank for it. 'What should we do?' Dan asks. 'I mean, do we tell her we know, or what?'

Catherine is quiet on the other end of the line for a moment, thinking. 'I don't think we can let her get away with it with *us*, you know?'

Dan is silent. He doesn't want her to get away with it at all.

Catherine says, 'Can you come over tonight? We have to let Jenna know we know and reassure her that we're never going to say anything.'

'Okay,' Dan says reluctantly. 'If you think that's wise. You know what a temper she has.'

The atmosphere is palpably tense in Catherine's house that evening.

Now that the moment has arrived, Catherine finds that she's nervous and glances at Ted for support. He looks on edge too. She doesn't know exactly what she expects – some sort of cold denial from Jenna – but they must reveal to her that they know. She and Dan will have to keep an eye on

Jenna and hope she will never have any cause to murder anyone else.

Irena, who had finally answered her call, had declined her invitation. She didn't want anything more to do with them. Irena told her she had decided to retire and move south when she got her bequest, that she would send her a Christmas card. And then she hung up. Catherine could hardly blame her. Her loyalty only went so far; she'd almost been framed for murder.

They are all here – except for Audrey – she and Ted sharing the sofa, Jenna in one armchair and Dan in the other, Lisa sitting beside him in the other chair Catherine has pulled up. Catherine has already poured everyone a glass of wine, and is nursing her fake gin and tonic.

Catherine aims to make her voice as neutral as she can and says, 'We found out, Jenna, that the detectives found your DNA in Irena's car, that they think it was you who murdered Mom and Dad.' She watches Jenna's expression grow cold, her mouth taking on an angry shape. 'But it's all right,' Catherine continues. 'Because nothing's going to happen. That hair in Irena's car – it's not enough to arrest you. It's going to be okay.' There's a moment of loaded silence.

'How *dare* you,' Jenna says in a menacing voice.

Catherine recoils. She's seen her sister like this

before; she's frightening. Catherine glances at the others for support. 'We *know*, Jenna. There's no point in denying it to *us*. We're not going to do anything.'

'They don't *know* anything,' Jenna says icily. 'They found a hair of mine in Irena's car. They don't know how it got there – but maybe *you* do.' She looks nastily back at Catherine and Catherine feels sick. *She can't mean to put this on her*. She glances up quickly at Ted, but he's staring at Jenna as if there's a snake coiled in the chair.

'Or maybe it was you, Dan,' Jenna says, turning to him.

Dan gapes at her.

Jenna says, 'I don't know who, but one of you killed Mom and Dad and put my hair in Irena's car.'

'No one else put it there,' Catherine says quickly, as the situation becomes clear to her and her nerves lurch crazily. This is what it has come down to – *Jenna* murdered their parents. But now Catherine's own husband will never be entirely sure that it wasn't her. She glances at Lisa, and she sees the desperate uncertainty there as Lisa stares at the side of Dan's head. Who will *she* believe? Then Catherine turns back to Jenna – but Jenna is looking at her more calmly now, her confidence restored.

Jenna says, 'I never left my house that night, although I can't prove it. But we all know each of *you* were out for *hours*.'

Catherine, silently panicking, thinks, *This fucking family.*

Chapter Sixty-three

JENNA DRIVES HOME from Catherine's, her headlights piercing the darkness along the dirt road, remembering that Easter night. She'd been in a murderous mood when they left. She dropped Jake at the train station – she didn't want his company, and he didn't try to change her mind. Then she went home and thought about it and put together a plan.

Jenna drove to Dan's house. Dan's car wasn't in the driveway. Wearing latex gloves from her cleaning cupboard, she snuck into his garage through the unlocked side door. Dan's car wasn't in the garage either. He'd gone out for a drive, she thought, because he's sick that way. She knows about his creepy habits. She used a small flashlight she'd brought – she'd deliberately left her cell phone at home – to collect the disposable coveralls and booties she already knew were there. Then she drove to Irena's house. As expected, her car was parked on the street, and her house was dark. Jenna parked her own car farther down the street, out of sight of Irena's house, and careful not to be seen, located Irena's spare keys in the back, under the planter. Then she drove Irena's car to her parents' house, arriving shortly before eleven, and killing the headlights, pulled in and parked at the end of the drive.

The night was dark and still. Probably no one would see the car parked here, but if they did, it would be Irena's car they'd see, not hers. She hadn't wanted to risk anyone seeing her own car, her Mini Cooper, anywhere near the place that night.

She got out of the car and stared at the house for a moment. There was a faint light coming from the master bedroom. Jenna walked to the backyard with her canvas bag of gear. There, she took off her shoes and jacket and pulled on the disposable coveralls, an extra pair of thick socks, and the booties. Once she was suited up, the hood pulled tight against her face, no hair escaping, she felt a strange sense of invincibility. She took the electrical cord she'd brought with her and went back around to the front and rang the doorbell. No one came. She rang the bell again. And again. Finally, she could sense lights going on, over the stairs and in the front hall, filtering out through the living-room windows to her left, and at last her mother opened the door, as she knew she would.

For a moment, her mother stood there, not getting it. Maybe she didn't recognize her with the hazmat suit covering her completely, even her hair, and changing her shape. Her mother didn't understand what she was here to do. And then she recognized her, and she knew. *The look on her face.* She backed up, turned and stumbled toward the living room. But Jenna was right behind her and brought the electrical cord up fast around her neck before she could even scream. She held the cord tight, dragging her mother farther into the living room, trying not to make too much noise, squeezing hard until her mother finally stopped struggling and sagged against the cord. It took longer than expected. Then she lowered her to the floor. Jenna felt nothing. She went back and quietly closed the front door. Then she returned to the body and struggled with her mother's rings, wrenching them off. It was difficult, with the gloves. She heard her father calling from upstairs.

'Sheila, who is it?'

There wasn't time to remove the tricky diamond studs from her mother's ears. Jenna moved quickly into the kitchen through the back of the living room, avoiding the front hall where her father would come down the stairs. She put the electrical cord and the rings down on the counter and withdrew the carving knife from the knife block. 'In here,' she called, hoping he wouldn't look inside the living room first. If he did, she would improvise. She would chase him down.

She stood like a statue in the dark kitchen and waited for him. She remembers grabbing him from behind as he passed by her and slitting his throat in one clean stroke, the blood spurting all over her hand. The rest is a bit of a blur – it was different from killing her mother. Something in her took over. By the time it was done, she was panting with effort, exhausted, and covered in blood. She sat on the floor for a minute, resting. She knew what she had to do next, and she had to be quick.

She grabbed a garbage bag from under the sink and put her mother's rings and the electrical cord inside. Then she walked down the hall and upstairs to the master bedroom. She rifled through the jewellery box, then decided to take everything, dumping its contents into the bag. She emptied their wallets and threw them to the floor. She left a bloody trail behind her, pulling open drawers, trashing the place as she went, upstairs and down. She went into the study, but left the safe alone. Last of all, she took the box of family silver from the dining room. Then she went out the back door in the kitchen to the backyard, which verged on a ravine. She knew no one could see her – it was pitch dark and the other houses were too far away, blocked by trees. She placed the box of silver in the canvas zip-up bag she'd brought. Then she stripped off the bloodied disposable suit and the booties and the thick socks and placed them carefully in the plastic bag, along with the electrical cord and the jewellery, cards, and cash, removing the gloves last of all. She wiped her face and hands thoroughly with wet wipes, then placed those in the garbage bag as well. Then she placed that bag inside the canvas bag, put on her shoes and jacket and a fresh pair of latex gloves, and made her way back to Irena's car. She drove back to Irena's, moved the canvas bag into her own car, and returned the keys.

On the way home, she got rid of the evidence. Somewhere no one would ever find it. She hid the canvas bag on a farm property along the same isolated country road she lives on. She buried it in the ground where a concrete floor was going to be poured for a new outbuilding sometime in the next day or two. It was a stroke of good fortune that she already knew this because she's acquainted with the woman who owns the property, and she had mentioned it to her.

Now, every time Jenna drives past that building, seeing it go up – it's progressing nicely – she feels a sense of satisfaction.

They will never find the evidence. She's the only one who knows it's there.

Catherine and Dan did not kill their parents, but Ted and Lisa don't know that for sure. Jenna smirks as she drives. If she wanted to, Jenna could tell Ted and Lisa things – things that were actually true – that would make their toes curl. Those earrings, for example – the ones they found in Catherine's jewellery box, the ones she 'borrowed' – Jenna knows her mother was wearing those same earrings the night she strangled her. She had long enough to notice them while she had the cord around her neck. She knows Catherine must have taken them off their mother's body that night. She wonders what Ted would think of that.

And Dan – does Lisa not wonder about her husband's compulsion to drive endlessly after dark? Where does she think he goes? Does she never try to call his cell? What does she suppose he's doing? *Classic serial killer behaviour, if you ask me*, Jenna thinks to herself.

It's too bad Audrey didn't die from the poison she put in her iced tea that Sunday morning, sneaking in the open back window while Audrey was out, but in the end, Jenna thinks, it doesn't really matter.

Epilogue

AUDREY DRIVES THE route from Fred and Sheila's house to Irena's house, then to Jenna's house, over and over again over the next weeks. She thinks Jenna must have dumped the bloody clothes or disposable suit along here *somewhere* that night.

She wants to prove that Jenna murdered Fred and Sheila. Catherine clearly doesn't – she wants to keep everything quiet, and to protect the family name. But Audrey suspects Dan feels the same way she does. Audrey can understand why. In the public imagination, in the press, obsessed with the Merton killings, Dan is the one everybody seems to think is guilty. He wants to be exonerated.

Audrey figures it was Jenna who tried to poison her.

She takes to following Jenna, but at a safe distance. One day she sees her stop in briefly at a home

427

along the country road that Jenna lives on. She doesn't stay long, but long enough for Audrey to notice, as she waits well back on the side of the road, that a new building is going up on the property, some distance from the house. Jenna comes out carrying something. Audrey is too far away to see what it is.

As Jenna drives off, Audrey stays where she is for a moment. Then she drives closer. She sees the sign: FRESH EGGS. Audrey gets out of her car and walks up the short drive. It's an old house, nicely redone to retain its original charm. Red brick, cream gingerbread trim on the porch. Audrey could see herself living in a place like this, out in the country, but not too far from town. Of course, she resents that she'll never be able to afford Brecken Hill, but it's true she loves it out here – so pretty and peaceful.

'Hi,' Audrey says, when a woman comes out the screen door. 'What a lovely place you have here.'

'Thank you,' she says. 'Did you want some eggs?'

'Yes, please,' Audrey answers. 'A dozen.'

As the woman packages her eggs, Audrey says, 'I notice you're putting up a new outbuilding.'

She nods. 'Poured the foundation just after Easter, and now it's almost finished.'

Audrey smiles at the woman and pays for her eggs.

Audrey has watched enough crime shows to know that it's smart to bury bodies under poured concrete, especially when it's the foundation for a building. Why not evidence? She visits Reyes and Barr and tells them what she thinks. But they explain that they can't dig up a building on someone's private property based on her suspicions, no matter how much it makes sense to her.

Somehow a full year goes by. Audrey's heard that Catherine has given birth to a baby girl, and that she and Ted and the baby now live in Fred and Sheila's old house in Brecken Hill. Audrey saw Ted recently at the grocery store, wearily pushing a cart, buying food and diapers. He looked haggard, unhappy. She turned away, avoiding him before he saw her.

One sunny day in early June, Audrey happens to drive by the lovely rural property again. This time she notices a FOR SALE sign out front. Audrey has just received her inheritance – a million dollars. She stops the car and stares at the sign for a long moment. Should be more than enough.

She picks up her cell phone and calls the realtor.

Acknowledgements

Writing a book and getting it to market – especially within the space of a year – requires a concerted team effort, and I'm extremely fortunate to have the best teams out there! Here we are at book six, and once again I give my heartfelt thanks to all the people who make my books the best they can be, every single time. Thank you to Brian Tart, Pamela Dorman, Jeramie Orton, Ben Petrone, Mary Stone, Bel Banta, Alex Cruz-Jimenez, and the rest of the fantastic team at Viking Penguin in the US; to Larry Finlay, Bill Scott-Kerr, Frankie Gray, Tom Hill, Ella Horne, and the rest of the brilliant team at Transworld in the UK; and to Kristin Cochrane, Amy Black, Bhavna Chauhan, Emma Ingram, and the entire team at Doubleday in Canada. Thank you all, with an extra shout-out to my much-appreciated, hard-working editors, Frankie Gray and Jeramie Orton!

Special thanks, again, to Jane Cavolina for being an exceptional copy-editor. I can't imagine having anyone else copy-edit my books.

Thanks again to my beloved agent, Helen Heller – especially this year, when the pandemic made everything seem so much harder. You always keep me going, and I am grateful. Thanks also to Camilla and Jemma and everyone at the Marsh Agency for representing me worldwide and selling my books into so many markets.

Thanks again to my adviser on forensic matters, Mike Iles, MSc, of the Forensic Science Program at Trent University, and also to Kate Bendelow, Crime Scene Investigator, in the UK. I'm very grateful for your help, both of you!

As always, any mistakes in the manuscript are entirely mine.

I'd also like to thank all the people in the book world who stepped up to do events virtually when we couldn't do them in person.

Thanks always, to my readers. I wouldn't be here, doing what I love, without you too.

And finally, thanks to my husband, my kids, and Poppy the cat. Manuel gets a special mention for endlessly solving technical problems over the past year.

Shari Lapena worked as a lawyer and as an English teacher before writing fiction. Her debut thriller, *The Couple Next Door*, was a global bestseller, the bestselling fiction title in the UK in 2017 and has been optioned for television. Her thrillers *A Stranger in the House*, *An Unwanted Guest*, *Someone We Know* and *The End of Her* were all *Sunday Times* and *New York Times* bestsellers. Shari's books are published in 37 territories worldwide, with global sales of over 7 million. *Not a Happy Family* is her sixth thriller.

Also by Shari Lapena

THE COUPLE NEXT DOOR

You never know what's happening on the other side of the wall.

Your neighbour told you that she didn't want your six-month-old daughter at the dinner party. Nothing personal, she just couldn't stand her crying.

Your husband said it would be fine. After all, you only live next door. You'll have the baby monitor and you'll take it in turns to go back every half hour.

Your daughter was sleeping when you checked on her last. But now, as you race up the stairs in your deathly quiet house, your worst fears are realized. She's gone.

You've never had to call the police before. But now they're in your home, and who knows what they'll find there.

What would *you* be capable of, when pushed past your limit?

'Entirely compelling and utterly realistic.
You will not see the twists coming'
DAILY MAIL

OUT NOW

A STRANGER IN THE HOUSE

Why would you run scared from a happy home?

You're waiting for your beloved husband to get home from work. You're making dinner, looking forward to hearing about his day.

That's the last thing you remember.

You wake up in hospital, with no idea how you got there. They tell you that you were in an accident; you lost control of your car whilst driving in a dangerous part of town.

The police suspect you were up to no good. But your husband refuses to believe it. Your best friend isn't so sure. And even you don't know what to believe . . .

'Shari expertly traps you, confounds you and leaves you gasping at the end. More, please'
FIONA BARTON

OUT NOW

AN UNWANTED GUEST

We can't choose the strangers we meet.

As the guests arrive at beautiful, remote Mitchell's Inn, they're all looking forward to a relaxing weekend deep in the forest, miles from anywhere. They watch their fellow guests with interest, from a polite distance.

Usually we can avoid the people who make us nervous, make us afraid.

With a violent storm raging, the group finds itself completely cut off from the outside world. Nobody can get in – or out. And then the first body is found . . . and the horrifying truth comes to light. There's a killer among them – and nowhere to run.

Until we find ourselves in a situation we can't escape. Trapped.

'Tense. Unpredictable. Unputdownable. Shari Lapena's novels are domestic noir at its finest'
SIMON KERNICK

OUT NOW

SOMEONE WE KNOW

It can be hard keeping secrets in a tight-knit neighbourhood.

In a tranquil, leafy suburb of ordinary streets – one where
everyone is polite and friendly – an anonymous note
has been left at some of the houses.

'I'm so sorry. My son has been getting into
people's houses. He's broken into yours.'

Who is this boy, and what might he have uncovered?
As whispers start to circulate, suspicion mounts.

And when a missing local woman is found murdered,
the tension reaches breaking point. Who killed her? Who
knows more than they're telling? And how far will all
these very nice people go to protect their secrets?

**Maybe you don't know your neighbour
as well as you thought you did . . .**

OUT NOW

THE END OF HER

It starts with a shocking accusation . . .

Stephanie and Patrick are recently married, with new-born twins. While Stephanie struggles with the disorienting effects of sleep deprivation, there's one thing she knows for certain – she has everything she ever wanted.

Then a woman from his past arrives and makes a horrifying allegation about his first wife. He always claimed her death was an accident – but she says it was murder.

He insists he's innocent, that this is nothing but a blackmail attempt. But is Patrick telling the truth? Or has Stephanie made a terrible mistake?

How will it end?

'Shari Lapena has done it again – another cracking domestic thriller, and trust me, "the end" will leave you clamouring for more'
CARA HUNTER

OUT NOW